Luke hurried into the barn ahead of Harriet and disappeared into the feed room. Harriet gathered Major's blanket and headed down the aisle. Simon was sitting in his chair in front of Major's stall, his back to her.

Oh, great, she thought. She'd been hoping to slip in, try Major's blanket on, and go home for her morning run. Simon undoubtedly was waiting for Luke, as she couldn't imagine what he'd want to talk to her about.

"Simon," she called when she was two stalls away. He didn't reply. She called out again, louder, as she continued closing the distance. He still didn't respond. She slowed her approach.

His head was leaning at an odd angle. She made a wide circle around his chair.

"Oh, Simon," she murmured as she pulled her phone from her purse and dialed 911.

He was slumped against the headrest of his chair, his skin gray-blue. He had an angry-looking red ring around his neck where something had clearly been used to squeeze the life from him.

"Yes, this is Harriet Truman," she said when her phone connected. "I'm at the Miller Hill Equestrian Center, and I've just found a dead man in front of our horse's stall... Yes," she replied when the speaker asked if she was sure he was dead.

She agreed to stay where she was and to not touch the body. She didn't need to be told. This wasn't her first dead body, after all.

ALSO BY ARLENE SACHITANO

The Harriet Truman/Loose Threads Mysteries

Quilt As Desired
Quilter's Knot
Quilt As You Go
Quilt by Association
The Quilt Before the Storm
Make Quilts Not War
A Quilt in Time
Crazy as a Quilt
Disappearing Nine Patch
Double Wedding Death
Quilts Make A Family
The 12 Quilts of Christmas

The Harley Spring Mysteries

Chip and Die
Widowmaker

The Permelia O'Brien Mysteries

Double Knit

A QUILT OF A DIFFERENT COLOR

A Harriet Truman/Loose Threads Mystery

ARLENE SACHITANO

ZUMAYA ENIGMA   AUSTIN TX

2021

A QUILT OF A DIFFERENT COLOR

© 2021 by Arlene Sachitano

ISBN 978-1-61271-429-5

Cover art and design © April Martinez

"Zumaya Enigma" and the raven logo are trademarks of Zumaya Publications LLC, Austin TX, https://www.zumayapublications.com

Library of Congress Control Number: 2021940602

For Michele Voorhees

Chapter 1

"Tell me again why this woman couldn't come to our meeting," Lauren Sawyer said as she got out of Harriet's car.

Harriet Truman locked up and joined her in the parking area of the Miller Hill Equestrian Center.

"Aunt Beth was right behind us when we left Pins and Needles." She looked around. "They must have stopped somewhere."

"Like we should have. I'll bet they got drive-through coffee. They figured out we were going to be freezing, standing around talking about whatever we got called here for. Remind me again why we're here?"

"Would you stop complaining? You know we're here to look at some sort of horse blanket. Makes more sense to me for us to come to the horses."

Harriet's aunt pulled up beside them in her silver Beetle and got out along with her friends and fellow quilters Mavis Willis and Connie Escorcia. Beth reached back into the car and brought out a carrier with three steaming cups. Connie and Mavis already held theirs.

"Here, I figured you two could use a hot drink, and I didn't see you stop, so I took the liberty of bringing you something."

Lauren stepped forward and took a cup. She sipped it with her eyes closed.

"Mmmm…" she said, "Hot cocoa."

Harriet took a cup.

"Thank you, so much."

Beth took the remaining one and tossed the carrier back into her car.

"Do you have any idea what the trainer wants to talk to us about?" she asked.

"Luke wasn't sure, but he said she was talking about some sort of saddle blanket a horse wears when they're riding it. He hasn't seen one."

"Your boy's horse is so big it undoubtedly needs a custom-made one, but one person could do that," Mavis said. "Marjorie said the new stable manager wanted to meet with all of us. That sounds like a lot of these blankets."

Lauren nodded at the open barn doors. A woman was walking toward them.

"I think we're about to find out."

"Hi," the tall, slender woman said as she approached. She was dressed in tan riding pants and a brown down vest over a long-sleeved white shirt. Her dark-brown hair was pulled back into a tight braid.

Aunt Beth extended her hand when the woman reached them.

"Hi, I'm Beth Carlson. These are my friends, Mavis, Connie, Lauren, and my niece Harriet. We're waiting for two more—Jenny Logan and Carla Salter."

"I'm Angela Tavarious, the new stable manager. Let's go on into the barn where it's warmer."

She led them to the center of the building, where the main aisle bisected another one. A large electric space heater glowed from the beams.

"Have any of you been to our equestrian center before?" Angela asked. "I'm sorry, being new here, I don't know who is who yet."

"Lauren and I have," Harriet volunteered. "My foster son Luke has his horse Major stabled here."

"The big gray guy?" Angela said and smiled. "He's not your usual saddle horse."

Harriet heard Major whinny from down the aisle. He must have recognized her smell, or more likely that of the carrots in her coat pocket.

"He's a former police horse," she said and pulled out the bag of cut-up carrot pieces. "I'm going to give him his carrots before he starts kicking the door."

Which he was already doing by the time she approached.

"Hey, settle down, big guy," she told him and opened his stall door. "Luke couldn't come yesterday—he has a cold, and we made him stay home." She held a handful of chopped carrots on her flat hand, and he picked them off with his soft lips. "James sent you these leftovers from the restaurant."

"That horse is even more spoiled than those two mutts you live with," Lauren said, coming up behind Harriet.

2

"Luke loves him, and he seems to love Luke, so in my book, he gets all the spoiling he needs."

"Which somehow leads to us having to make whatever this lady wants us to make, to make Luke happy."

"You don't have to participate, you know. Loose Threads quilting projects are always voluntary."

Lauren ran her hands through her long blond hair, sweeping it back on her shoulders.

"Don't listen to me, I'm frustrated with an impossible client right now. I haven't stitched on a quilt or anything else because of his increasing demands. He calls all hours of the day and night asking for changes that are meaningless. His product is finished, but he's unwilling to launch it."

"I'm sorry," Harriet said.

"Well, it is what it is. Look, Jenny and Carla have arrived. Let's go see what's going on."

"This is all of us," Aunt Beth was saying. "Now, what is it you need?"

"Well, as I said, my name is Angela Tavarious, and I'm the new manager of Miller Hill Equestrian Center. With my husband Simon. We'll be running things here.

"We were brought in without much warning. The stable we had been working at unfortunately burned down, and the owners decided not to rebuild. I gather something happened here that resulted in the former manager being removed with little warning.

"Now, it appears there's a horse show in the works, six weeks from now. That puts it at the last week in February, which means it's likely to be cold. I'm not sure how things were done here in the past, but I like horses to wear a quarter-sheet to keep their kidneys warm to make it easier to remove the lactic acid buildup that can occur when horses are working. This is only a worry when it's forty degrees or below, but since our show is in February, it could be an issue."

"I'm guessing these quarter-sheets are quilted?" Harriet asked.

"They can be. They can be made of wool, flannel, or even crocheted. Some people buy ones that cover the rider's legs as well. Those, of course, aren't appropriate for a horse show.

"I like ones with a narrow shape that fits under the saddle and then spreads out over the horses' hips. When I heard from some of the local people about an active quilt group in the area, I wondered if you could make quilted quarter-sheets. They could even have designs on the part that covers the flanks.

"I'll completely understand if it's too much trouble. In my mind, it would look very striking. Look, I'm going to go check on my stall cleaning crew and see how things are progressing. Will that give you enough time to decide if you'd like to take on this project?"

"That will be fine," Beth assured her.

They watched as she turned down the side aisle and out of sight.

Harriet sipped her cocoa. "What do you think? Anyone?"

Jenny rubbed her hands together briskly.

"I think it sounds interesting."

"How do we figure out the shape?" Carla asked.

"We'll have to think about it," Harriet said, "but right offhand, I think I would take a piece of muslin and lay it over the horse and then pin darts into it until it lays flat. Then I'd use that as the pattern."

"If we're going to machine-quilt them, we should probably mark the dart lines on the muslin but not cut them. That way, we can maintain the rectangular shape. We can cut away the batting and backing after it's quilted and then sew the darts," Aunt Beth suggested.

Mavis sipped her latte and then raised her cup.

"I'm in."

"Me, too," Connie said, doing the same.

One by one, the rest held up their cups, tapping them against Mavis's in agreement.

"I'll call Sarah and see if she's interested," Jenny said.

Connie sat down on a bench by the wall.

"I wonder what sort of design she's thinking about."

Mavis joined her.

"Some sort of appliqué, no doubt."

They debated the merits of machine-stitched appliqué vs. fused appliqué vs. needle-turned appliqué as it related to durability in this particular situation.

"Can I assume from your discussion you're at least considering my request?" Angela asked, joining them again.

Mavis stood up.

"I think we've agreed we will try. To my knowledge, none of us has ever attempted anything like this before."

"And there's no guarantee we'll be successful," Beth added.

"But we're willing to give it our best," Connie finished.

"We'll go back to the quilt shop and do some figuring," Mavis said.

Harriet tossed her empty cup into a trashcan beside the bench.

"Do you have an average-sized horse we can measure to get started? I'm thinking measuring Major wouldn't do us much good."

Angela chuckled.

4

"Very true. Wait here. I'll bring one of the school horses out."

Connie and Jenny pulled retractable tape measures from their purses, and Lauren took her tablet computer from her messenger bag and turned it on. Angela led a tall bay gelding into the aisle and attached cross ties to his halter on each side.

"Nick here is a very gentle beginner's horse, so feel free to do whatever you need to do to get your measurements."

Harriet took the end of Connie's tape and unwound a few feet before walking carefully behind him and stretching the tape over his back. Lauren tapped numbers into her pad until they'd recorded every possible dimension on Nick.

"Do we need to custom-make each one to fit a particular animal?" Jenny asked.

Angela attached a lead rope to Nick's halter and detached the two cross-tie ropes.

"They don't need to be that precise. Maybe a small, medium, and large option?"

"We can do that," Harriet said.

"Do you need Nick for anything else?" Angela asked, and when no one said anything, she led him back to his stall.

Chapter 2

Harriet was in her studio sketching design possibilities for the quarter-sheets when Luke came in from the kitchen. He held the sandwich she'd made for him in one hand and a glass of milk in the other.

"Hey, how was school?" she asked him.

He laughed. "You never quit trying, do you."

"I know you're never going to love it, but I hope things are a little better."

"Actually, things *are* a little better. A few people from school have signed up to take riding lessons at the stable since the new management took over. We've started having lunch together to talk about the horses."

"That sounds good."

"A couple of guys who are still living in bad foster homes aren't too happy about it."

Harriet set her grid paper pad on the table.

"You're in a tricky situation. You got to leave a crowded, miserable place to come live with us, and those other kids didn't. That's not your fault. And we would like to help every kid living in a bad situation, but we can't. If you went back to living in an overcrowded, neglectful home, it wouldn't help those other guys at all."

"So, what am I supposed to do?"

"You make the best of every opportunity you're given. You grow up to be a productive member of society and do what you can to make the world a better place. Do things like James does feeding the homeless, or the quilters do, making warm blankets for the kids, or teach people to read, like Connie does–whatever you can do to make the world a better place. But for right now, take care of yourself."

"Sometimes I feel guilty about…" He spread his arms wide, "…all this."

"I think that's called survivor's guilt. I'm not sure how you feel about religion or church. I mean, I know you've been coming with us, but your beliefs are just that—yours. Having said that, if you're comfortable at church, you could try talking to Pastor Hafer. I've found him to be pretty helpful when I've been confused about things. I'm sure he'd be able to help you with this."

"He won't think I'm being a selfish ingrate?"

Harriet smiled.

"I promise he will not judge you."

Luke took a bite of sandwich and chewed thoughtfully.

"I guess it can't hurt. I'm getting nowhere with it, and Major hasn't been much help on this one."

"Give the pastor a call when you're ready, and let me know if you need a ride somewhere to meet him."

"Will do, for now, though, can I get a ride to the stable? The new manager's husband wants to talk to Emily and I and the other therapy volunteers this afternoon. I guess he ran a program where they were before, and he wants to tell us about it."

"What time do you need to be there?"

"Four o'clock. He said to plan on being there for about two hours."

Harriet looked at her watch.

"It's three now, so finish your snack, and I'll take the dogs for a quick walk before we go."

At the mention of the words *dogs* and *walk*, Scooter and Cyrano got up from their beds in the studio and started jumping at her leg.

Harriet smiled.

"I guess I better get the leashes."

✂-- ✂-- ✂

Harriet texted Lauren while the dogs circled her legs, tangling her in their leashes.

> *Luke has a two-hour meeting at the stable. Want to meet for coffee?*
> *When and where?*
> *Steaming Cup 4:20*
> *See you there.*

Lauren was at a table, drink in front of her, when Harriet arrived. She ordered a London Fog tea latte and headed for the table to wait while it was being made.

"Who is Luke's meeting with?" Lauren asked when Harriet was settled.

"Apparently, the new stable manager's husband ran a therapy-horse program at their previous location, and he plans to bring his program here."

"That's good, right?"

"Assuming the people who were already doing horse therapy under the old manager are on board."

"Speaking of the stable people, I went over there a couple of days ago to review the security system with them. I had written a program for the previous manager so the old cameras and the new ones they added on could all be viewed on one screen. It's on a desktop system in the office in their house."

"Did you get a sense of what they're like while you were working with them?"

"They were both uncomfortable with the level of surveillance at the barn. I explained the problems at Christmas time that led to the enhanced system, and they said they understood; but they both said they were going to talk to the owners about backing off a little if things go well under their care."

"I guess I can see how cameras everywhere accessible by the boss could be a little intimidating."

"I told them the logs indicate the owners hardly ever access the files, but I don't know if that helped any."

The barista delivered Harriet's drink, and she blew on it then took a small sip.

"I'm sort of glad we have this blanket-quilting project that will give us an excuse to visit the barn. I know Luke is almost an adult, but I'll feel better if I see for myself that everything is going okay. Especially, as you were saying, in light of the troubles they had a few weeks back."

"You can't wrap him in bubble wrap."

"I guess."

"I wonder if Simon, the manager's husband, will be making any modifications to the arena if he's going to run the therapy program?"

"Why would he need modifications?"

"I guess you haven't met him yet. He's got some sort of disability. He uses an electric wheelchair."

"That must uniquely qualify him to develop and run a therapy-horse program." Harriet watched as people entered and lined up at the counter. "I guess a lot of people have the same idea as we did."

"It's because of this wacky weather. We're supposed to be in one of the most temperate locations in the Northwest, if not the country, but suddenly, for the last two years, we're having real winter."

"And people are trying to say climate change isn't real," Harriet said with a chuckle.

"I guess our horse blankets will be timely."

Harriet sipped her tea again. "I've been thinking about that."

"And," Lauren prompted when she didn't say more.

"I haven't come to any conclusions, but I'm trying to imagine what sort of design we can use. I'm thinking a patchwork background with some sort of appliqué in the hip area.'"

"That sounds good so far."

"It's the appliqué I'm struggling with. A horse blanket is a functional quilt with a capital F."

"Don't they just put it on the horse right before the saddle goes on? That doesn't seem too complicated."

"It's not the time the blanket's on the horse I'm worried about. It's when they take it off and toss it in the direction of the saddle they've just taken off, and then carry all their gear to the tack room."

"That rules out ribbon embroidery and beads," Lauren said.

Harriet sipped her tea latte and smiled.

"If your heart is really set on it, you could cover your embellishments with sheer netting."

"Wouldn't that flatten my fabulous work?"

"Not if you're careful. Seriously, though, we need to figure out something that will be decorative but sturdy."

Lauren leaned forward and tilted her head to the side to see out the front window.

"Is that your aunt's Beetle that just drove in?"

Harriet turned and looked. By this time, the car was parked, and she could see her aunt climbing out of the driver's seat and Mavis exiting on the passenger side. She waved when the pair came in, and they joined her and Lauren.

Beth took her hat off and ran a hand through her short white hair.

"If you two are going to be here for a while we could join you."

"Go get your drinks," Lauren said, "We're waiting for Luke, who's at a meeting at the stable."

"What's going on at the stable?" Beth asked when she'd returned with her coffee.

"Luke says the manager's husband ran a therapy program at their previous location. He uses a wheelchair himself, so he has his own ideas about how it should be done, I guess," Harriet told her.

Mavis brought her latte to the table and sat down.

"Have you guys figured these horse blankets out yet?"

Harriet set her cup down.

"We've been mulling it over. It seems like you'd want something decorative in the hip area, but it would have to be durable, since these are functional quilts."

Aunt Beth blew on her coffee.

"That's what Mavis and I were thinking. We can either do a complicated patchwork pattern or a simple appliqué."

Lauren ripped at the edge of her napkin.

"That's where we were ending up."

"Since I've got access to Major whenever I need him, I was thinking I might try a few options," Harriet said. "Just to get the basic shape and see how it fits when you add the quilting to the mix."

"That's a start, anyway," Mavis said.

Aunt Beth mentioned that she'd run in to Freida from the Small Stitches, who was recovering from a broken leg she'd suffered during the Christmas holidays, which led to a thorough discussion of the troubles that had befallen the Small Stitches and how they were all recovering.

Chapter 3

H arriet and Luke had only been home for a few minutes when James came in, carrying a quilted hot-food carrier. He set it on the kitchen island and turned around to kiss Harriet.

"That smells really good," Luke said with a grin.

"I'm not sure you can smell anything the way I've got it wrapped."

Luke laughed.

"It's going to smell good once you unwrap it."

James unwrapped the covered pan.

"Tonight, we're having pot roast, which was the special of the day at the restaurant. This being the after-holiday season and a weekday, things are very slow."

Harriet put the pan in the oven and turned it on *warm*.

"I like pot roast."

Luke laughed. "I like anything James makes."

"Turn the other oven on to four hundred," James told him. "I'm going to get some rolls from the freezer."

Fifteen minutes later, the trio was seated at the kitchen table with their dinner.

"How was the meeting at the stable?" Harriet asked Luke.

"If they actually do everything they talked about, it should be great."

Harriet briefly wondered if Luke would ever stop being so guarded. He'd seen so much disappointment in his young life.

James passed the basket of rolls to her.

"What are they planning?"

"The therapy program before was mainly for children. Now, they're adding more adult programs, like for veterans. And Simon said they found out some of the people at the homeless camp are veterans, so he's thinking of inviting any of them who want to come to participate."

"Wow, do they have enough horses for that?" Harriet asked.

"I guess someone with farmland took in the horses that survived the fire at their previous place. They have a big trailer, and will bring the horses over when they need extras."

Harriet set the basket of rolls in the middle of the table.

"That's convenient."

"Yeah," Luke said around a mouthful of pot roast. "Simon has a contraption for helping paralyzed adults mount up. The horses from the previous place are used to having people hoisted onto their backs, he says."

"Have you learned anything more about the quarter-sheet blankets we're supposed to be making?"

Luke smiled. "Not really. I saw one, but it just looked like a funny-shaped saddle blanket."

"Do you think Major would be willing for me to make samples and try them on him?"

"I think Major would love that. Especially if you keep bringing him carrots."

"I can do that," Harriet said with a smile.

"By the way," Luke said after he'd eaten most of his first serving. "You probably already know this, but Raven is taking riding lessons and is volunteering with the therapy-horse program."

Harriet set her fork down.

"I *didn't* know that. I guess I didn't realize she was interested in horses. Jenny hasn't mentioned anything."

"I'm pretty sure she wasn't until her popular girlfriends started taking lessons."

James cut a small piece of roast up into three parts and slipped them to the two dogs and Fred the cat.

"I wonder if Jenny and Brian will buy her a horse," he said.

"Probably," Luke said. "They buy her everything she asks for."

James raised an eyebrow. "Is that a note of jealousy I detect?"

"Not even a little bit. I shouldn't have said anything."

"So, why did you?" Harriet asked. "You know you can tell us anything. Or, at least, I hope you know that."

Luke sighed. "All I meant was since Raven went to live with Jenny and Brian, she's been…I don't know how to say this right."

"Just spit it out, we won't judge you," James encouraged.

"You know how you guys wanted to buy me everything in sight at first? Only I kept saying no to most of it." His face turned red. "You finally got the hang of it after a while. Well, Raven says yes to everything they offer and then some. She's got a bigger wardrobe than anyone at school, they've bought her an electric guitar and a drum kit, a designer purse, three phones already, and two tablets, and a stereo system for her bedroom, which she says is decked out in all new furniture and designed by an interior decorator.

"I guess what I'm saying is, I think she's taking advantage of them, big time."

Harriet sat back in her chair and smiled.

"Don't worry, Jenny's got a handle on things. She says Raven is testing them. She doesn't believe they could possibly care for her, and she believes showering her with possessions is equal to caring. Jenny thinks Raven is waiting for her to say no to something to prove her belief that they don't really love her."

"All she has to do is ask for something they can't afford—an airplane or something, doesn't she?" Luke asked.

Harriet twirled her fork between her fingers.

"It's all complicated. Raven deliberately isn't asking for anything out of financial reach, because she wants to believe Jenny and Brian love her. She doesn't really want them to refuse her. But she keeps asking for stuff to reassure *herself* it's true. Jenny believes she will eventually believe they care and stop asking for stuff. And she thinks it's slowly starting to happen already."

Luke got up and started taking dishes to the kitchen peninsula.

"By the way, if you want to volunteer with the therapy-horse program, especially the veterans' part, since that will be new, the orientation meeting is next Wednesday at four."

Harriet looked at James, and he smiled.

"I might just do that," she said and smiled back at him.

Chapter 4

Robin McLeod, DeAnn Gault, and Lauren met Harriet at the stable the following Tuesday at nine. The weather remained cold and clear, so they all were clad in down jackets or vests and knit hats.

"Major will give us an approximation for our trial run although he's a lot broader than the dressage horses. Wait here, and I'll get him out of his stall."

Robin pulled a folded piece of muslin from her bag.

"Is Major going to be bothered by four women hanging fabric on his backside and pinning in darts?"

Harriet chuckled.

"He's a decorated veteran of the Seattle Police Mounted Patrol. He's probably seen it all. He retired when he was stabbed, don't forget. I'm not sure he'd flinch even if you stuck him with a pin."

She turned and went down the aisle to Major's stall, snapping on his lead rope and bringing him back to one of the side crosstie stations, so they wouldn't block the main aisle. Robin pulled a yellow legal tablet and pen from her purse before setting the bag on a bench.

"Okay, I'll take notes. When you pinch up a dart, measure how deep it is and how long it is. I made a rough sketch of what I think the blanket will look like."

Lauren got her retractable tape measure from her messenger bag.

"We should measure the darts twice, and if the two measurements don't match, we can do a tie-breaker."

"I'm not sure it's quite that precise," Harriet said with a grin.

✂ -- ✂ -- ✂

Robin flipped the top page of her tablet over the numbers.

"Okay, I'm going to swing by the Steaming Cup on my way to the Loose Threads meeting. Anyone want anything?"

Harriet and Lauren ordered drinks, and Robin and DeAnn took off.

"Do you mind if I brush Major a little before I put him back?" Harriet asked. "He was so patient with us, he deserves a reward."

Lauren rolled her eyes. "Do what you need to do."

Harriet pulled a bag of cut-up carrots from her pocket and fed a handful to the horse, and then spent fifteen minutes brushing him.

✂ -- ✂ -- ✂

Harriet had just latched the door on Major's stall when a compact gray-haired woman led a tall dark-bay horse out of the stall next to his. The bay was favoring his left front foot. She led him a few lengths and then stopped, turning around and walking backward, trying to look at his foot.

"Would you like me to lead him so you can watch?" Harriet asked her.

"Thank you," the woman said, and handed over the leather lead strap. She smiled at Harriet. "I'm Stella Bren, and this fellow is Milo's Second Season."

"I'm Harriet Truman. The big fellow in the next stall in my son's horse Major."

Stella walked behind the horse, and Harriet led him the length of the aisle, turned and brought him back in a straight line.

Stella looked puzzled.

"He was favoring that foot a few weeks ago, but then it cleared up, and he was fine. We went to a show last weekend outside Seattle. He got two firsts. Everything was great, but now he's lame again. I don't understand."

"That *is* curious."

"I wonder if something's wrong with his shoe?" Stella lifted the foot up and looked at the bottom of the hoof. "I can't tell if anything is wrong."

Harriet looked. She didn't see an obvious wound.

"Maybe I should call the farrier," Stella said.

"I think I'd try the vet. He might have a navicular bone problem, or maybe a coffin-bone break."

"I don't know what I'd do if he went lame. We imported him from Germany and spent a fortune having him work with a trainer and learn his commands in English. It would be really hard to lose that sort of investment."

15

Harriet patted the horse's neck. "I wouldn't write him off just yet. See what the vet has to say."

"You're right. I shouldn't think so negatively. Thanks for helping me."

"You're welcome. I'll see you around."

✂-- ✂-- ✂

Lauren looked at her watch as Harriet got in the car.

"You must have given that nag the full spa treatment."

"There was a woman trying to check her horse's injured foot. She need-ed someone to lead it down the aisle and back, so I helped her out."

"We're going to have to hurry."

"Are you afraid your drink will be cold?"

Lauren laughed.

"No, that's what microwaves are for. I'm worried we're going to miss all the best gossip."

"When have you known the Threads to only discuss a hot topic once? If they've got anything good, they'll still be dissecting it when we get there."

"Who was the woman you were helping?"

"I've never seen her before today. Her name is Stella Bren."

"Is she related to Milo Bren?"

"Possibly—the horse's name is Milo's Second Season."

"Milo Bren started a very successful software company. He made a lot of money and then suddenly dropped off the radar. There's been a lot of speculation as to what happened. Some think he had a mental breakdown, some think he has a terrible disease."

"What did you think?"

"I didn't think anything. His company stayed open; the new CEO is competent. Their stock has maintained its value, and they still hire me to do freelance work."

"Very interesting. That explains how they could afford to buy an ex-pensive Warmblood horse in Germany and have it trained to learn Eng-lish commands." She pulled her car to the curb in front of Pins and Nee-dles. "Here we are."

✂-- ✂-- ✂

"Do you want me to reheat your drinks?" Robin asked when Harriet and Lauren entered the classroom/meeting room inside the shop. "I kept them wrapped in a dish towel in the kitchen, but you could microwave them if they're not hot enough."

Harriet went in and got her London Fog latte.

"This is still plenty warm," she said and carried it into the classroom.

16

"Did we miss anything?" Lauren asked.

Mavis pulled her coat up over her shoulders and shivered.

"The only time anything happens in this town, you and your sidekick are in the middle of it."

"So, let us ask *you*, did we miss anything?" Aunt Beth added.

"Geez, I was only asking," Lauren said.

Mavis reached over and patted her hand.

"I'm sorry. I'm just tired of all this cold. I don't need to take it out on you."

"You might not be interested in my next announcement," Harriet said, "but Luke was telling me the new stable managers are expanding the horse therapy program to include veterans and people from the homeless camp. They're looking for volunteers."

Aunt Beth pulled a piece of black wool from her bag, along with a sandwich bag filled with colorful wool circles and triangles. She took a threaded needle from the background and positioned a red circle before beginning to whipstitch it in place on the black wool.

"Do you have to be able to ride a horse?"

Harriet sipped her tea.

"I don't think so. They usually have volunteers who walk along beside the horse and rider on both sides to keep them balanced. Someone also leads the horse. I think they have some clerical tasks, too. Checking people in for each session. I don't know if they plan on offering food, but I'd assume if they're bringing people from the homeless camp, they'll feed them before they take them back."

"They must have some sort of training for the volunteers, too," Lauren added.

"They do," Harriet said.

Jenny got out her quilt block and began stitching a green leaf onto a gray background.

"I'd like to have an excuse to spend some time at the stable. Raven's out there almost every day, and I'd like to see what she's doing."

Lauren smiled.

"I like it— trust but verify."

Connie took a cookie from a plate in the center of the table.

"I think Grandpa Rod would babysit Wendy if you want to come volunteer with me," she told Carla Salter, the group's youngest member.

DeAnn slipped her needle free from her quilt block.

"I'll need to see the schedule. If they need help with daytime programs when the kids are in school, I could do that. Our nights are pretty busy with kid activities."

"Same for me," Robin said.

Marjorie Swain, the owner of the quilt store, came to the doorway.

"I heard you say you were making some sort of quilted saddle blankets for the horses at Miller Hill, and I thought I'd offer to sell you the fabric at cost as my contribution to the project."

"Are you sure?" Mavis asked. "We can pay for our fabric."

"I wouldn't offer if I didn't mean it, and besides, it'll help me move fabric to make space for the spring stock."

Harriet stood up.

"I'm going to go look at fabric so I can get started when I get home. I'm making a muslin template for fitting purposes."

Lauren got up and carried her empty cup to the wastebasket.

"I'm fabric-shopping, too."

Chapter 5

James came home early from the restaurant the next night so they could eat dinner before the volunteer meeting. He brought chicken breasts with mushroom gravy and rice pilaf with roasted root vegetables.

"I thought I'd come with you to the volunteer meeting. I can't really spend time out there, but if they're going to feed people when they bring the homeless and veterans in, I can help with that."

Luke filled three glasses of water and carried them to the table before sitting down.

"Simon said he's going to have Emily and me work with the horses that are coming from the other stable. He wants us to lunge them all before the therapy clients ride them."

"What's lunging?" James asked.

Luke looked at Harriet.

"You can explain it to him," she encouraged.

"You put the horse on this long rope and hold a buggy whip and have it go in circles around you."

"It's a technique for warming a horse up," Harriet added.

James took a roll from the breadbasket and handed the basket to Harriet.

"I guess I'm going to have to learn all the horsey lingo if I'm going to have two horse people in the family."

✂-- ✂-- ✂

The orientation meeting took place in the indoor riding arena at Miller Hill Equestrian Center. Emily Roberts met them at the door. She worked cleaning stalls to help pay the boarding fees for her horse, and she and Luke rode their horses together whenever they could.

"Hi, Luke," she said with a nod to Harriet and James. "Can you come help me? Angela's going to use Fable to demonstrate how we work. You and I will show what the volunteers do."

He looked at Harriet. "Will you two be okay?"

"I think we can manage on our own," she said with a smile. "You go ahead."

Lauren was already sitting in the bleachers with Connie, Carla, Mavis, Aunt Beth, and Jenny when they climbed the steps.

"Come on in, glad you could make it," Lauren said with a grin. "Apparently, we're waiting for the van to arrive with the people from the homeless camp."

"I hope it doesn't take too long," Connie complained. "It's cold in here."

Beth unfolded the blanket she'd brought to cover her legs with and handed Connie a corner of it.

"Here, I'll share. We're going to have to figure out a warmer outfit if we decide to volunteer."

Harriet leaned forward so she could look past Lauren and down the row to her aunt.

"When you volunteer, you'll be moving the whole time, so I don't think you'll have to worry. If you're still cold, though, a trick I learned at boarding school in Switzerland was to wear tights or panty hose under my jeans. They aren't as bulky as long underwear so you can still move around easily, but they're warm as an under layer."

"I'll try it," Connie said. "I rode horses on my uncle's ranch when I was young, but that was in Mexico, so I didn't have to worry about being cold."

Their discussion was interrupted by the arrival of Jorge, followed by half a dozen residents of the homeless camp at Fogg Park, including the acknowledged leader of the group Joyce Elias. Jorge climbed the bleachers and took a seat beside James. Joyce and her friends sat several rows above Harriet and the Loose Threads.

"Were you thinking about feeding the veterans' and homeless groups when they are here to do their therapy?" he asked.

"Something like that," James replied.

"Great minds think alike, my friend."

A few more people Harriet only recognized as having met in passing filtered in and took seats before Angela stepped out into the center of the arena, a microphone in her hand.

"Thank you for joining us this evening," she began and, after welcoming them, described the program, emphasizing the changes there would be from the previous one. Her husband made a grand entrance, riding in on a vehicle that seemed to be a hybrid of a motorized wheelchair and a quad bike. Behind him walked four teen-aged girls, including Jenny's foster daughter Raven. When Simon stopped his chair beside his wife, the girls arranged themselves around the chair like princesses at court; each with a hand on the side or back of the vehicle.

Harriet glanced at Jenny, who had a look of disgust on her face.

"What is he doing with those girls hanging off his chair like some sort of sultan with his harem?" Jenny said.

"Didn't you ever have a crush on an older teacher?" Mavis asked her.

Probably not the right question to ask Jenny, who had spent her teen years in a commune, Harriet thought.

Connie tucked the blanket tighter around her knees.

"It could be the little-mother syndrome. He's crippled, so they all want to take care of him."

Lauren leaned closer to Harriet.

"Look at the way the blonde has her hand on his shoulder, stroking his hair. That doesn't look motherly to me," she whispered.

"I'm with you. Look at the way he smiles at them."

Lauren shook her head. "Creepy."

Emily led Fable out, and Luke followed, carrying a set of steps he set beside the horse when they'd stopped a few feet short of Angela.

Angela spoke about preliminary meetings the participants would have where they would learn how to groom the horse, how to walk around the horse, how to take care of it, etc. Only when they were comfortable with their mount would they begin to ride.

When she got to the part of the demonstration that involved riding, Emily mounted Fable using the stairs, and Luke led the mare. Two of the girls left Simon's chair and moved to either side of Fable, each holding onto one of Emily's legs while Luke led the horse in a slow circle.

"Okay," Connie said, "I can do that."

Luke brought Fable to a stop in front of Angela, and Emily dismounted.

"As people progress with their riding skills, they can eventually ride without people on either side, if they wish. No one is pushed to advance further than they feel comfortable."

Luke picked up the steps and followed Emily as she led Fable out of the arena.

"Before we take questions, I'd like to introduce my husband, Simon Tavarious. He'll be working with the children's therapy group in the mornings, but you may see him helping with the evening groups occasionally."

Simon wheeled his vehicle to her side, and she handed him the microphone.

"I hope you will all sign up to volunteer with our program. I think you'll find it to be quite a rewarding experience.

"When we work with veterans, we have a meal after our riding session each week. If you would like to volunteer to help provide, prepare, or serve food, please meet with me after this meeting." He handed the microphone back to his wife.

"Now we'll break up into groups. Simon will talk to people who want to help with food, and then he'll talk about his riding classes. He'll stay in the arena. I'll meet the therapy class volunteers by the entrance at the base of the bleachers. If you folks don't mind waiting, I'll meet with the people from Fogg Park when I'm done with the volunteers."

Harriet heard Joyce Elias muttering. She thought she heard her say, "Where else would we go?"

She smiled. Joyce was an independent woman. It probably galled her that they would be dependent on the stable for transportation if they participated in the program. Joyce prided herself on her ability to bike or bus anywhere she needed to go. This was a situation where neither of those options was going to work for her.

Jorge, James, and three women went to the middle of the arena, while Harriet, Lauren and the rest of the people in attendance climbed down the bleachers and reassembled in the entrance hall. A stout blond woman walked beside Harriet.

"Hi, I'm Crystal Kelley, and that beautiful girl in the blue jacket beside Simon is my daughter Paige."

"Harriet Truman," Harriet said.

"Oh, I've read about you in the newspaper. Aren't you the one who found Daniel hanging in the back of the Print Shop at Christmas time?"

"Sadly, yes,"

"Well, I always wondered about him."

"Oh?" Harriet said.

"You know," the woman said with a knowing smirk.

Lauren was walking on Harriet's other side.

"Oh, you mean because he was gay, he deserved to be hanged?" she asked.

"That's not what I meant," Crystal said and shoved her hands in her pockets, speeding up so she was no longer beside them.

"That wasn't very friendly," Harriet said, trying hard to suppress a grin.

"She deserved it. Besides, I don't have a kid who's going to be riding with her kid."

"Thanks, that helps a lot."

"Admit it, you didn't like her, either."

Harriet shook her head. "It is not for me to judge."

They reached the gathering spot, where Angela was handing out packets of information and taking people's names and contact information. Lauren and Harriet pulled the pages out of their envelopes and reviewed them.

"It says here I need to wear riding boots of some sort, English or Western." Lauren shook her head. "I've followed you into a number of interesting situations since you've moved back, but this one may take the cake."

"Don't knock the boots until you try them. You may find you like them."

"That'll be the day."

Chapter 6

J ames and Jorge were still talking to Simon when Harriet's group broke up.

"For crying out loud, how long does it take to arrange for food?" Crystal complained. She had volunteered for the veteran's group, and apparently was now waiting for Simon to talk about lessons.

"She could keep this adventure interesting," Harriet commented quietly to Lauren.

"Finally," Crystal said in a loud voice when James and Jorge came out of the arena. The men were still talking, so Harriet and Lauren watched as Crystal and several other parents stood in a semicircle around the front of Simon's wheelchair.

"I teach intermediate and senior riding classes in two student age groups each," Simon explained.

"If I sign my daughter Paige up for private lessons, can she enroll in the intermediate class?" Crystal interrupted.

"What level is she now?" Simon asked.

"The previous trainer wouldn't let her move out of the beginner class, but that was because she wanted me to buy a horse from her. I know if you work with her a little, you'll see she's really an intermediate."

"I'm sure the previous manager had a reason to not advance her, but I can take a look. Of course, I'm happy to teach private lessons to any student at any level, but I can't make any promises as to placement level."

"I think you'll see that my daughter is exceptional. Those other people just didn't like her."

Simon looked uncomfortable.

"Does anyone else have any questions before you sign up for classes?" No one did, so he handed the closest mother a clipboard with class signup lists on it. "I may choose to move people up or down after I see everyone ride, but for now, sign up for whatever class you were in before, whether you took classes here or elsewhere."

Harriet and Lauren watched Crystal. Her face was red, and she clenched her hands into fists.

"Wow, she's really mad," Harriet said.

"What do you call a stage mother when it's horses, not acting?" Lauren wondered.

Harriet turned so Crystal couldn't see her laughing.

"I don't know, but she's it, whatever you call it."

Lauren feigned coughing to cover her laugh.

"This is too painful to watch," Harriet said. "I'm going to go check on Major."

"I'm going to head for home. I've got to talk to an East Coast client early tomorrow morning."

"I'm going to be working on my muslin mock-up tomorrow. Stop by in the afternoon if you want to see how it looks."

"I'll see how my workday goes."

✂ -- ✂ -- ✂

Harriet had almost reached Major's stall when Stella led Milo out into the aisle. The horse was now noticeably favoring his front foot.

"I don't understand," Stella said when she saw Harriet. "He was doing so well at the show, and now he's getting worse and worse."

"What did the vet say?"

"He didn't see any obvious injury on the bottom of his hoof. Since he was better at the show, he said we should rest him for a week and re-evaluate. I thought Essy was looking a little better, but I guess I was fooling myself. I'm going to call the vet first thing tomorrow."

Harriet attempted a reassuring smile. If she had spent that much on a horse, she'd want more than a wait-and-see. She'd be asking for an x-ray, at least.

"You call him Essy?"

"My husband picked him because they share a first name, but it would be too confusing for them to both go by Milo, so we shortened 'Second Season' to SS or Essy."

"That's clever," Harriet said. "Let me know what the vet says."

She continued on to Major's stall. The horse nickered as she approached, probably smelling the bag of chopped carrots in her pocket.

Luke approached, skirting Stella and Essy.

"Are you going to sign up to do therapy?" he asked when he reached the stall.

"I need to read all the information in the envelope they gave us, but yes, I think I will. I'm pretty sure Lauren is going to, also."

"That's cool."

Harriet started back down the aisle to go find James, but Luke stopped her.

"Before you go, do you think…? I mean, I was wondering if…"

"Are you wondering if you and Emily could go to the coffee shop in town?"

He let out a relieved sigh.

"Yeah."

"Yes, as long as your homework is done."

"It is," he said quickly.

"And Emily's mother agrees. We can drop you both off, but either James and I or Emily's parents need to pick you up in an hour."

"Okay, I'll go ask her." He said as he hurried on his way to find her.

"Fine," she said to his fleeing back.

✂ -- ✂ -- ✂

Joyce and the rest of the homeless group were just finishing up with Angela when Harriet returned to the arena.

"I'll be right back, and then we can get you folks home to the park," she told them. Then: "What do you think?" she asked Joyce.

Joyce gave her a weary smile.

"It's a grand idea, but there are some logistics to deal with. Angela wants us to wear cowboy boots, and she's gotten Vern to agree to sell them to us for twenty dollars, which is, as you well know, below cost. Most of us have a little income, so it's not a problem for us, but a few of the younger people haven't gotten their banking straightened out yet."

"I'd be happy to fund them, if they wouldn't be offended."

"That's very kind of you. They can pay you back when they get their lives organized. I think they need the therapy the most. The fellows I'm thinking of are war veterans who came home with a hard case of PTSD."

"I'm happy to help, and I can take you to town to get your boots, if you wish. I'm bringing James's leftovers out to you tomorrow afternoon, in any case. And I can call Vern and see if that works for him."

"You are a godsend, Harriet Truman. You really are."

Harriet's cheeks turned pink.

"I'll see you tomorrow afternoon."

26

"I'll have the group ready."

James finished talking to Jorge and started in Harriet's direction.

"Goodbye, Joyce," Harriet said, and then turned to James to explain Luke's plan.

Chapter 7

*H*arriet called her aunt when they got home from the stable. She knew Beth would want to come along to deliver food to the homeless camp; and she was pretty sure she needed to buy boots for volunteer work at the stable.

"I think we should invite Mavis and Connie, too," Beth suggested. "We already talked about all of us needing boots. We have hiking boots, and Connie has boots from when she was in her twenties; those are past their prime by a few decades. None of us have anything like what Angela described."

"Do you think Connie will be willing to drive? I'm not sure how many people are joining this venture, and with you and I in my car, I can technically manage six more, but they'd be packed like sardines."

"Good idea. I'll call her and Mavis. I need to talk to them anyway about the clothes closet at the church."

"Great, I'll see you tomorrow."

"Why don't I come to your house?"

"Perfect," Harriet told her and hung up.

James came up behind her and wrapped his arms around her.

"You are a good person, Harriet Truman."

She turned around, still within his arms and kissed him.

"You're not so bad yourself," she said and smiled.

"Shall we walk these little beasts?" He asked and indicated their dogs, who were circling their feet. "And then go get our son?"

"Sounds like a plan"

✂ -- ✂ -- ✂

A cold air mass still had Foggy Point firmly in its grip when Harriet got up the next morning. She pulled on her fleece-lined running tights and a long-sleeved wool shirt, then stretched in the garage before going out into the cold, damp morning.

The first few steps were torturous, but she knew with a chef for a husband running to burn the extra calories was going to have to be a lifetime habit. She went four miles before returning home and jumping in a warm shower.

"I don't see how you can stand to go running in this weather," Aunt Beth said when Harriet came back downstairs. "I took the liberty of making some tea and heating up the chocolate croissants I brought from the bakery."

"Those wonderful smelling pastries are why I force myself out the door on these cold mornings. If I didn't work at it, I'd weigh three hundred pounds."

"I'm glad you're keeping an eye on it."

Harriet's aunt had ridden her pretty hard about her eating habits when she'd first come back to Foggy Point, and she still wasn't quite sure what that had been all about. She was a few pounds heavier than the insurance charts wanted her to be, but not enough to warrant the comments her aunt sometimes still made. Maybe Aunt Beth was worried about her own health.

She hadn't thought of that before; she'd have to file that idea away for more consideration later.

"Can anyone join this party?" Mavis asked as she came into the kitchen.

Harriet got another mug from the cupboard and handed it to her.

"There's a pot of tea on the table, and I can make coffee, if you'd prefer."

Mavis joined Beth at the table.

"Tea's fine." She held her cup out, and Beth filled it. "What did you both think of the meeting last night?" she asked.

Connie arrived, took a mug from Harriet, and joined the others at the table.

"I thought that blond woman, Crystal was pretty pushy. She's the classic mom who's trying to relive her youth through her child. Her poor daughter will suffer for it."

Mavis took a croissant and a napkin.

"I'd keep an eye on the manager and her husband."

Harriet poured herself a cup of tea.

"What are you thinking?"

Mavis took a deep breath and let it out.

"I'm not sure. Something about the way the girls stood around Simon's chair. Like he was the Pied Piper."

"I'm reserving judgement until I see a session or two of horse therapy," Harriet said. "I'd like to see everyone in action."

✂ -- ✂ -- ✂

Vern Jenkins met Harriet and her carload of people at the entrance to The Outdoor Store, his shop in downtown Foggy Point.

"Come in, come in," he said, and waved them on to the back of the store. "I've set out samples of all the colors and styles in the boots I can offer at a reduced price. And I've brought out a variety of the most common sizes in each style. I checked with Angela at Miller Hill to be sure these meet her requirements, and she assured me they do. I do have more sizes in the storeroom, so if you don't see a pair in your size, just ask and I'll see if we have it."

Beth strode directly to a pair of purple cowboy boots sitting on a stack of boxes.

"I am in love," she said. "Can I try them on?"

Vern laughed.

"Let's measure your foot and see if we have them in your size." He guided her to one of the benches that sat in a semi-circle in the middle of the footwear area. "Everyone is going to need their feet measured. This basket of boot socks is for you to use. Each of you take a pair, and they're yours to keep. They may be thicker than you're used to wearing, but they'll protect your feet from blisters while you break your boots in."

He picked up the basket and handed it to the closest man, then set about measuring Beth's feet.

"I'm Stanley Oliver," a muscular man next to Harriet said to her quietly. "I have a question. If this horse thing doesn't work out for us, can we keep the boots? I mean, I know twenty bucks isn't much to most folks, but it's a lot for some of us."

"Yes, you can keep them," Harriet said, glancing at Vern as she spoke. He nodded slightly and went back to fitting Aunt Beth.

Connie, Joyce, and Mavis measured their own feet, and Joyce then helped the other guys in her group. The people from the homeless camp were reticent at first; but after a few minutes, everyone was trying on boots, looking at them in the mirror, and test-walking them around the store.

Harriet slipped her debit card to Vern when it was time to pay, and after everyone who could pay did, he discretely ran the remaining three sales on it. Then, he held up a small white plastic jar.

"I've given you each a sample of mink oil. Rub this on your boots and set them by the fire or a heater and let it soak in. When they're dry, rub them with an old tee-shirt. Repeat this two nights in a row, and your boots will be well-protected. They'll be fairly waterproof, too."

Joyce picked up the shopping bag that held her boots.

"Thank you, Vern. I think I speak for everyone when I say how much we appreciate your generosity." She turned to Harriet. "And yours as well."

"I'm happy to help," Vern said. "And it wasn't all me. When I talked to my supplier, he gave me an additional discount when he heard what we were doing."

✂ -- ✂ -- ✂

"I love my boots," Aunt Beth said when they'd returned to Harriet's house.

"We bought cowboy boots for our trip last Thanksgiving. The reservation we went to in Arizona is home to a number of venomous snakes, and cowboy boots are very helpful in protecting against bites. I did buy some mink oil, so if you want to stay and slather your boots up, we can let them sit on the floor vent in the studio."

Beth took a newspaper from Harriet's recycle box in the garage and spread it over the kitchen table before unboxing her boots and setting them on it while Harriet went upstairs to get hers

"Mine aren't quite as fancy as yours, but they kept my feet safe from snakes, and I'm sure they'll do equally well preventing damage from horses stepping on my tootsies."

Beth laughed.

"I'm hoping mine will keep me safe from snakes at the stable."

"I don't think…" Harriet started to say. "Oh, got it."

They slathered the paste-like oil on their boots and carried them to the studio, returning to the kitchen for tea and ginger snaps when they'd finished.

"This should be fun," Beth said as she slipped into her jacket and picked up her purse.

"I hope so. One of the homeless guys, Stanley Oliver, asked me if he got to keep the boots if he dropped out of the program. Seemed like he was planning on it being a failure before it even started."

"Let's hope all of them don't have that attitude," Beth said before kissing Harriet's cheek and heading out the door.

Chapter 8

$\mathcal{T}$ he first horse-therapy session was at three o'clock on a cold and foggy afternoon. Harriet had wool socks on with her cowboy boots as well as a down vest and wool flannel shirt.

Simon came into the arena in a different model three-wheeled all-terrain wheelchair.

"Volunteers, you can sit in the stands for the first part of our session. Participants, you will each be assigned a horse. This will be your mount for the duration of your time in the program."

Raven led a chestnut gelding into the arena. She smiled as she walked past Simon.

"We will not be riding today, or at your next session, for that matter. Before we start riding our horse, we need to get to know him or her."

He continued describing the process of haltering and grooming a horse, and then the participants were taken to meet their mounts. For this part, they used volunteers who had experience around horses, including Harriet, Luke, and Emily.

Harriet was paired up with Stanley Oliver. Each volunteer and their participant walked up to Simon, who was now positioned just outside the arena. He referred to a list on his clipboard and then announced the name of their horse and which stall number it could be found in.

When Harriet and Stan stepped up to Simon, the two men glared at each other, neither one speaking.

"I take it you two know each other," Harriet finally said.

"You could say that," Simon said. "Stanny and I served in the Marines together."

Stan scoffed.

"One of us did, anyway." Stan took in Simon's chair. "I see karma's finally caught up to you."

Simon referred to his list, his eyes cold, then looked up at Harriet.

"He's assigned to Lily." he said. "Next."

Luke walked up to Simon with Mateo, and Emily accompanied Joyce. Joyce and Emily approached, and Stan finally stepped away with one last glare.

"So, you and Simon served with each other in the Marines?" Harriet repeated as they walked down the aisle of the barn.

"Simon didn't serve anyone but himself, but yeah, we joined up together."

Stan stopped in front of a stall with a name plate that read *Lily*.

"Is this my nag?"

Harriet tried not to laugh.

"Yes, this is your horse. Let me show you how to put the halter on."

Stan was either the most natural horseman ever born, or he had previous experience he wasn't willing to own up to. He slipped the halter on Lily without missing a beat and led her out of the stall like he'd been doing it every day.

Harriet picked up a green tote sitting outside the stall door. It contained a brush, curry comb, mane-and-tail comb and hoof pick. She followed Stan and Lily into the arena, where they were all to line up while Simon instructed them in their next moves.

Simon and Angela took turns instructing the group in basic horse grooming; and then everyone practiced leading their horse around the arena, the participant on the animal's left and a volunteer on the right. Harriet noticed that when more than a few steps were involved, Stan had a noticeable limp. She'd have to remember to ask Joyce what the story was, as she was certain he wouldn't be forthcoming.

They were learning how to present snacks to the horses by keeping their hand flat, so as to not get bitten, when Harriet spotted James and Jorge carrying foil-covered pans along the front of the bleachers to the food service area. The volunteers took the horses back to their stalls while the participants retreated to enjoy whatever James and Jorge had brought them.

"How did it go?" Lauren asked when Harriet returned from the barn.

Harriet sat down next to her and the other Loose Threads.

"Stanley Oliver is an interesting guy."

"How so?"

"He obviously has experience with horses he isn't owning up to. He's way too comfortable handling his mare. But the more interesting thing is his previous relationship with Simon."

"I'm guessing it wasn't a good one."

"He wouldn't own up to whatever the problem was, but apparently something happened when they were in the Marines together. And Stan has a noticeable limp when he walks very far. I'm wondering if that's something that happened while he was in the service."

"I noticed he was limping."

"I was so busy with Stan I didn't see how everyone else was doing. Anything unusual with the rest of the crew?"

Lauren laughed. "Other than Diandra being scared to death of her horse, no."

"This must have been pretty boring for you and the rest of the Threads, since you don't have to help until they're actually riding."

"I think we all wanted to see what we were getting ourselves into."

Harriet stood up. "Shall we go see if there are any leftovers?"

Aunt Beth gathered her bag and got up.

"Connie and I were thinking the same thing. You know Jorge and James will have brought enough food to feed half the town."

"Lead the way," Mavis said from behind Connie.

✂-- ✂-- ✂

James was putting packages of leftovers in the chest freezer in the garage when Luke and Harriet got home.

"I guess the people at the homeless camp are getting enough to eat," he said as he came back into the kitchen. "They barely made a dent in their dinner."

Harriet put her arms around him.

"I think that's because you and Jorge brought enough food for a whole army."

James smiled.

"Now we have dinner for the next week."

She kissed him, and he went to the sink to wash the serving utensils he'd used.

"What do you think of the new people?" he asked as he ran hot water into the sink.

"I think the jury is still out. She seems nice enough. A little cold, but maybe that's her being professional. There's some sort of tension between the veteran I was helping and Simon."

"Weren't you helping Stan? I've talked to him several times when I've brought food to the camp. He's the most easygoing guy out there. Nothing ruffles his feathers."

"Believe me, Simon does."

"Huh. That's weird."

James swirled his hands around in the soapy water to make sure he hadn't left any utensils behind and then rinsed the whole batch with hot water.

"I'm going to go take a shower," he said when he was finished.

Harriet filled the kettle and put it on to boil.

"I'm going to go sit in my studio and stare at the horse blanket pattern I made from muslin. I need inspiration to strike, and so far, it's deserted me."

James peeked from the kitchen, past the stairs and into the dining room, where Luke was pacing, his phone at his ear.

"Looks like a serious discussion is going on in there. Let me know if anything's up."

"What makes you think he'll tell me?"

"Oh, please. Boys always talk to their moms."

He grinned and pulled her into his arms. She smiled and gave him another quick kiss.

"If you say so."

✂ -- ✂ -- ✂

An hour later, Harriet tossed her colored pencil onto her worktable and sat back in her chair. She was about to crumple up her latest design failure when Luke came in, plopped down in a wheeled work chair and slid over to her table.

"Is this Major's quarter sheet?" he asked, picking up her drawing.

Harriet ran her hand through her hair.

"It's one more drawing that isn't quite right. I've looked at pictures of quarter sheets on the internet, but none of them are anything like what we're making."

Luke looked troubled.

"Oh, don't worry, I'll think of something really amazing."

"I'm not worried."

"If it's not Major's blanket that put that frown on your face, something else must be bothering you. Do you want to talk about it?"

He hung his head.

"It's Emily." he said.

"What about Emily?" she prompted when he didn't continue.

"I don't know if I should be talking about it."

Harriet reached across the table and took his hand.

"It must be bothering you a lot, or you wouldn't be in here looking so miserable."

He took a deep breath.

"You know how we have the new barn managers."

"Yes," Harriet said, trying not to smile.

"Well, Angela is okay. I mean, she's a little strict, but she just wants the barn to run perfectly."

"But Simon…?"

"I know he's disabled and everything, but I think he uses that to get overly friendly with the girls."

"What do you mean, 'overly friendly'?"

"Well, first of all, he calls them *sweetheart* and *honey* and stuff like that. He calls us guys, 'hey, you' and once he called me 'boy'."

"He didn't!" Harriet said, shocked.

Luke's face turned pink.

"That's not the point. I don't care what he calls me. But tonight he asked Emily to bring him something, and when she did, he reached his hand under her shirt."

"I hope she told her parents."

"She's afraid to tell her parents because her dad will make her sell Fable. He already thinks riding is stupid and a waste of money. Her mom supports her, but if she hears what Simon did, she might change her mind about it. I'm not sure Emily could survive without Fable."

Harriet thought for a moment.

"My first answer has to be she should talk to her mom." Luke started to protest, and she held her hand up to silence him. "But, if she's unwilling to do that, there are a couple of options. He's in a wheelchair, so she could take the passive approach and stay out of his reach. I'm not a real advocate of that method.

"I think if he tries something like that again, she should say very loudly and very firmly, 'Stop, that is not okay'."

"Do you think that will work?"

"Unfortunately, most men are bigger and stronger than women, so simply saying 'stop' isn't always going to work, especially if no one else is around. But since there are likely to be people around when Emily is at the stable, and he can't get out of the chair, it should work in this case. I still think she should tell her mother, though."

"I'll let her know you said that."

He stayed in his seat.

"Is there more?" Harriet asked.

"I haven't seen Simon do anything bad to the younger girls, but he does give them candy all the time. And he makes them come right up to his chair. He straightens their braids and adjusts the chin straps on their helmets. It's just a little creepy."

"Would it be creepy if he hadn't made a move on Emily?"

Luke thought for a minute.

"Maybe not, but I think it would. If he was someone's grandpa or something like that it might be okay, but there's just something about the way he looks at females of any age."

"If your instincts are telling you something's off, it probably is. Tell you what, since the Threads and I are working on the horse blankets, we'll make a point of spending some time at the stable and see what we see. If nothing else, it should put a damper on his grabbiness while we're there."

The tension in Luke's shoulders relaxed.

"Thank you so much. And you guys can use Major for a model as much as you want. You may have noticed how much he likes attention. I'll ask Emily if you can use Fable, too. I'm sure she'll say yes. And Fable is normal-sized."

"If we do observe anything, you know I *will* have to take action."

Luke's brow furrowed.

"What's that mean?"

"It means I'll talk to Angela. It undoubtedly won't be a surprise to her if he's as blatant as you've described."

"Don't worry, he is."

"I'll call Aunt Beth and Mavis, and some of us will go out tomorrow."

Luke came around the table and gave her a hug.

"You're the best," he said and retreated back into the kitchen.

Chapter 9

$\mathcal{H}$arriet waited until Luke went upstairs before calling her aunt. She explained what Luke had observed and Emily's unwillingness to tell her parents.

"So, you're thinking we need to be out at the stable to see for ourselves what's going on," Beth said.

"I have no doubt, if Luke and Emily are this distressed, there's something going on. What we need to see is the degree. And I'm worried about the younger kids. They are much more vulnerable. Not that Emily isn't, but she told Luke right away. The little kids won't know what he's doing is wrong."

"We better call the rest of the Threads," Beth said thoughtfully. "It will be a little too obvious if we're all out there all the time, but we can take turns bringing our projects to try on the horse and take more measurements."

"We can take snacks to Major, too. And Luke is pretty sure Emily will let us measure and fool around with Fable."

"Doesn't Jenny have a horse Raven is riding for her lessons?" Beth asked.

"She does. I was thinking I'd call Mavis and Lauren. Could you call Connie and Jenny?"

"Sure, and I'll ask Connie to pass the word on to Carla. I think she was signing Wendy up for pony riding at the stable, so she may be out there in any case. I can ask Jenny to call Deann and Robin, too."

"That should give us coverage. I wonder if any of Robin's or Deann's kids are taking riding lessons. I thought I heard Simon say something about doing some sort of activity with the middle school."

"That would be handy. The more legitimate reasons we have to go out there, the better."

"Okay, let's talk tomorrow morning and see how we did on recruiting."

"It's a plan," Beth said and rang off.

✂ -- ✂ -- ✂

Luke was in the kitchen eating the next morning when Harriet came in from her run.

"I called Emily, and she said you can use Fable as a model for blankets or whatever."

Harriet took a glass from the cupboard and filled it with water from the tap.

"Are her halter and lead easy to find?" she said and drank her water.

"It's in the tack room, and there's a name plate over the peg her halter hangs on."

"Perfect. Do you want a ride to school? I'm meeting the Threads at the coffee shop to discuss our plan. I'll just take a quick rinse off." She glanced at her watch. "We've got plenty of time."

"Sure, if it's not out of your way."

"I'll be down and ready to go in a few minutes."

Luke opened the kitchen closet door and got the dogs' leashes.

"Come on, you lazy bums. Let's take a quick walk while your mother is cleaning up."

✂ -- ✂ -- ✂

"Simon really put his hand up Emily's shirt?" Lauren asked when Harriet had gotten her latte and bagel and sat down at the big table at The Steaming Cup.

"He did."

Connie stirred her tea and put her spoon down.

"That's terrible. I know a riding school is different, but if he was at a public school, he'd be out on his ear for that sort of behavior."

Jenny set her mug down hard.

"Chair or no chair, Brian was ready to go break Simon's head when I told him how he was treating the little girls, and that was without Raven being in the mix. If David were to find out he'd been inappropriate with her, I'm not sure what he'd do."

"That's kind of harsh," Lauren said. "I mean, I know Simon's a jerk, but he *is* handicapped. It might be an ego thing."

39

Jenny shook her head.

"Brian's sister was date-raped in college. It took her years to get back to some semblance of normal. And she's never married or had children. I think she was a little unstable before the rape, but he's convinced it's all due to a jerk she encountered at a party."

Harriet sipped her latte.

"I'm sorry for his sister. That's terrible."

"It *was* terrible," Jenny agreed, "but as I said, she was having problems in college, and according to his mother, she wasn't making very good choices during that period. I know that's no excuse for what happened to her, but she was drinking pretty heavily and using drugs, so her self-protective instincts might have been nonexistent. Anyway, it left Brian with a real hatred of men who prey on vulnerable women."

Connie reached over and patted Jenny's hand.

"*Diós mio.* This makes it especially important for us to be sure he doesn't try any of his tricks on Raven."

"What did I miss?" Mavis said as she joined the group. "Beth and I got sidetracked on our way here. Did we miss anything."

"Nothing important," Jenny said. "Get settled with your food. We were just to the part where we make a plan."

Robin bustled in and in a few minutes sat down with her cup of tea. "What did I miss?"

Lauren sipped her mocha. "Is there an echo in here?"

"I'll take notes," Robin said, ignoring her and pulling out her ubiquitous yellow legal tablet and pen.

"So, what do we think we're doing here?" Mavis asked.

Harriet sat back in her chair.

"I think we're going to try to be enough of a presence at the stable that Simon won't be able to pull anything with the young women there. And if we do see him doing anything untoward, to call him out on it."

"So, how are we going to figure out when the kids will be there?" Connie asked.

Lauren pulled her iPad from her messenger bag and fired it up.

"The stable has a web page that lists the classes they offer and when."

When she had the page open, she turned it toward Robin, who began writing the class dates and times in a column down one side of her tablet.

Aunt Beth broke off a piece of her orange-cranberry scone and popped it in her mouth.

"Can you add up how many hours per week that amounts to? Then we can look at how many hours each of us can volunteer and see how that matches up."

"I'm thinking we won't have to do it forever," Harriet said. "If there's an observing adult hovering around the barn whenever kids are there, I think he'll get the message. After a couple of weeks, we should be able to cut back."

"And if we cut back in an irregular way, he'll never know when we're going to be there." Beth added.

Connie sipped her tea.

"I read a book some years ago that said it took twenty-one days to form a habit. Maybe we can retrain him in twenty-one days."

Lauren chuckled.

"I have no doubt this crew can get their message across, and I'll bet it won't take twenty-one days for him to get the message."

"Okay," Harriet said. "Let's start with the little-kid times first. They're the most vulnerable."

It took almost two hours for them to get their schedules sorted out. Carla joined the group late, but she was also up for taking shifts around Wendy's riding lessons.

Harriet, Beth, and Mavis carried used cups and napkins to the garbage can.

"I hope we're not fooling ourselves thinking we can protect these girls," Mavis said.

Beth wiped her hands one last time on a napkin before tossing it into the can.

"I don't think we're going to change who he is, but I think we can get the message across that he's to keep his hands off our kids."

"That will be a good start. If he really is as grabby as Luke described, we're going to have to do more than just guard our kids."

"I'm a mandatory reporter," Connie told them. "I may be retired from teaching, but my license is still current, which means I still have an obligation to report."

Harriet sighed. "We may need to talk to Detective Morse about this."

Robin stood up and gathered her purse and coat.

"Right now, as much as we believe Luke, it's hearsay. We need to see the situation for ourselves before we decide the next course of action."

Chapter 10

"Did you buy a new outfit for this activity?" Harriet asked Lauren as they got out of her car at The Steaming Cup the following morning.

"As a matter of fact, I did get a new outfit, but not just because we're on a spy mission at the stable. It's been so cold lately my usual jacket-and-sweater scheme isn't cutting it. I've tried walking Carter in my ski jacket, but that's too hot; and besides, it's a bit bulky."

"That long vest is very slimming."

"Beth has given you a complex about weight."

Harriet laughed. "I'm not sure if it's her Jekyll-and-Hyde behavior, nagging me about my weight one moment, then bringing over baked treats the next, or living with two guys who never gain weight, no matter how much they eat."

"On a totally different and more relevant topic, what are we supposed to be doing today?"

"Didn't you listen during the meeting yesterday?"

"I did, kind of. I get that we're supposed to keep the creep from making moves on the kids, and *we* have the little-kid class today, but what are we actually doing?"

Harriet pointed to a canvas bag on the floor of the back seat.

"I brought a piece of muslin and the safety pins for us to make a blanket pattern to fit Emily's horse. I figured we could make her pattern, which will be useful in any case, then we can watch the kiddie class. Emily helps with it, so we can easily watch under the guise of talking to her about Fable's blanket."

"Makes sense."

"Now, can we go in and get our drinks?"

"Lead the way," Lauren said and followed Harriet into the coffee shop.

✂-- ✂-- ✂

Harriet got Fable from her stall and clipped the cross-ties to either side of her halter in the center of the aisle. She had just unfolded the piece of muslin onto her back when Stella Bren came into the barn and strode over.

"Would you mind helping me again? Since you saw how Essy was limping the other day, you'll have a better perspective on whether he's better or not."

"Stay with Fable," Harriet said to Lauren.

Lauren was about to protest, but when she saw Harriet's face, she closed her mouth.

Harriet waited while Stella put Essy's halter on and brought him out of the stall. She didn't need to lead the horse down the aisle and back to see he was limping worse than before, but she went through the motions.

"Do you think it's any worse?" Stella asked when Essy was back in his stall.

Harriet latched the stall door.

"Has the vet been out to see him since last week?"

Stella's shoulders sagged.

"No. He said he'd come this week and bring his portable x-ray."

Harriet put her hand on the other woman's arm.

"Is there some reason you don't want to call the vet? Essy needs to be seen today."

Stella looked away.

"Milo told me I had no business buying such an expensive horse when I don't know what I'm doing. But I insisted. I do know how to ride. I figured if I kept him at a stable, the managers could help me with feeding and the stuff I didn't know as much about."

"He's not going to get better without help, and the sooner the better."

"I'll go call now."

✂-- ✂-- ✂

"That's weird," Harriet said in a low voice when she got back to Lauren and Fable.

"What?"

"That woman's horse cost more than both our cars put together. He's gotten worse and worse for days, and yet she's hesitating to call the vet. A horse is only as good as his feet. If he can't carry a rider and therefore can't be shown, his value will drop to dogfood level."

"I suspect it's one more example of someone having more money than sense. Just because you can afford the most expensive horse in the barn doesn't mean you have the skill to take care of it. Check and see if I've got the darts where you think they should go."

Harriet tugged on the corners of the muslin square.

"I'm making this up as I go, but it looks like it's lying flat on her back and rump and the bottom edges seem square."

Lauren removed the fabric from the horse's back and folded it up, stowing it in the canvas bag. Harriet returned Fable to her stall just as Emily joined them.

"Did she behave herself?" Emily asked.

"Of course," Harriet assured her. "Do you mind if Lauren and I watch your riding class?"

Emily held her gaze for a long moment.

"I think that would be great," she finally said.

Harriet put the canvas bag back in her car and joined Lauren on the bleachers on the near side of the arena. A group of anxious parents were gathered along the rail on the outside of the work area.

Simon appeared in his all-terrain wheelchair.

"Parents and teachers, you are going to need to retreat to the bleachers. Don't worry, our ponies are well-trained, and your children are not in danger." His voice was enhanced by a portable microphone and speaker setup attached to his chair.

The adults shuffled up to the second row and sat down. When everyone was settled, Simon waved, and Emily, with two other young women, led in two ponies each. When they had tied them securely to a side rail, Angela arrived leading a dozen children, each wearing a sturdy helmet on their head.

She assigned two children to each pony, and Simon began talking the kids through basic grooming and saddling of the animals.

"Have you been watching his face?" Harriet asked Lauren.

"Yeah, I've noticed. He has no inappropriate interest in the little ones. Which is a relief, I guess."

"And clearly he keeps his eyes where he should when Angela is present."

"We should have brought stitching. He's not going to do anything in front of all the nervous parents."

"Let's go give Major a treat, and then figure out where they keep the ponies. That'll be Simon's next opportunity to harass Emily."

✂-- ✂-- ✂

44

Harriet and Lauren took the opportunity to explore the area on the other side of the arena while they waited for the class to finish. There were stalls the previous managers had reserved for visiting horses during shows. They could tell by how low the hay nets hung this was where the ponies were kept.

They moved beyond the stalls into the practice arena and were surprised to see Paige Kelley walking around kicking the footing.

"What's she doing?" Lauren whispered.

"Looks like she's looking for something. Do you need help?" she called to the girl.

"My retainer fell out somewhere. I don't even know if it happened here, but my mom said to retrace my steps."

"Don't you have school?"

Paige bent down and picked something up, then tossed it away again.

"I'm homeschooled with tutors so I can concentrate on my riding."

"Okay, we'll leave you to it, then," Harriet said, and they continued out of the practice arena.

"Shall we watch the end of the pony class from this side?" Harriet suggested as they headed back into the large arena. There was a two-tier bleachers on one side of the doorway, and they climbed up to the top.

"Those costumes most of the kids have on look expensive," Lauren said.

"They are, and it's sort of silly to spend that much money when they don't even know if their child is going to like riding. Not to mention, they're going to grow out of them before they wear them out. They could buy sturdy leggings, and those would do just fine."

"Is this another one of those 'living through their children' situations?"

Harriet chuckled. "Pretty much."

They watched as the children climbed onto the ponies and the helpers led them around the arena, one person holding the pony's lead and two others walking on either side, a hand on the child's leg.

Lauren pointed to the middle of the line.

"Look, Mavis and Beth have joined the party."

"That will make it easier to follow Emily to the pony barn without looking suspicious."

The kids rode around for another fifteen minutes before the helpers took them off the ponies and they ran to their parents with excited tales of their first riding lesson.

"Do these kids not realize their parents watched their every move?" Lauren asked.

"Apparently not," Harriet replied and headed for the pony barn.

It turned out they hadn't needed to worry about Emily. A few minutes after the ponies left the arena, they heard the motorized buzz of Simon's chair. He didn't even pause as he rolled into the practice arena. They could hear him talking to Paige.

Mavis came over to where they stood.

"Looks like the girls are safe this time. Simon didn't even give Emily a second glance."

Harriet tilted her head toward the practice arena.

"He may be after a different target right now. I think I'll go see how Paige is doing, looking for her retainer."

"Me, too," Lauren added.

At first, Harriet didn't see Simon or Paige, but then she spotted them in the far corner. Paige was sitting on Simon's lap in his chair. The back of Simon's chair blocked Harriet's view of Simon's hands.

Lauren coughed loudly, and Paige jumped to her feet like she'd been burned.

"Simon was helping me look for my retainer," she blurted as she headed toward them.

Simon sped out the doorway and into the pony barn.

"Paige, you need to not be alone with Simon. And definitely not sitting in his lap."

"That's not what my mother says. She says the more Simon likes me the more he will teach me."

"That's not how it works," Lauren told her. "He's a lecherous jerk getting his jollies at your expense. He's going to keep you right where you are if it keeps you sitting in his lap."

Paige glared at Lauren.

"We'll just see," she spat and hurried back toward the main arena.

Lauren shrugged and looked at Harriet.

"I tried."

Chapter 11

The children had returned to their ponies, and Aunt Beth stood to one side as Emily showed the young riders how to undo the cinch on the saddle and remove it from the pony's back.

"Make sure nothing's trailing on the ground as you carry the saddle and bridle to the tack room," Emily instructed. "Take it to the rack marked with your pony's name, and then bring back a curry comb and a brush from the green tote beneath the saddle rack."

The girls shuffled off to the pony barn's tack room, struggling with the saddles and bridles.

"How'd it go?" Harriet asked her aunt.

"That dirt stuff on the arena floor is like walking in sand, but otherwise, it was okay."

Harriet laughed. "That 'dirt stuff' is called footing. It's a special blend of ground-up tires and dirt."

Mavis joined them.

"Wow. Who knew? I thought it was plain old dirt."

Beth brushed some of the footing off the leg of her jeans.

"Simon behaved himself during the little kids' class, as far as we could see."

"We watched a little, and he didn't appear to have any interest in the little kids as far as we could see, either," Harriet said.

"Different story with Paige Kelley," Lauren added. "We found her sitting on his lap."

"He dumped her off and took off when we showed up," Harriet concluded.

"Sounds like we've found the lower limit of his interest group, then," Mavis said.

Emily showed her two charges how to use the circular rubber-toothed curry comb and the wooden-handled brush, and then came over to join them. They all turned as Simon buzzed across the aisle back toward the practice arena; he made the opposite trip a few moments later.

"He must have been hoping Paige was still there," Lauren muttered.

"Are you okay here?" Harriet asked Emily.

Emily unclipped Robby, the pony she'd been handling, from the crosstie and attached a lead rope to his halter.

"Can you lead him back into his stall?" she asked the two little girls assigned to him.

They nodded, and got on either side of Robby's head and headed for his stall. Emily watched until they were out of sight.

"I'll take these two to their mothers, and then I'm going to brush Fable. I can do it in her stall."

The two girls came back after shutting Robby's stall door and hanging his lead rope on a hook beside the hinge. Emily took them each by the hand. Lauren and Harriet, Mavis and Beth followed the trio into the path around the large arena.

"Open your shoulders," Angela called to a woman riding a sleek black mare around in a circle. "Barbara, your shoulders. Open them up."

Emily looked up as Barbara rode past on the other side of the barrier.

"She's a new student," she told Harriet. "I don't know where they advertise, but Angela has a lot of new private students."

"Do they all board their horses here?" Lauren asked.

"Not all of them, but the barn is filling up."

"That's good, right?" Harriet asked.

Emily looked off toward the main barn.

"I guess so."

✂ -- ✂ -- ✂

Beth, Mavis, and Lauren opted to sit on a bench at the front of the barn while Harriet made one last visit with Major. Stella was standing outside Essy's stall when she approached. Major began nickering and poking his door with his hoof.

"Settle down, big guy," she said and emptied the bag of chopped carrots into her hand.

"I've got the vet coming this afternoon," Stella said.

48

Harriet put the empty bag back in her pocket.

"I think that's wise."

"I do feel bad for him," she said defensively, "It must hurt."

"Hopefully, the vet will have good news for you."

They chatted a few more minutes. The woman was obviously worried about her horse and didn't want to be alone. She went on about Essy's breeding and the long search process they'd gone through to find him.

Harriet's mind wandered as she watched Emily return and take Fable from her stall. She was probably imagining things after all this talk with Stella, but now it looked like Fable was limping.

"Excuse me a minute," she said to Stella.

"I thought since Mrs. Bren was here, it would be okay to bring Fable out of her stall," Emily explained when Harriet came up.

"That's fine, and you're right. What I came over here for—it's probably my imagination, but when you led Fable out, it looked like she was limping. Could you lead her down the aisle so I can reassure myself it *is* my imagination?"

Emily unhooked the cross-ties and reattached Fable's lead. She walked the mare down to the end of the aisle, turned her, and brought her back.

Lauren had joined Harriet.

"Is her horse limping?"

"Unfortunately, yes."

Emily looked at Harriet worriedly.

"She *is* limping, isn't she."

"It's not bad," Harriet said carefully. "But, yes, she's limping. Stella has a vet coming this afternoon. You might ask her who it is, and see if they can look at Fable while they're here."

"Do you think it's bad?" Emily asked, her face showing even more distress.

Aunt Beth and Mavis had come close enough to hear the discussion.

"Don't go borrowing trouble," Mavis advised.

"Wait until the vet has a look," Beth added.

"Do you want us to wait with you?" Harriet asked her.

She gave a weak smile. "Thanks, but I need to clean stalls when I'm done brushing her."

"Okay, well, let us know if you need anything."

Emily led Fable back to the cross-ties.

"Anyone want to stop at Annie's for coffee?" Aunt Beth asked. "I need to get fabric for my horse blanket."

"I need to look at fabric, too," Lauren said. "And how can we not stop at Annie's when we're that close?"

"Well said," Mavis agreed.

"I'm in," Harriet said and led the way back to the parking area.

✂-- ✂-- ✂

Aunt Beth took a tentative sip of her tea and set the steaming cup back down.

"I never would have guessed what a soap opera this horse business is turning out to be."

Harriet sat down beside her at the big library table in the middle of Annie's coffee shop.

"There's potential for drama any time you get a group of people together, but I agree, this bunch has more than the average amount going on."

"You think?" Lauren said with a chuckle. "Let's see—we have the manager's possible pedophile husband, bad blood between one of the homeless veterans and the same husband, the rich horse owner who has an expensive horse with a bad foot, the veteran who is pretending he knows nothing about horses when he clearly does. Am I forgetting anything?"

Harriet laughed.

"Don't forget the overbearing stage mother—Crystal."

"These horse blankets are going to create drama all on their own if I can't come up with a plan," Beth added.

Mavis took a bite of her cinnamon twist.

"I think the solution to my problem is going to be to use a solid-colored fabric in the areas where the darts go. I originally was going to do a patchwork background, but I think when you get to the dart areas, the piecing will really make the darts obvious."

Beth leaned back in her chair.

"I've been worrying about those darts, too. I'm thinking I'm going to do the shaping in a background color and then figure out some appliqué that can go over the darts, to distract your eye from the straight line."

Harriet picked up her mug to warm her hands.

"Very clever, Auntie."

"I'm going to have to do a plain version in muslin so I can envision what the issues will be," Lauren said.

Harriet set her mug down again.

"Good idea."

Everyone looked up as the bell on the door chimed. Jenny came in, bundled up against the cold.

"Can anyone join this party? I was just stopping in to get something warm to drink before I go to Pins and Needles."

50

Harriet pulled out a chair.

"That's what we're doing. We're all trying to get serious about our horse blankets."

"Oh, good, let me get my drink, and you can tell me what you-all are doing."

Harriet sipped her tea as she watched Jenny go to the counter.

"I hope we can pull this off."

Beth patted her hand.

"Have faith, girl. Have the Loose Threads ever failed?"

Harriet pressed her lips together.

There's always a first time, she thought.

Chapter 12

*H*arriet was guiding the head of her long-arm machine through a complicated series of loops and lines when Luke got home from school. He came into her studio with half of the sandwich she'd left in the refrigerator for him and a glass of milk. He stood beside her machine and watched her work, a troubled look on his face.

She reached a stopping point and turned the machine off.

"What's up?"

"Emily texted me while I was on my way home."

"And?" she prompted when he didn't say more.

"This is a little tricky, and it's okay if you say no."

"Let me be the judge. What's the question?"

"Well, Emily said you noticed that Fable was limping." He paused again.

"Yes, and I suggested she talk to Stella Bren about having her vet take a peek at Fable. Did she do it?"

"No, I mean, yes, she asked, but Mrs. Bren's vet came from Seattle, and Essy's foot problem is complicated, so they called the farrier to bring a special shoe, and then they got Angela involved, and I guess the vet left before Emily could ask."

"That's too bad. Did she call our local large animal vet?"

"This is where you come in. Dr. Billings had to have his gallbladder removed—today. Needless to say, he isn't seeing anyone for a while."

"So…" Harriet said, pretty sure where this was going.

"I know you have a difficult relationship with Dr. Jalbert, but Emily said she'd heard that when he was in Africa, he did all animals, not just dogs and cats, and maybe if you asked him, he could come look at Fable. I know it's a big ask, but…"

Harriet looked at the ceiling.

"That is a big ask. The last time I talked to Dr. Jalbert, it didn't go so well."

"Was that at Christmas?"

Harriet nodded, thinking of Aiden's disastrous proposal to his never-before-seen-by-anyone girlfriend during the Christmas dinner that was supposed to be the setting for his best friend's proposal to *his* long-time love.

"Yeah, that would be the last time." She sighed.

"Emily is really worried," Luke said when she didn't speak.

"Okay, fine," she finally said.

Luke set his milk down and hugged her, lifting her off her feet.

"Uff," she groaned.

He set her down quickly, his face turning red.

"Sorry…" he stammered.

She reached out and put her hand on his arm.

"No, honey, it's okay. You just surprised me and squeezed the breath out of me."

Luke sat down on one of her work stools.

"I don't know where that came from."

Harriet took his hand in hers.

"Sweetie, you don't ever have to apologize. You've had such a difficult family life you haven't had much experience with expressing your positive emotions. Hugging when you're happy or feel gratitude is perfectly normal. You don't want to overdo it and go around hugging everyone you meet, but when you're happy, it's okay to let it out."

"It's all so confusing. I mean, I know I've been happy and sad before. More of the latter, I guess. But now that I live with you guys and have Major and Emily…" His face reddened again. "I just feel things so much stronger, and it feels weird, like I'm out of control."

He hung his head and looked at their hands; she squeezed his.

"I think you've protected yourself from feeling too much because you've been so disappointed in your life. Believe me, when I was growing up in boarding schools, it was easier to not feel anything than it was to feel how lonely I was without real parents. I mean, I had parents; they just weren't accessible. I think yours weren't, either, just in a different way.

"And you had all the violence and neglect to deal with, too. So, I'm thinking you shut down instead of feeling how sad you really were. It allowed you to survive, but now that you don't have to worry about your safety, or where your next meal is going to come from, that protective wall is starting to slip, and that's a good thing."

"So, you don't think I'm weird?"

She pulled him into a hug.

"No, I don't. I think you are a perfectly normal young man. And as much as I don't look forward to it, I will call Dr. Jalbert and see if he will go look at Fable's foot."

Luke stood and picked up his glass.

"I'm going to go call Emily."

Harriet smiled.

"Okay, and I guess I'm going to call the vet."

✂ -- ✂ -- ✂

Aiden was with a patient when Harriet called, so she left a message describing the circumstances. She took the dogs out for a walk, and when she got back, Aiden had left messages on her house and her cell phone, which was plugged into the charger on the kitchen peninsula.

"I have to say I'm surprised you called me, but you're right, I am qualified with large animals as well as the small animals I do here. I imagine I'll have a number of requests once word gets out about Billings's surgery. I'd be happy to go out and look at the horse's foot. Can you meet me there in an hour?"

Harriet's shoulders slumped. Of course he'd use Fable as an excuse to see her. But he was doing her a favor, so she couldn't complain.

"Sure," she told him, and rang off. "Luke," she called up the stairs.

He appeared on the landing.

"Aiden…Dr. Jalbert, that is…will see Fable at the stable in an hour. Call Emily, and we'll head out there in about thirty minutes." She went to her cell phone and texted Lauren.

Aiden coming to check Fable's hoof - one hour - need moral support.

Her phone buzzed to signal an incoming text a few moments later.

Okay??? See you there…

She looked down at Scooter.

"Well, this should be interesting."

Scooter whined.

"I know, it's not about me, it's about Fable."

Chapter 13

$\mathcal{H}$arriet called James and filled him in on what had happened, and to warn him she might need emotional support after seeing Aiden.

"I'm sure Aiden will be a changed man now he's engaged to be married," he said and laughed. "You're just another notch on his belt."

"Hopefully, he won't make a scene in front of the kids."

"I suspect since he's there to treat a horse, he'll be in professional mode. You'll be fine."

"Thanks, that's what I needed to hear. It will all be fine. He's moved on and will be professional."

"Call me when you get back."

Harriet assured him she would and rang off. Luke came downstairs as she finished her call, and they headed for the stable.

✂-- ✂-- ✂

Emily and Luke were brushing Fable in her stall when Aiden drove up in the vet clinic's large animal truck. Lauren had arrived moments before.

"Gird your loins, it's showtime," she said with a wicked grin.

Aiden strolled up and stopped in front of Harriet. Her body had tensed, but she relaxed when she realized his presence no longer elicited an unbidden physical response.

"Good afternoon, ladies," he said in his professional voice. "Where's our patient?"

Harriet gestured to the opposite end of the barn.

"The kids are with her in her stall. They weren't sure if you wanted her out in the aisle."

"Let's have them bring her out so I can see her walk."

Lauren took off toward Fable's stall before Harriet could move. Harriet glared at her back as she went. She'd have a few choice words for her friend when Aiden had left again.

"Can you tell me what happened?" Aiden asked, still in doctor mode.

"I'm not sure we know. Emily said her horse was fine when she put her back in her stall yesterday, and this morning, she came out limping."

They both watched as Emily and Luke brought Fable out and walked her slowly up the aisle. Aiden folded his six-foot three-inch frame into a crouch and studied the horse's gait.

"She's definitely favoring her left front foot." He looked up at Emily. "Put her in the cross-ties while I bring the truck around."

He went back to the truck and backed it up to the barn doors, then opened the back. He pulled on a worn leather apron with a split up the middle and grabbed a wooden tray containing various tools before approaching Fable.

"Let's see if we can figure out what's making your hoof sore," he said to the horse.

Luke and Emily stayed by the horse's head, rubbing her face and murmuring calming words to her while Lauren and Harriet moved around to the side so they could see what Aiden was doing.

The first thing he did was walk around her, viewing her stance from all angles. Harriet was pretty sure he was looking to see if she had her weight distributed evenly. When he finished that, he moved in closer and ran his hand over her neck and shoulders and then down her leg, checking for swelling.

"Okay, can you walk her down the aisle and back?" he asked Emily. "Keep her lead rope loose so her head can move freely."

She took Fable from the cross-ties and led her down the aisle. They repeated this exercise several times, trotting and then walking again after Aiden had held her ankle in a flexed position for a minute.

Lauren leaned closer to Harriet.

"So, what do you think?" she whispered.

"She's definitely limping, but it looks like it's only her hoof, not her shoulder or ankle or anything else."

When Fable was clipped into the cross-ties again, Aiden ran his hand down her leg and then picked up her hoof, holding it between his knees.

"Can you slide my toolbox closer?" he asked Harriet.

When the box was in reach, he picked up a tool that looked like a cross between pliers and ice tongs. He gently closed the tool over Fable's hoof, one piece on the outside and the other on the bottom, pinching the hoof between the blades. He moved it around her hoof bottom. Harriet watched closely as he pinched the frog, the triangular-shaped soft area in the middle. Fable didn't flinch.

She let out a breath she hadn't been aware she was holding.

"Was that good?" Lauren asked.

"Yeah, you don't want damage in that area."

Finally, Aiden pinched a spot halfway between the frog and the outer wall of the hoof, and Fable grunted. He set the pincers back in the toolbox and picked up a hoof knife. He carefully brushed the dirt from the bottom of her hoof, and then used the knife to scrape off more. Revealed was a pink spot with the end of a nail sticking out of it.

Aiden rubbed his finger over the nail and bent his head to look closer before setting Fable's foot back on the ground. He put the knife back in the box and chose a pair of pliers. He carefully grabbed the nail head and pulled it out. He held it up so Emily could see it.

"It looks like Fable stepped on a piece of shoeing nail. It's been in there long enough to create an abscess."

Emily's face had gone pale as he spoke.

"What do we do about that?"

Aiden reached out and patted her arm.

"She's going to be fine. We just need to put a soaker bandage on her foot so the abscess can drain. I'm sure Dr. Billings has what I need in the back of the truck—it will just take me a minute to locate it."

Lauren nudged Harriet.

"What's a soaker bandage?"

Emily stepped closer to hear the answer.

"If it's what I've seen before, he'll cut the end off of an IV bag and fill it with water and maybe Epsom salts or something like that. He'll put a disposable diaper over that on her foot and wrap that with rolled cotton. That will be wrapped with something called Vet Wrap.

"The bag will be sealed to her leg with another kind of elastic bandage called Elasticon and the whole works wrapped in duct tape. Usually, they leave that on for twenty-four hours. When you take it all off, it will be obvious if the abscess has drained."

"How?" Emily asked.

Harriet laughed.

"It will stink to high heaven. Most of the time once is enough. Rarely, you have to do it a second time."

"Won't she try to take it off?" Emily asked.

"No, her foot won't feel good enough to try to kick around and get it off."

Aiden returned, his hands full of supplies.

"He had everything we need. Emily, can you stand by her head and talk to her while I put this on? I think she'll feel better if you give her a little sympathy."

Emily stood on one side of Fable's head, stroking her face. Lauren and Harriet stepped back so Aiden could work.

"He seems to know what he's doing," Lauren murmured.

"There's never been any question about his competency as a vet," Harriet whispered back. "It's all the other stuff he struggles with."

"Okay, that's all there is to it," Aiden announced as he stood up, stretching his back. "I'm going to give her a tetanus booster and an antibiotic shot." He returned to the truck to prepare the injections.

"Are you going to ask him?" Lauren whispered to Harriet.

"Ask him what?" Harriet whispered back.

"When he's getting married, of course."

Harriet shook her head.

"Of course not. What am I supposed to say—Thanks for helping Emily's horse, now how about that wedding'?"

"You could be more subtle, but enquiring minds need to know."

"No, they don't."

Aiden returned with the two injections. He ran his hand over the mare's back, and when he reached her rump, held one hypodermic in his mouth and one in his right hand while he patted her with his other. After a slightly harder slap, he quickly injected first one then the other shot. Fable swished her tail but otherwise didn't react.

"Call me if anything changes," he told Emily. "Go ahead and put her back in her stall, stay off her for a week, and if you have a treat, she's earned one."

He carried the empty hypodermics back to the truck, putting the needles in a red sharps container before putting everything else in a small garbage can. He took his leather apron off and threw it into the truck before closing the back doors.

"How are things going out here with the new managers?" he asked. "Dr. Billings has picked up a few patients. Seems like some of the horses came from a fire situation."

"Luke told us that," Harriet said. "The new managers worked at a stable that burned and brought the surviving horses with them."

"Are we sure they didn't burn it for the insurance money?"

"That's kind of harsh," Lauren said.

"It may sound harsh, but not unheard of. These horse folks are the sort that have insured animals put down if they have an injury that prevents them from performing. A horse that could be saved but would be blemished. This is a business, and they treat it as such."

"Wow," Lauren said with a grimace.

Aiden stepped closer to Harriet. Her first reaction was to back up, but she stood firm. He lowered his voice.

"I'm not going to put this in my official report, but that horse's hoof looked like a nail had been driven straight into it. She either has a really incompetent farrier or someone did it deliberately."

"Couldn't she have stepped on the nail by accident?"

"Possibly." He looked down at the ground. "But look how clean the aisles of this barn are. And it would have to have been sticking straight up out of the ground—not impossible, but also not likely.

"That's just my opinion. Maybe horses step on nails here all the time. This one just looks like a perfect nail impression, as if the nail was driven straight in."

"We'll keep our eyes open. I have to say, I'm not impressed with the managers so far. The woman isn't particularly warm and fuzzy, but she hasn't done anything suspect yet. Her husband, though, is a real piece of work."

"Billings said something to that effect, and he's not one to gossip." He looked at Lauren and then Harriet. "I know it's not my business anymore, but you two need to be careful."

"We always are," Harriet said and stepped back.

"How are things with you?" Lauren asked, with a glance at Harriet. "Are you busy working on your upcoming nuptials?"

Aiden's face flamed red.

"I'm surprised Jorge hasn't told you. The wedding's off."

"I hadn't heard," Harriet said cautiously. "I'm sorry."

"Don't be. It was stupid. Everyone knew that but me. She went home, and her parents told her she'd be disinherited. I told my brother, and he threw a fit. He told me I had to go to therapy."

"Wow," Lauren said. "That's harsh."

Harriet looked into his ice-blue eyes.

"Did you? Or are you?"

He stared back at her.

"Actually, I did. I've just started."

"I'm going to go check on the kids," Lauren said and backed away, leaving them alone.

"I'm starting to realize that the problem with our relationship was me," Aiden said when she'd gone. "I've got to do some work before I'm ready to have a relationship with anyone."

"That's good, I guess."

He reached out and took her hand.

"I still care about you, but I get it now, and I'm really sorry for all the grief I gave you."

Harriet pulled him into a hug. She no longer cared about him in the way she once did, but she did feel for him. He'd been through a lot with his family, and it was going to be hard coming to terms with it all.

"Come on, kids," Lauren shouted from down the aisle. "Let's go get a snack before it's time for the veterans to get here."

Harriet was thankful for Lauren's warning, and was standing a respectable distance from Aiden when Luke and Emily came out of Fable's stall.

"I'll come back in a week to see how she's doing," Aiden called over his shoulder to Emily as he headed for the truck.

"Let's go get that snack," Harriet said, and led the way to her car.

Chapter 14

"**W**here do you kids want to get your snack?"

In the back seat, Luke and Emily looked at each other.

"Tacos?" Luke said tentatively.

Emily smiled. "Works for me."

"That will work for me, too. We can swing by home to let the dogs out first."

"My neighbor has Carter for the evening, so I'm good," Lauren said. "I had a feeling things might go this way. And he loves to visit her."

✂-- ✂-- ✂

The waitress at Tico's Tacos seated the group at a large table and instead of giving them menus, she stepped aside as James came from the kitchen carrying a tray of tacos along with a stack of small plates.

Lauren sat back in her chair.

"Okay, now I'm confused. There are only four of us and what are you doing here?"

Harriet smiled. She had called James to tell him about the interaction with Aiden and to let him know they were coming to Tico's.

"Jorge and I are working on dinner for the veterans tonight. Harriet told me you guys were coming here, and I told her I was here, and Jorge would have your snack ready. I know you don't have too much time. And the other half of your tribe had the same idea as you all did."

As if on cue, Jorge arrived with a big bowl of guacamole in one hand and a large basket of chips in the other.

"I figured you wouldn't mind sharing with the rest of your group," he said and set the snacks down.

James re-tied his white apron.

"We have to get back to work," he said. "Jorge is making chili that will be served in bread bowls that I made. They'll be topped with grated cheese, sour cream, and chopped green onions assuming we get busy chopping."

He went back into the kitchen.

The other four Loose Threads came in as Harriet and Lauren were eating their tacos. Lauren waved them over, as she finished her mouthful of taco.

Beth sat down beside Harriet.

"May we join you?"

Harriet set her taco down. "We were waiting for you," she said with a smile. She looked at her taco. "Well, I guess we didn't wait, but Jorge did tell us you were coming."

Mavis sat next to Lauren.

"How did you like helping with the kids and ponies today?" Lauren asked her.

"It was fine. The ponies' legs are short enough it's easy to keep up with them. I have to admit I'm a little worried about being able to do the same with the big horses. That footing stuff is like slogging through sand. Do you think they'll be riding tonight?"

"Ask these two," she replied, gesturing to Luke and Emily.

Emily set her second taco down on her plate.

"I think they will. They all did pretty well with walking their horses on a lead and grooming them."

"They won't let them ride alone at first. We'll lead them, and you guys will walk along on either side," Luke added. "They have a mounting contraption the horse walks into. We mainly use it for people who are physically unable to mount from the ground. It has an arm with a harness attached to put the person in the saddle if they're paralyzed, and stairs so someone can easily get on if they're not strong enough to lift their own weight onto the saddle."

Emily picked up her taco again.

"I'm pretty sure Simon brought that with him. He uses it so he can still ride."

"Angela said she plans on adding a class for disabled kids once things get going with the veterans and the school kids," Luke added.

Harriet glanced at her watch.

"Finish up, kids, we need to stop and get gas on our way back to the stable."

When they were done, Harriet stood up.

"We'll see you ladies out there," she said, and followed Lauren and the kids out to the car.

✂-- ✂-- ✂

Harriet and Lauren were feeding carrots to Major when an olive drab-colored van pulled up outside. A side door opened, and the residents of the Fogg Park homeless camp climbed out.

A man dressed in army fatigues, his gray hair cut in that military style Harriet had heard referred to as high-and-tight, got out of the driver's door. He closed the side panel, and she saw the Army National Guard emblem painted on it. She wondered if Simon had worked his military connections to get free transportation for the group.

The man looked at his watch.

"I'll be back at twenty-one hundred hours," he said before driving off.

Luke and Emily led two horses out of their stalls and into the big arena.

"I guess that's our signal to go find out who we'll be helping," Harriet told Lauren.

When the first two horses were handed off to volunteers, Luke and Emily returned to the barn for two more. Angela came over to the cluster of Loose Threads and other volunteers with a clipboard in her hand.

"Okay, Harriet, you'll be leading Blue—the roan gelding. Mavis?" Mavis raised her hand. "You'll be on one side of Blue's rider, and Beth…" Beth gave a little wave. "You'll be on the other side."

She continued reading names, assigning leaders and side-walkers for each horse.

When Luke and Emily had all the horses lined up, Simon had the veterans and homeless people return to the animal they'd been assigned the previous week. They brushed them down and then were instructed on saddling. Simon buzzed around in his chair, checking the placement of the saddles and the tightness of the girths.

When everything was done to his satisfaction, he had the first horse and rider approach the mounting structure. Joyce, who had been assigned a petite mare named Fancy, used the stairs to mount. One of Angela's students held the mare, and when Joyce was aboard, Jenny and Connie took their places on either side, a hand on her leg. They set off along the rail.

Harriet's charge was a man she knew as Tim.

Finally, Crystal led Lily into the mounting structure and Stanley prepared to mount. As he dropped his weight onto the saddle, Lily took off like a racehorse from the starting gate, her eyes bulging, the whites showing. The lead rope was ripped from Crystal's hand, and she fell back onto her rear end.

Harriet looked away from Crystal in time to see Stanley pull Lily into an increasingly tight circle until her nose was nearly to his knee and she had to stop. As soon as she did, he jumped off and undid the saddle cinch, pulling the saddle off and tossing it to the ground.

"Hold this," Harriet said to her aunt, and handed her Blue's lead rope. Then, she ran to Stanley and Lily.

He was running his hand over the horse's back. He held it up to show her his palm was covered in blood. Harriet picked up the saddle blanket and spotted the thistle that had been attached. She attempted to pull it free, but it wouldn't come loose. She inspected it closer and saw what looked like glue around the edge.

She showed it to Stanley.

"Simon," he spat.

"Why would he harm one of their own horses?"

"He's trying to send me a message."

"And what message is that?"

He stared at her. "None of your business."

Simon buzzed up in his wheelchair.

"Is there a problem?"

Stanley threw the saddle blanket at him.

"Lily didn't like her blanket." He picked up the saddle and Lily's lead rope and led her back to the railing.

Harriet followed him.

"Lily's done for the night. And she'll need some ointment for the sore on her back."

Angela joined them and took Lily's lead.

"Raven, give your horse to Paige and go get Speck for Stanley."

Harriet went back to Blue. Beth was rooted to the ground where she'd left her.

"That wasn't so bad," she said with a strained laugh, animated now that she was no longer holding the horse.

After about five minutes, Raven returned with Speck, Angela helped Stan get mounted, and class resumed.

"Now that we've all seen the expert display of horsemanship by our 'novice rider' Stan," Simon said, his voice dripping with sarcasm, "I'd like you all to begin a slow walk along the arena rail. Side walkers, please keep your hand loosely on the rider's leg and keep up with the pace of the horse.

"Mrs. Kelley?" he called out to Crystal as the horses began circling. "Are you okay?"

Crystal stopped. "I'm afraid I've twisted my ankle."

Simon looked over at the bleachers.

"Emily, take over for Mrs. Kelley." It wasn't a request. Emily hurried to take the lead rope from Crystal.

From then on, Harriet's attention was consumed with leading Blue. She kept the big gelding at a snail's pace until Tim finally relaxed. When Simon finally called a halt, she stayed with Tim and Blue, grabbing Beth's sleeve as she and Mavis started to leave the arena.

"Keep an eye on Lily's saddle blanket over there." She nodded toward the rail where the offending blanket was hanging. "Someone glued a piece of thistle on the underside. See if anyone fiddles with it before it gets taken to the tack room."

Beth and Mavis positioned themselves a few yards away from the saddle blanket in question, slowly gathering up grooming tools that had spilled from a tote box when Crystal fell.

✂ -- ✂ -- ✂

Harriet joined the rest of the Loose Threads volunteers in the bleachers when the homeless veterans headed off to eat.

"Did you see anything?" she asked her aunt.

"You were right about someone messing with it," Beth said.

"How did you know?" Mavis asked at the same time.

"Who was it?"

"Simon," they both answered.

"Just like you figured," Beth continued, "when everyone was busy taking their saddles and bridles off and putting them in that wagon they use to haul them around—"

"Simon came over and used a knife to cut something off the blanket," Mavis concluded.

"It had to be the thistle piece," Beth added.

"Yes," Mavis agreed. "Why else would he be digging around with a knife on the underside of a saddle blanket. He put whatever it was into his pocket, and then took the blanket over to the wagon and put it in with the rest of the stuff."

Lauren brushed dust off the leg of her jeans.

"There doesn't seem to be any love lost between Simon and Stanley. You can tell from their body language."

Carla twisted a strand of her long black hair around her finger. A sure signal the shy girl was about to say something significant.

65

"Stanley sure seems to know how to ride. He knew just what to do when his horse took off."

"You're right," Harriet said. "Lauren, do you think you could dig up any info about Stanley?"

"What's his last name again?"

"If the name on the camo shirt he's wearing is his, it's Oliver," Jenny said. "I noticed when he walked by me."

"Yeah, that's what he said when he introduced himself," Harriet added.

Lauren took her phone from her vest pocket and made a note of the name.

"Will do. If anyone wants to meet for coffee in the morning, I'll let you know what I find," Lauren told the group.

"Steaming Cup at eight?" Jenny asked.

"Works for me," Harriet said.

"I'll see you all then," Connie said. "Carla and I need to go home and rescue Grandpa Rod."

Chapter 15

It was cold and gray when Harriet went out for her run the next morning. It would have been a good day to stay in her studio with the heater on. Instead, when she finished her five miles, she went inside, showered, and after tending to the dogs, bundled up and headed for The Steaming Cup.

She arrived a few minutes early, but Lauren was already at the big table, her laptop open and a large cup of steaming liquid in her hand.

"How's it going?" Harriet asked when she'd ordered her drink and a bowl of oatmeal.

Lauren looked at the oatmeal.

"I see you're going with the hearty breakfast. Are you preparing for a Nor'easter or something?"

"I got cold running this morning. It feels like it's going to snow. And we're about to go stand around the stable for two more hours in the cold."

Lauren slipped her thumb under the armhole of her down vest.

"Wear more down."

Aunt Beth, Mavis, and Connie came in and went to the bar.

"Did you find anything on Stanley?" Harriet asked Lauren.

"I'll tell you when everyone gets here, but yes, I did."

Jenny, Robin, and DeAnn arrived moments later. Carla was right on their heels.

Lauren waited until everyone was settled with their drinks. She closed her laptop and sat back.

"Okay, just so we're on the same page, yesterday when the veterans were having their therapy session, Stan Oliver's horse took off, bucking and running as soon as he mounted her. Harriet discovered a thistle glued to the underside of the saddle pad, which was later, under the watchful eye of Beth and Mavis, removed by Simon Tavarious. Clearly, there is some sort of history between Stanley Oliver and Simon. I went digging to find out what it is."

She paused to take a sip of her coffee.

"Those of you who have seen Stanley Oliver may have noticed he has a pretty pronounced limp. It turns out he was injured when his Marine unit was ambushed while resupplying a forward operating unit in Afghanistan. Stanley and four of the Marines were injured, three more were killed, and the rest of the convoy survived."

"How does Simon figure in?" Beth asked.

"Is that how he lost the use of his legs?" Mavis wondered.

Lauren took a bite of her toasted bagel and cream cheese while the Loose Threads pondered the story so far.

"Okay," she said, and set her bagel down. "I'm on a task force that works on a military contract, so I was able to get one of my contacts from that group to take a peek at some after-action reports. He said it was heavily redacted, but it appeared that Simon was the guy in the unit who was in charge of communications. He was supposed to be monitoring satellite information, making sure the road across the desert was clear.

"Apparently, he missed the report that a small group of locals had come in on horseback and set up on either side of the road. What was redacted was what Simon was doing instead. The nomads placed roadside bombs and took off, and the first two vehicles were hit, including the one Stan was in."

Harriet sipped her hot tea.

"I wonder if Stanley knows what Simon was doing?" Harriet mused.

"I don't know what Stanley knows or doesn't know," Lauren said. "In addition to his leg injury, he also sustained a brain injury. There wasn't any information on that, so I don't know if his memory was impacted or not."

Connie stirred a spoonful of sugar into her coffee.

"It must not have wiped his memory. He knows enough to resent Simon."

Harriet ate a bite of oatmeal.

"Did you learn anything about where he got his horsemanship training?"

"I did," Lauren replied.

"Do tell," Harriet encouraged her.

"It turns out our friend Stanley is a graduate of Texas A&M University, where he was not only a cadet in the ROTC program but also a member of the Parsons Mounted Cavalry."

"So, he knows how to ride," Mavis said.

"Oh, yeah," Lauren said. "The ROTC is also a leadership program, and only about forty-five percent of the graduates go on into the military."

Harriet put down her spoon.

"He must have some pretty major skills. I assume he graduated."

"He did," Lauren said. "I think it said his bachelor's degree is in business management. Makes you wonder how he ended up in the homeless camp."

"I'm guessing PTSD might be involved," Jenny suggested.

Mavis nibbled on an oatmeal raisin cookie.

"With both a head injury and a leg injury, he must have some sort of disability pension."

Lauren sipped her coffee.

"I'm sure he does. They have formulas to figure out combined disability rankings. I didn't ask my friend for that info. Military pensions for the average soldier aren't enough to live on unless you're pretty thrifty, but they do help a lot."

Harriet ate her last bite of oatmeal and put her spoon in her empty bowl.

"Lauren, you never answered Mavis's question about whether the bombing in Afghanistan is where Simon lost the use of his legs."

"It is not. He was in a car accident a year or so ago. Apparently, a stoplight malfunctioned after a storm, and someone in a big truck plowed into his sports car. It was determined to be neither driver's fault, and according to the news reports I was able to find, Simon settled with the county for an 'undisclosed' sum."

Beth sipped her tea thoughtfully.

"If Simon did something that contributed to Stanley's injuries, you have to wonder why he's antagonizing Stanley by putting a burr under his saddle."

Mavis put her cup down.

"I'm wondering why Stanley is in a therapy program as if he's never seen a horse before."

Connie put her cookie remains on her napkin.

"If he has a brain injury, he might not remember he knows how to ride, or he might not be confident in his skills, or maybe he needs the therapy part of the program and he can't get access to a horse any other way."

"Good point," Jenny said.

The group was silent for a few minutes, digesting the new information.

"How are everyone's horse blankets coming?" Beth finally asked.

This started a conversation that lasted until it was time to leave.

Chapter 16

The young riders wore pastel-colored puffy coats as they filed into the barn and headed toward the pony stalls. Harriet, Lauren, Beth, Connie, and Mavis sat in the arena bleachers under a ceiling heater.

Harriet pulled a sandwich bag from her pocket.

"I'm going to go give Major his carrots. I'll be back in a flash."

Beth pulled a piece of fabric from her tote bag.

"I'll be here appliquéing something that may or may not be part of my horse blanket."

Mavis and Connie pulled sewing from their bags, too.

Harriet could hear Major stomping and snorting as soon as she came into the barn aisle.

"Hey, big guy," she called. Normally, she stood outside his stall and fed him his snack; but Fable's hoof injury was on her mind, so she decided to go inside so she could look around and see if there were any stray nails in his bedding. She chuckled to herself, realizing she was literally looking for a needle in a haystack, but went inside anyway.

His stall had been recently mucked out and top-dressed. She didn't see anything suspicious and was about to go back out when she heard the buzzing of Simon's wheelchair.

"What, exactly, were you playing at last night?" she heard Angela say. The buzzing stopped. They must be right outside Major's stall.

"Keep your voice down," Simon said in a harsh tone. "What I do is my business."

"Not when it involves my class horses. Lily is going to be out of commission for several days, if not a week."

"So what? You have plenty of horses here."

"And I need all of them. You know as well as I do that the last manager was fired because of problems she couldn't even control. We're still on probation here."

"That's your problem. I'm just the hired help."

"You know that's not true."

"They aren't going to fire you. If they give you any trouble, we cry bias against the crippled guy."

"Why are you trying to antagonize Stanley Oliver, of all people?" she demanded, changing topics.

"You know darn well what he cost me. If he'd kept his mouth shut, I would have retired with a nice pension. Instead, I was demoted and kicked out."

"You're lucky that's all that happened."

He gave a harsh laugh.

"On the other hand, if I'd been in the brig, I wouldn't be in this chair."

"Leave the horses and the class people alone. We need this job."

"Yes, ma'am," he said. From the tone of his voice, Harriet could imagine him giving her a mock salute.

"I'm not kidding, Si. No more funny business. Not with the horses, not with the riders."

Simon didn't say anything else. She heard the buzz of his chair again and waited in the stall with Major for another five minutes before she came out and returned to the arena. Lauren slid over so Harriet could sit beside her.

"We were about to send a search party."

"I went inside Major's stall, and while I was in there, Simon and Angela got into an argument right outside. I didn't want to interrupt, so Major and I stayed quiet and listened. I'll tell all later."

"Anything happening we need to worry about?"

"Not really."

The little kids each took a turn leading their pony under the watchful eyes of Emily and her cohorts. Once again, the class went off without a hitch, and Simon showed no interest in the little riders. Harriet stood up and stretched as Emily and the other teenagers led the ponies back to the stalls, followed by the young riders.

Paige was riding in the small arena when Harriet and Lauren walked past on the way to the pony barn. Simon buzzed past them, pausing to watch her. She made eye contact and slowed her horse to a walk. Simon spun around and headed toward the stall where Paige's horse was kept. As he went, a black leather bag fell off the back of his chair.

Harriet waited until he turned the corner and then walked over and picked it up. Beth, Mavis, and Connie joined them.

"I think maybe we should go see what Simon's up to," Beth said. "Clearly, there is no interest in these little ones."

"I think Lauren and I will hang out here with Emily for a while," Harriet said; then, when they'd gone, she turned her attention back to the leather bag.

"What do you have there?" Lauren asked.

Harriet unzipped it.

"Wow, I wonder what this is?" The bag held a row of hypodermic syringes on one side and slender drug vials on the other.

Lauren got her phone out and activated the camera. Harriet held the bag flat while she snapped multiple photos.

"Rotate the end vial so I can get the label," Lauren directed, and then took two more pictures. "Okay, got it."

"Time to return it to Simon, then," Harriet said.

"I'm going to stay here with Emily. I know if you're with him she should be fine, but just in case you don't find him..."

"I'll be back in a flash."

✂-- ✂-- ✂

Harriet went to the small arena, but no one was there. No one was around Paige's horse's stall, either, so she moved on to the main arena. Paige and another girl were riding along the rail. Simon was in the center of the arena. His chair had a feature that allowed him to assume a nearly vertical position, giving the illusion he was standing.

"Keep your weight evenly distributed," he barked at Paige. "Megan, ride toward the bit, don't pull back."

Harriet had taken her share of riding lessons when she was in boarding school, and from what she could see, the girls and their horses were doing well. She noticed Angela observing from the bleachers and walked over to where she was sitting.

"The girls look good," she commented.

"They're never good enough for Simon," Angela replied without taking her eyes off the girls.

Harriet held out the black case.

"I think this fell off Simon's chair. By the time I was able to catch up to him, he was already in the arena."

"Thank you," Angela said and took the bag. "Simon gets pain from muscle contracture as a consequence of being in his chair; these injections

73

are for when he can't bear it. He tries not to, but they come on suddenly, and sometimes, he needs help."

She turned back to the riders, and it was clear Harriet had been dismissed.

She was walking back to the pony barn when she literally ran into Crystal, carrying Paige's coat and not looking where she was going. If Harriet hadn't caught her with both hands, she would have fallen.

"Oh, I'm sorry, I wasn't paying attention," Crystal said. "My mind was elsewhere."

"How are you feeling after your tumble last night?"

Her cheeks turned pink.

"My tailbone is a little sore, but mostly my pride was injured."

"I'm glad it wasn't worse. I was just watching Paige in the arena. She looks very good."

"I know everyone thinks I'm being a stage mother, but Paige really is a better rider than Simon gives her credit for. He wants all the students to ride in beginner classes in the show until he's seen how they do. I think he and Angela just want the kids to get a lot of firsts to make the stable look successful so they can attract more students. I don't know what it will take to convince him she belongs in a higher-level class."

"Can't you enter her in whatever class you want?"

"We risk them dropping her as a student, and with the other stable in reasonable driving distance having burned down, we don't have a lot of options unless we move."

"That's tough."

"Yeah, well, I'm not giving up on convincing him."

"Good luck with that," Harriet said, and continued to the pony stalls. She hoped Crystal would give up on pushing Paige to throw her young body at a man who was clearly a pedophile.

Chapter 17

Because of their duties at the riding stable, the Loose Threads decided to have a dinner meeting. Harriet dropped Luke off at the restaurant with James before heading for Pins and Needles. Marjorie was keeping the store open late to accommodate them.

"I've got tea and coffee made," she said as Harriet came in carrying her quilting tote.

"Good, I need something warm. It is so cold outside."

Marjorie looked out the front window.

"The forecasters say we may get snow again by the weekend."

"I guess we better get busy on the horse blankets, then," Harriet said and went into the classroom to get settled.

"I'm working on my appliqué piece," Connie said as she arrived a few minutes later. "My exercise ball is similar in size to the horse's rump, and when I put my first blanket attempt on the ball, it looks lopsided, so I must have measured something wrong. I couldn't figure it out, so I decided to work on an appliqué to put on the blanket when I get it right."

"I'm piecing my background," Harriet said. "I haven't tried to put the darts in yet."

"This is a little harder than it looked at first," Connie said and sighed.

Robin came in carrying two large pizza boxes.

"I figured DeAnn and I should bring dinner, since we haven't been able to do guard duty at the stable this week. I have pizza, and DeAnn is bringing salad."

Marjorie went into the kitchen.

"I've got plates and napkins and plastic forks," she called.

Carla, DeAnn, and Jenny arrived and set the salad, a pan of brownies Jenny had made, and a plate of cookies Carla had baked on the table.

Harriet took a piece of pizza and some salad and sat down. She watched until everyone had their food and was settled.

"Does anyone have any observations they'd like to share now that we've had a few days to watch Simon with the kids?"

Connie set her fork down on her plate.

"I'm not sure where his age cutoff is, but clearly he's not interested in the little pony riders."

"That's what I'm seeing, too," Mavis said. "He's all over Paige, but I haven't seen him show any interest in the littles."

"Does everyone else agree with that?" Harriet asked, and looked around the table. "Okay, shall we concentrate our attention on the young teens?"

Beth sipped her tea and set her mug down.

"I think that would be wise. Connie and I have dropped by some of the bigger-kid classes, and Simon is definitely interested in them. He swatted one girl on the rear end, and then noticed Connie and I watching."

"He had the audacity to look up at me and smile," Connie added.

Robin chewed her bite of salad thoughtfully.

"I wonder if we could get any of the girls to back us up if we reported him?"

Harriet thought for a minute.

"I could ask Luke and Emily and see what they think."

Jenny was twisting the edge of her napkin into a rope.

"I'd rather not involve Raven. She's doing well in therapy, but she's still struggling with setting boundaries and respecting her own body. I don't think she's ready to represent the whole group yet."

Mavis patted her hand.

"Don't worry, we understand. Raven went through so much in her young life before she came to you and Brian. She needs to concentrate on herself."

"Unless Raven's one of the girls he's preying on," Harriet said.

The group ate in silence for a few minutes, each Thread lost in her own thoughts.

Lauren came in.

"What have I missed?"

"Get your pizza, sit down and we'll tell you."

Harriet caught her up as she filled her plate and started eating.

"So, no more little kids, and we'd like to report Simon, but we're not sure any of the girls will back us up. Is that about it?"

"Pretty much," Beth confirmed.

Robin pulled out her yellow legal pad and dug in her purse for a pen.

"Let's work on our new schedule of observation. Lauren, can you pull up the class schedules on your tablet."

Lauren did, and they put together a new schedule of observation.

✂ -- ✂ -- ✂

Luke and James were both home when Harriet returned. James came into the kitchen where she was taking off her coat and scarf and hanging them in the closet. He waited until she was done and then took her into his arms.

"How was your meeting? Did you make any progress on saving the world's children?"

"Are you mocking me?" she asked.

He held her tighter.

"Of course not. I would never," he said with a grin.

"We've determined the little kids aren't in any danger, and we're moving on to the teenagers. How was dinner with Luke?"

"I made an executive decision in your absence."

Harriet pulled loose from his arms and looked at him.

"What did you do?"

He pulled her back.

"Relax, it's nothing drastic. I told Luke it was time we had Emily's parents over for dinner."

"That's probably a good idea. I've waved at them when we dropped Emily at her house, or when we've crossed paths. Should we meet them at the restaurant or at home?"

"I've been debating. I could dazzle them with a gourmet restaurant meal, but that might be overwhelming. Or I could cook at home, but then they might be insulted because I own a restaurant and didn't think they were worthy of a restaurant meal."

Harriet laughed and kissed him.

"That *is* a tough one. I'm glad you care enough about Luke to be worried about what his girlfriend's parents think."

"Thanks. That doesn't help solve my problem."

"We could ask Luke. He's met the parents. Or we could ask Mavis. With five sons, she's had lots of meet-the-parents opportunities."

"Good idea. You ask her, I'll ask him."

Chapter 18

$\mathcal{H}$ arriet had just finished her after-run shower the next morning when her phone rang.

"There's been some sort of incident with Major," Angela Tavarious said. "Can you come to the stable?"

"Is Major okay? Do I need to call the vet?"

"Nothing like that. Can you just come down here?"

"Sure, I'll be right there." She immediately dialed her aunt. "I'm going to be late to our date at the church clothes closet," she told her, and recounted the call from Angela.

"That's fine. Should I meet you there?"

"I thought I'd call Lauren and see if she's busy, but I probably don't need help until I see what I'm dealing with."

She hung up after promising to call when she knew anything. She waited until she was in the car to call Lauren with the speaker phone.

"Are you in the car?" Lauren asked her immediately. "I can hear a whooshing noise in the background."

"I am in the car, but listen."

She explained the call from Angela. Lauren was available and agreed to meet her there.

✂ -- ✂ -- ✂

Lauren pulled into the equestrian center parking lot right behind Harriet.

"Did you stop and take a nap on your way?" she asked as Harriet was getting out of her car.

"You shouldn't harass me, I stopped and got us lattes. I did a longer run this morning and was just getting out of the shower when Angela called." She handed Lauren a cup.

"Well, thanks for this."

Harriet smiled.

"You're welcome."

✂-- ✂-- ✂

As they approached Major's stall, Harriet could see the splintered door hanging by a single hinge. The horse was tied on the far side of the stall. Harriet climbed past the broken door and went over to him.

"What's happened here?" she asked him, handing him a few carrot bits from the bag in her pocket. He nickered softly as he gently picked the pieces from her palm.

She checked his front legs and didn't see any damage.

Angela arrived just as Harriet came back out of the stall.

"As you can see, Major seems to have had a fit during the night, completely destroying his stall door."

"Was anyone here?" Harriet asked her. "Did someone try to go into his stall?"

Angela pressed her lips together before speaking.

"I reviewed the security camera footage. Two of the lights are out in the aisle, so there's a deep shadow along one side. You can see his door open slightly, but it's too dark to see if anyone went in. The next thing you see is the door exploding outward."

"Can you hear anything?" Lauren asked.

"You can hear Major snorting, and a person grunting, but I couldn't tell if it was a man or a woman."

"I'd like to copy the footage," Lauren told her.

"Be my guest." Angela held out the keys to the office, and Lauren took them and walked away.

"What do you think happened?" Harriet asked Angela.

Angela looked down at her feet while she thought for a moment.

"All I really know is someone went into Major's stall, and he didn't like it."

"He's not normally like that," Harriet protested.

Angela put a hand on her arm.

"Don't worry, I don't think Major did anything wrong. He's always been very friendly to our staff when they take him out to clean his stall or take him to the paddock. I have to conclude whoever went into his stall was trying to harm him in some way."

"What are you going to do about it?"

"First of all, I'm going to call the handyman I called last week, and tell him we can't wait any longer for him to come change the lights. If they weren't so high up, I'd change them myself."

"Next, I guess Simon and I will have to take turns walking the aisles all night."

"We can talk to Lauren, but I imagine you could put a motion detector alarm across the main aisle to alert you to anyone creeping around after dark."

"That's a good idea. I've been trying to figure out how we could afford to have a security guard at night."

"I'd be willing to pay for motion detectors for across the aisle on each side of Major's stall."

"I'll ask Lauren how much that would cost," Angela said. "If it's not too terrible, we can handle it."

Harriet stepped back over to the broken door and looked into Major's stall.

"What about him?"

"I've called a local carpenter, but he said he can't come until next week. The big stalls are all occupied. We have some spaces in the pony barn. You probably know the previous managers used those stalls for horses staying overnight at shows, but they're small, and for a big guy like him would be way *too* small. I worry that if he laid down and then tried to roll, he might get stuck."

"Are they that small?" Harriet asked.

"They really are. People kept their horses tied."

"If I can find someone to come fix the door, would that be okay?"

Angela looked at her.

"Seriously? If you can get it fixed, I'd call that a blessing."

"No promises. I'll let you know."

Lauren rejoined them.

"If Harriet can't get the door fixed, what will you do?"

Angela sighed.

"I suppose we could lock him in the small arena. It's not ideal. We could park the trailer in front of the outside door and the pickup across the inside door. As big as he is, if he put his mind to it, he could jump over the sideboards. I don't think he would, though."

Harriet pulled her phone out and tapped in a number.

"Let's not worry about that until I see what I can do."

She turned her back and walked down the aisle as she spoke on her phone, dialed a different number, and then talked again. She returned when she was finished and slid her phone back in her pocket.

"Okay, James's dad will be here in a few minutes to measure the door and then go buy the stuff to fix it. I can take Major out for a walk when he starts doing the work."

Angela looked relieved.

"Thank you so much. And Lauren, do you think we should put motion detectors in the aisles? And can you help figure out what we need?"

"Hardware isn't my main skill, but yes, I can give you some opinions."

Angela looked at her watch.

"I'm sorry, but I've got a lesson."

"No problem," Harriet told her. "I'm going to wait for Will to arrive."

Lauren rubbed her hands together.

"Can we sit in your car and warm up until he gets here?"

Harriet laughed.

"Yes, we can. Even holding this warm cup, my fingertips are frozen."

Chapter 19

"**W**hat's our big fellow been up to?" Will asked when he arrived and joined Harriet and Lauren at Major's stall. "Don't they have security cameras in the barn?"

Harriet and Lauren looked at each other and shook their heads.

"What?" Will asked.

"They have cameras, but they didn't show enough because two of the lights in this section are out. All you can see is his stall door opening a little, and then a moment later, the door exploding," Harriet said. "Unfortunately, his side of the aisle was in a deep shadow."

Will swung what was left of the door forward and back.

"Sounds like someone went inside and did something Major didn't like. Has anything been going on with the horses here?"

Harriet shrugged.

"Not that I know of. Course, we have a pretty limited knowledge of what goes on out here. Luke hasn't said anything. Lauren and I and some of our friends have just started volunteering with the horse therapy program, and so far, we haven't seen or heard anything involving people who don't belong here going into stalls."

Will pulled a tape measure from his overall pocket and started measuring the door opening. He made some notes on a small spiral notepad with a stub of a pencil he pulled from another pocket.

"I threw some wood I had left over from another project in the back of the truck. It should be enough for this. The aisle is wide enough I can back the truck in. Can you take Major somewhere else for a little while? He probably isn't going to want to be close when I plug the saw in and start cutting."

Harriet picked up the lead rope hanging outside the stall.

"They don't have a spare stall that's big enough for him, so we're going to take him for a walk."

Lauren chuckled.

"By that she means she's going to walk him, and I'm going to come along at a safe distance to keep her company."

Will patted Lauren on the back.

"You don't have to worry about Major. He's a big pussycat. I've come out to watch Luke ride a few times, and he's let me take him for a spin. He's very well-behaved."

This was news to Harriet, but she was glad Luke was developing such a close relationship with James's father.

She went into the stall and clipped the lead to Major's halter, then led him out while Will held the remains of the stall door aside.

"Come on," she said to Lauren. "Let's take him out behind the barn and see if there's any grass worth munching on."

There was a door to the outside on the far side of the small arena, and Harriet was headed inside when Raven called to her from the aisle past the pony stalls. She was wearing heavy Lycra riding pants, a long-sleeved sweater, and a fitted down vest. Harriet wished there was a less revealing option for the young women who had to work with Simon.

"Can you watch how Nick is walking? I was supposed to put him out in the paddock, but as I was leading him out it looked to me like he's limping. Angela is giving a lesson, and I don't know where Simon is. I'm not sure if what I'm seeing is normal or not."

"Let's go into the small arena," Harriet said. "Here," she told Lauren when they reached it. "Hold him for a minute."

Lauren's eyes got big, but she took the lead.

"Okay," Harriet told Raven. "Bring him out to the middle and then walk him straight away from me."

Raven did, leading him away from Harriet and then back again. He was definitely lame. Not as severely as Essy, but limping all the same.

"You're right. He's limping."

"What should I do?" Raven asked.

"Let me look at his foot."

Raven held him still while Harriet picked up his right rear foot. She ran her finger over his foot bulb—the leathery area at the back of his foot right where the hard hoof stops. There was a two-inch-long cut across it.

"He's got a cut on his foot bulb. It'll need to be cleaned, and he'll probably need some antibiotics. Put him back in his stall, and then tell Simon or Angela, whoever you can find first."

She rejoined Lauren and Major, and Lauren handed her the lead-rope as soon as she was in reach.

"Shouldn't she be in school?" Lauren asked.

"She and Luke have work-study arrangements this term. They have to write papers about the horse business and what they learned here."

"Is it normal for so many horses to be limping in one stable?"

"Horses get stone bruises sometimes, or they can step on a shoeing nail. In this case, they'll probably never know what cut his foot. If he goes outside, there could be something in his paddock. With as many horses as they stable here, more than one could have a foot injury at the same time."

"You'd think you'd be careful about your nails if shoeing horses was your business."

"A horse might have kicked out while the farrier was shoeing it, causing him to drop his nails, or he could have dropped a box. It was only one nail that caused a problem so far."

"Yeah, but still."

Major poked Harriet with his nose.

"Okay, big guy. Let's go outside."

✄ -- ✄ -- ✄

Major was happy to be outside. Angela hadn't been letting most of the horses out into the paddocks because of the frigid weather. Major didn't have a heavy blanket yet, so he'd been kept inside. She was pretty sure neither Major or Luke cared if going outside caused his coat to become long and fuzzy for the winter, but Angela and Emily were both encouraging Luke to enter the beginning class in the upcoming show, which would mean Major's coat should be as sleek as possible.

Major found a patch of grass he liked and grazed, pulling Harriet along as he mowed a section at a time.

Finally, Lauren looked at her phone. They'd been outside for thirty minutes.

"Can we go into the arena or the aisle or something? I'm freezing."

Harriet pulled Major's lead, struggling to get him to raise his head.

"I'm a bit chilly myself. We can check and see how much more time Will needs then walk around the little arena as long as no one has a lesson there."

Will reported he needed about thirty more minutes. Harriet and Lauren were on their way to the small arena when they turned the corner into the pony aisle and came across Raven and Simon. She was trying to ask him about Nick, and he was running his hand up the inside of her leg as she stood beside his wheelchair.

"Raven," Harriet called out.

"Oh, hi, Harriet," she answered, as though nothing was wrong.

"I'll get the vet out here to check Nick," Simon said, and buzzed off in the opposite direction while Raven came over to Harriet and Lauren.

"Sweetie," Harriet began, trying to figure out what she could say that wouldn't alienate the girl. "I know you like being here learning to ride, and I know Simon is a trainer, but that doesn't give him the right to touch you like that. If he can't keep his hands off you, I'm sure Jenny can find you other places to ride."

"I don't want to ride somewhere else. I want to be here with Luke and Emily and the other kids. Besides, it's no big deal. Men always act that way. Unless I go to a convent, and I'm not sure they have horses."

"Raven," Lauren tried, "not all men act that way, and you don't have to put up with it."

"Look, I have to go do my chores. Thanks for your advice, but really, I'm fine. I've dealt with creeps much worse than Simon. He's nothing. Besides, he can't get out of that chair, so he can't really do anything." She turned to go.

"Him being in a chair doesn't make it okay," Harriet said.

They watched her go down the aisle in the same direction Simon had gone.

"He is such a slimeball," Lauren said.

"I don't even want to know what has happened in Raven's past that makes her think an adult groping her, just because he can, is okay."

Lauren shook her head.

"The real question here is what, if anything, do we say to Jenny?"

Harriet rubbed her free hand over her face.

"That's a tough one. We need to tell her, though. I know she has Raven seeing a therapist. If she reacts badly, and takes Raven out of her riding classes and the upcoming show, Raven will be devastated."

"Maybe we should run it by one of the elders before we talk to her."

"We can talk to my aunt or Mavis or both. I can text Aunt Beth and see if they're available after this, if you're free."

"Let me check my emails, and I'll let you know."

✂-- ✂-- ✂

Mavis was picking up dropped branches in her front yard and carrying them to a rusted wheelbarrow nearby when Lauren and Harriet arrived.

They'd had to wait for Lauren to go back to her office for a few hours, and for Aunt Beth to finish cooking food for the local Meals on Wheels program.

Harriet parked by the fence in front of the cottage, leaving room for her aunt's VW beetle closer to the sidewalk.

"I don't see that we have an option here."

Lauren arranged her wool scarf so it covered her neck and chin.

"I guess it's just a matter of how we say it. I'm with you—we can't not tell her no matter what we think her reaction will be."

"Go on ahead in," Mavis called. "I've got tea laid out on the table. I need to dump this last barrow full before I join you."

"Can I help?" Harriet asked.

"No, no, I need the exercise. Go in before you freeze to death."

They went, and were settled at the dining table when Mavis came in, followed by Beth.

"Has something else happened?" Beth asked. "Your text was rather cryptic." She took off her coat and hung it on the back of her chair before sitting down.

Harriet picked up her mug of tea to warm her hands.

"It's a bit of a delicate situation, and Lauren and I want some advice about how to handle it."

Mavis finished washing her hands and joined them.

"Tell us what's going on."

Harriet let out a breath.

"I was looking for Raven," she began.

"We were at the stable walking Major while Will was fixing his stall door," Lauren interjected.

"Raven asked me to look at one of the horses that was limping, and I suggested she find Simon or Angela to let them know the horse had a cut that needed attention. When I saw her again later, she was talking to Simon, telling him about the horse, and he was running his hand up her leg in a very inappropriate way."

"You have to tell Jenny," Mavis said as soon as Harriet had finished.

Lauren stirred her tea.

"We figured out that part."

"We know Jenny has to be told, the question is, exactly how? Raven begged us not to say anything for fear they'll not let her ride anymore," Harriet said.

Aunt Beth leaned back in her chair and studied the ceiling.

"That's a little harder. I'm not sure there's an easy way to say 'someone's groping your daughter, but don't do anything'. She's going to go ballistic."

"Would you like us to go with you?" Mavis asked.

Harriet sipped her tea for a moment.

"No," she finally said. "I think having all of us show up will just make it seem even worse than it is."

"You're probably right," Beth said.

"Let's finish our tea and go get it over with," Lauren said grimly. "It won't be easier if we wait."

Mavis stood up.

"I've got some double chocolate chip cookies I made this morning. You'll need fortification before you go." She fetched her cookie jar and set it next to the napkin holder that always occupied the center of her table.

"These are really good," Harriet said around a bite of cookie.

"You two need to quit stalling." Beth said and picked up their empty teacups. "Mavis can pack you a couple of cookies for the drive over to Jenny's."

Mavis bagged the cookies and sent them on their way.

"Call us when you're done," Beth said as they walked out the door.

Chapter 20

"**H**ello, come in." Jenny was clearly confused. "Did I forget a meeting?" she asked, looking from one to the other.

Harriet stood just inside the door with her hands in her coat pockets.

"No, and we should have called before we came over."

Jenny held her hand out.

"Let me take your coats. We can talk in the living room."

They handed off their coats then followed her to her formal living room. Harriet sat on the edge of a chintz-covered sofa. Lauren took a matching side chair, hands in her lap.

"You guys are scaring me," Jenny said as she sat down beside Harriet.

They heard a door open somewhere in the house.

"Brian is about to go pick up Raven at the stable."

"Actually, that's what we wanted to talk to you about. We were just out there, and saw something disturbing," Harriet said.

"And there's not an easy way to tell you about it," Lauren added.

"Raven asked me to look at a horse," Harriet explained again, "and I did and told her she needed to tell either Angela or Simon they needed to take care of the horse. A little later, we found her telling Simon."

"That doesn't sound troubling," Jenny interrupted.

"The troubling part is Simon. He was groping her leg, and not in an innocent way. He stopped and took off when he saw us," Harriet continued.

"We told Raven it wasn't okay," Lauren said.

Harriet put her hand on Jenny's arm.

"She begged us not to tell you. She doesn't want you to pull her out of the riding classes."

Lauren sat back in her chair.

"It was sad. She basically said that's the way men are, and it didn't bother her."

"I'll talk to her," Jenny said. "And her therapist. The question is, what to do about him. Do I call the police? Do I talk to the wife?"

Jenny's husband came down a hallway, stopping briefly to grab a jacket from the hall closet, then stormed out the front door, mumbling as he went.

"Did he just say, 'I'll kill him'?" Lauren asked.

"That's what I heard," Harriet said and stood up. "We better get out to the stable."

"I'm coming, too," Jenny said.

"I think we better call Detective Morse," Lauren said.

Jenny got in the back seat of Harriet's car while Lauren and Harriet climbed in the front.

"Do we have to?" Jenny whispered.

Lauren turned around and looked at Jenny.

"It's for his own protection."

Tears filled Jenny's eyes as Lauren dialed and Harriet drove to the stable.

✄ -- ✄ -- ✄

Jenny jumped out of the car as soon as it stopped. She was halfway across the parking lot before Harriet had the car parked and locked. She and Lauren ran to catch up.

"Hey, wait up," Harriet called out.

Jenny paused.

"We don't want to go running into the stable. We could spook a horse and cause an accident if someone is in the aisle." Harriet put a hand on Jenny's arm, holding her back. "Besides, we don't know if anything is going on."

At that moment, they heard a loud male voice—Brian.

"You sorry excuse for a human. How dare you put a hand on my daughter!"

Jenny broke away and hurried into the barn. The main aisle was empty. She ran on toward the pony barn, while Harriet stopped and listened. Simon shouted back at Brian.

"Maybe you shouldn't send your foster daughter to the barn tarted up in skintight clothes and sexy makeup."

"Don't you dare try to make this about the child. She's an innocent."

Harriet and Lauren arrived at the arena entry from the barn. Detective Morse had already arrived, and was on the opposite side of the arena with Angela. They all watched in horror.

Brian stood over Simon in the middle of the arena. He grabbed the front of Simon's jacket with one hand and delivered several hard blows to his face with the other. Angela shrieked, and Simon clutched blindly for the controls to his chair. Brian's face was red with rage. He reared his fist back to deliver another blow, then grabbed Simon instead and pulled him from his chair, throwing him down on the dirt footing.

"Keep your hands off Raven," he shouted and whirled around toward the exit.

Detective Morse hadn't waited for the episode to play out. She jumped the arena side wall and hurried to the center of the arena, but she only arrived in time to grab Brian as he turned. She pulled his left arm around his back and clipped a handcuff to his wrist before he could react. She quickly grabbed his other arm and hooked the second cuff on.

"Brian Logan, I'm arresting you for assault. You have the right to remain silent…"

Harriet put her arm around Jenny's shoulders as Morse continued reciting Brian's Miranda rights.

"Come on," she said. "We'll meet them at the police station."

Lauren had her phone to her ear. She spoke briefly, then disconnected and put it in her pocket.

"Robin will meet us there. So will Mavis and Beth."

Jenny started crying.

"Thank you."

Harriet guided her toward the parking lot. Lauren came up on her other side.

"I can't believe Brian did that. I knew he had issues with abusers, but he's never been violent. Do you think they'll take Raven from us? They can't do that, can they?"

"Let's take it one step at a time. We'll get you to the police station and see what Robin says," Harriet said.

They passed an ambulance and a patrol car as they pulled onto Miller Hill road. Harriet hoped for Brian's sake the ambulance was just a precaution taken by Detective Morse.

✂ -- ✂ -- ✂

Beth and Mavis were sitting in the FPPD waiting room when Harriet, Lauren, and Jenny arrived. Mavis stood when they came in.

"Robin is in with Brian and Detective Morse."

Jenny slumped into a worn plastic chair beside Beth.

"I can't believe he hit a man in a wheelchair."

Lauren poured a cup of coffee from a carafe that sat on a table across the room and brought it to Jenny.

"Just because he's in a wheelchair doesn't make him a saint. I suspect Simon was a jerk before his accident, and it didn't change after."

"Anyone else want coffee?" Harriet asked.

Mavis and Beth did, so Harriet and Lauren both returned to the coffee table.

"Unless Robin has a judge in her pocket, I can't see how this can turn out any way but really bad," Lauren whispered.

"I don't think she does," Harriet whispered back. "I think his only hope is to get a judge who is hard on child abusers and sympathetic to the victims' parents."

Lauren stirred sugar into Mavis's coffee.

"Maybe."

Harriet gave her aunt the coffee and then pulled her phone from her pocket and typed in a text.

"James will go out to the stable and pick up Raven," she said to no-one in particular.

Jenny drank her coffee and began shredding the edge of her cup, while Mavis pulled a plastic sandwich bag containing a stitching project from her purse. The bag contained pre-cut pieces that were already pinned together and waiting to be stitched. A piece of felt held half a dozen pre-threaded needles.

Beth took the cup from Jenny, and Mavis handed her a pinned piece and a needle. Jenny took the project and began carefully stitching it together. The colors were the rusts and greens favored by Mavis as opposed to the pastel colors Jenny usually worked with, but Harriet guessed Jenny didn't even notice.

It was another hour before Robin came back into the waiting room.

"Brian is going to have to stay here overnight. He'll be arraigned tomorrow. What happens after that will depend on how seriously Simon is injured. If his injuries are considered minor, and he chooses not to press charges, this could be all over."

"If Simon is injured?" Harriet asked.

"Chances are it will be fourth-degree assault, which is a gross misdemeanor. At worst, Brian would be sentenced to up to ninety days in jail, but that's unlikely. Usually, a person is given probation. Especially if he has no other record."

"Of course, he doesn't," Jenny said indignantly.

"He should be good, then. I'm going to strongly argue the child-abuse motivation," Robin assured her. "That being said, there's nothing more we can do here. Everyone needs to go home. I'll let you know what time his arraignment will be when I find out."

"I need to see Raven," Jenny said and stood up.

"James is bringing her here," Harriet stated again, and Jenny sat back down, covering her face with her hands.

"This is such a mess."

Chapter 21

Harriet made a big plate of peanut butter and jelly sandwiches and set it on the kitchen table. She poured a glass of milk for Luke and carried it to the table with her cup of tea.

"So, what happened after Lauren and I took Jenny home?"

James sat down with his cup of coffee.

"I talked with one of the paramedics as I came in. Simon refused a trip to the hospital. Apparently, he wasn't badly injured. Black eyes, cut lip. He said Brian could have hurt him a lot worse if he'd wanted to."

Luke tore his sandwich half into two pieces and stuffed a piece into his mouth, chasing it with a big gulp of milk.

"He deserved it. Now maybe he'll keep his hands off Emily."

"I wouldn't count on it. That's not the sort of behavior that leaves a person very easily, I would think."

Harriet sipped her tea then set her cup down.

"Hopefully, Brian will get out of jail tomorrow, since Simon wasn't hurt that bad."

"Especially in light of Simon's poor behavior," James said.

"Do you think they'll make Raven go somewhere else?" Luke asked.

She knew the "they" he referred to was Children's Services. The same people who had controlled most of his life.

"I think they'll talk to Brian and Jenny and give them a warning, but I don't think they have enough families willing to take teenagers to just eliminate them as foster parents after one incident," Harriet said.

"Especially since he was protecting Raven, not harming her," James added.

"I hope not. I think they're good parents for her."

Harriet stood up.

"We'll know more tomorrow." She set her mug in the sink. "I'm going to take the dogs out and then go ponder my horse blanket."

"I'm going to find out how good Luke is at video hockey, once he runs out of PB and J," James said with a grin.

Luke grinned back at him.

"Better than you, old man," he said, grabbing the last sandwich half and racing up the stairs to the TV room.

✂-- ✂-- ✂

It was cold and gray when Harriet woke the next morning. She was tempted to just bury herself in her covers, but then she thought of all the tea and cookies she'd been consuming lately and dragged herself out. She did pull on an extra shirt over her usual outfit before going downstairs and putting on her running shoes.

She didn't break any speed records, but she did manage to complete five frosty miles without incident. As she rounded the last turn before heading for her driveway, her aunt's silver beetle pulled up beside her. Harriet jogged in place as Beth rolled down the window. Mavis, in the passenger seat, leaned toward the open window.

"Good morning, do you mind if we join you for coffee?"

Harriet smiled. "You don't need to ask."

Mavis held up a foil-covered baking pan. "I made cinnamon rolls."

"Of course you did."

Beth looked over the top of her glasses.

"We invited Connie, too."

"Let me get in and get a quick shower while you wait for her," Harriet said and then took off running.

✂-- ✂-- ✂

"There she is," Beth said as Harriet came into the kitchen.

Harriet went to the cupboard and selected the mug Luke had given her for Christmas.

"What are you three up to?" she asked as she prepared her tea.

Mavis had already set plates at each of their places, and now took the foil off the rolls.

"We wanted to talk about what happened at the stable yesterday, and we weren't sure if Jenny or Raven would be there today."

Harriet sat down with her tea and put a roll on her plate.

"Connie, did Beth and Mavis catch you up on yesterday's events?"

"They said Brian punched Simon and threw him onto the ground."

"According to Luke, Simon has black eyes and a cut lip. I'm guessing maybe a broken nose, too, but he didn't go to the hospital."

Mavis ate a forkful of roll.

"That should help Brian. If Simon isn't badly injured, I mean. Robin says people in cases like this usually get probation, anyway."

"I suppose it's too much to hope Simon will drop the charges," Connie said.

Harriet sipped her tea, savoring the warmth.

"I think there's a good chance he'll drop the charges. It can't possibly be good for a business where most of the clients are female children to have one of the instructors involved in an altercation where an angry dad is accusing him of molestation."

"You're right," Mavis agreed. "Angela will want it swept under the rug."

"How can we help Jenny and Raven?" Harriet asked.

Connie set her teacup down.

"I'm not sure we can. Raven might not see what Brian did as a good thing. Jenny is going to be mad at him for losing control. And Brian is going to be confused as to why the women in his house see *him* as the villain."

"All we can do is listen," Mavis said.

"Anyone want to split a roll?" Harriet asked.

Aunt Beth put a roll on her plate and cut it in half.

"Here," she said, and handed Harriet the larger half and then laughed. "I'm going to have to start running with you if I keep this up."

Mavis laughed.

"That'll be the day."

✂-- ✂-- ✂

Mavis smoothed the foil over the cinnamon roll pan, crimping it around the edges.

"Do you think Simon will be teaching his morning lessons? Connie and I are supposed to be monitoring."

Harriet carried the empty mugs to the sink.

"We might as well go find out. The veterans are supposed to be riding after that session, and I'd like to see how Major did with his new stall door and also check in on Fable and her sore hoof before they arrive."

✂-- ✂-- ✂

The group split up when they reached the arena complex, with Harriet going to the barn and the other three to the arena. The barn was a hive of activity.

Aiden was bent over Fable's wrapped hoof, removing layers of packing and dropping them in a bucket, while Emily stood at her head, rubbing her face and crooning at her. Farther down the aisle, Stella stood by Essy's head while a man Harriet didn't recognize—presumably the Seattle vet—held the horse's hoof between his knees.

Harriet stopped at Major's stall and went in, feeding him a handful of carrot sticks and examining his new door. There were no marks on it.

"Good boy, you didn't kick your new door."

He nickered a response. She didn't speak horse, but imagined he was pointing out that no one had tried to get in his stall during the night.

"Hey," Aiden said when she approached Fable.

"How's the patient?"

He stood up, rubbing his back as he straightened.

"Much better. The abscess drained, so that's good. We'll clean it out and put a wad of cotton soaked in iodine into the hole, and then put a treatment plate on it. She can be ridden with the treatment plate, but if it were me, I'd give her another day or two just to be really careful."

Harriet noticed a tear on Emily's cheek.

"Sweetie, she's going to be fine."

"But what if she wasn't? I don't know what I'd do."

Harriet hugged her, and Aiden looked at her wide-eyed.

"Luckily for you, Dr. Jalbert was able to fix her sore, and she'll be just fine." Harriet stepped back. "I'll stay here with Fable for a minute while you go to the restroom and splash some water on your face and pull yourself together."

Emily smiled through her tears and left for the bathroom.

"Whew," Aiden said when she was out of earshot. "I'm not used to teenage girls."

Harriet smiled.

"Everything's a little dramatic at that age." She glanced down the aisle. "Do you have any idea what's going on down there?"

"That guy is a specialist from Seattle. He and I got here before the owners did, and he showed me the x-rays. He's pretty sure they were riding the horse after he suffered his initial injury. His coffin bone is broken, and it's kind of messy."

"Stella said he was limping, and then he quit limping, so they went ahead and took him to a horse show. When they got back, he was *really* limping."

"There's no way he stopped favoring it with that sort of break."

Harriet held her hands out.

"I'm just the messenger. It's what Stella told me."

"I wonder if she told her fancy vet."

"Who knows."

Emily came back and let Fable out to eat some grass. Aiden pulled a note from his pocket.

"I'm supposed to look at another horse—Nick? The stable manager called me last night. Apparently, her husband had some sort of accident, so she was busy taking care of him and couldn't deal with the horse."

"I'll show you where he is." Harriet turned and went to the front of the barn. She went into Nick's stall, clipped on his lead rope, and led him out. He was definitely favoring his foot.

"He seems to have cut the foot bulb," she said.

Aiden pulled a pair of fresh disposable gloves from his back pocket, donned them, and picked up Nick's right rear foot. He brushed the dirt off the area and poked around at it before setting the foot back down.

"Your diagnosis is correct, Doctor," he said and laughed. "If I remember right from my days at school, this is a fairly common injury. It doesn't look too deep. If they keep it clean, he can probably get by without stitches." He handed Harriet his phone. "Will you take a couple of pictures for me while I hold his foot up and point at it. I'd like to double-check with Dr. Billings to be sure he doesn't think we need to do more."

Harriet cross-tied the horse and took the pictures, handing the phone back when she was finished.

"I'll call the manager after I talk to Billings," Aiden said.

Harriet put the lead back on Nick and unclipped him from the crossties. She started to walk him away but stopped and turned back to Aiden.

"Is it just me or does this stable have more than your average number of foot injuries?"

Aiden thought for a minute.

"Hoof injuries aren't uncommon, but this many this close together *is* a little unusual."

"Thanks for taking care of them," she said, and led Nick back to his stall.

When she returned, he was gone.

Chapter 22

$\mathcal{H}$arriet washed her hands and then went to the large arena, where Simon was working with a woman who looked to be in her late thirties or early forties. Even with Luke's warning, she was shocked by his appearance. His left eye was swollen shut, and that whole side of his face was black-and-blue. His lip had a poorly applied butterfly Band-Aid, attempting to hold an ugly slash closed.

"Lacy, look where you're going," he called out.

Lacy was clearly a beginner. She was riding a dark-bay horse who was looking around the arena, not paying attention to her rider at all.

"Lacy," Simon called and then again, louder. "Lacy, make sure your horse is looking where *you're* looking. Right now, he's watching the audience and thinking about the hay back in his stall."

Harriet continued watching as she climbed the bleachers and sat down next to Mavis.

"How are things?"

Mavis shook her head.

"According to the schedule, this was supposed to be a group of girls from the high school."

"I guess they don't reflect every change they make on their website," Connie said.

Aunt Beth leaned across Connie so she could speak quietly.

"Does he know what he's talking about?"

Harriet gave a small sigh.

"As much as we don't like him as a person, he seems to be a good trainer. The rider shouldn't have so much slack in her reins, she shouldn't be slumping, the horse should be paying attention to the signals she's giving him, if she was actually giving him any. She's clearly a beginner."

Simon pulled a cell phone from a side pocket in his chair and began making a video of the rider.

"I'm going to send you a video of how you look riding around here. I'll also send you a link to our YouTube channel. You can subscribe and then watch videos of experienced riders. Start with the one labeled *Beginner Class*, and you'll see what we're trying to achieve here."

"Wow, they have a YouTube channel," Connie commented. "Do all stables do that?"

Harriet laughed. "Who knows, but I'm not surprised. Technology is everywhere."

The veterans arrived as Lacy finished her lesson. They sat in the front row of the bleachers, waiting for their session to begin. Simon, in his chair, was blocked from view by Lacy and her horse. When Lacy led her horse from the arena, Stan started laughing loudly.

"What happened to you, Simon? Karma finally catching up to you? Couldn't happen to a more deserving guy." He laughed and clapped his hands.

Harriet was positioned in just the right spot she could see the laugh was forced, not reaching his eyes.

Simon glared at him with his one eye.

"Shut up, Stan, just shut up." He spun his chair and crossed to the opposite side into the pony barn.

"I'd sure like to know exactly what happened between them in the Marines," Harriet said quietly.

"Clearly something traumatic," Aunt Beth replied. "At least from Stan's point of view."

Emily brought the first horse in and tied it to the side rail before returning to the barn for the next one.

Harriet stood up.

"I'm going to go see if I can help Emily. I haven't seen Raven this morning, so she might be doing this solo."

She found Emily in the barn putting a halter on Blue, the roan horse that had been assigned to Tim.

"Can I help you bring horses out?"

Emily smiled.

"That would be great. Raven isn't here this morning. I guess that's not surprising, but no one called, so we couldn't get another helper."

"Who shall I bring?"

"Can you get Lily? Dr. Jalbert gave us a moleskin circle to put around her sore so she can be ridden without making it worse."

"Perfect," Harriet said, and headed to the mare's stall. She'd wondered what they would do for sufficient mounts, given the spate of hoof injuries.

Angela was in the arena when Harriet brought the last horse to the rail.

"Any sign of Simon?" Harriet asked her aunt while the veterans were brushing their horses before saddling them.

"None. Angela came out and announced that, due to an unfortunate injury, Simon wouldn't be working with their class this time."

Apparently, Simon wasn't up to another confrontation this morning.

With him out of the picture, the group made quiet progress. Joyce appeared to have some riding experience, but Diandra remained terrified of her mount.

Harriet noticed Jorge come in with a cooler as the session was coming to a close. Lunch, she assumed.

✂-- ✂-- ✂

The veterans were eating in the dining area off the end of the arena and the horses had been put away when Robin came breezing into the entry where Harriet, Beth, Mavis, and Connie stood waiting so Beth could talk to Jorge.

"Oh, good, I caught you," Robin said. "I thought you'd want to know about Brian. He and Jenny said it was okay to tell you. He's home, and no charges will be brought. As we suspected, Simon wasn't interested in pursuing them, and given his bad behavior, the court didn't want to pursue it, either. They warned Brian to call and report Simon if any further incident happened with Raven." She shook her head. "What a mess."

Beth pulled a paper from her purse and scanned it.

"If this schedule is correct, there should be a level-one class taught by Simon when the veterans clear out."

"Jenny was trying to talk Raven into staying away from the barn for a few days," Robin told them. "I don't think Raven was willing, so I'm not sure how that's going to shake out."

Lauren came in from the parking lot.

"Sorry I had to miss the veterans. I called Angela and told her this morning, I had a client emergency." She turned to Harriet. "Don't we have a class to watch in a few minutes?"

Harriet rubbed her hands together.

"We do, and I'm going to need a cup of something hot to hold onto from the vending machine before it starts."

Lauren made a face.

"That stuff is poison. We have a few minutes before the class starts. They have to move the therapy stuff from the arena first, which should give us just enough time to go get a real drink from the drive-through on Miller Hill Road."

Harriet grinned.

"Works for me. Is anyone else staying for the next class?"

Aunt Beth shook her head.

"The three of us have to come back later, so I think we're out of here as soon as I talk to Jorge."

"I need to stitch on trial three of my horse blanket," Mavis said.

Robin wrapped her knitted scarf more snugly around her neck and pulled her gloves on.

"I've got to go teach a chair yoga class at the church."

Lauren chuckled.

"That's the one I need to take."

Connie zipped her down jacket up to the collar.

"Let us know if anything else develops before we get back."

Harriet gave her a mock salute as she and Lauren left to search for warm drinks.

Chapter 23

Harriet and Lauren ended up driving all the way back to town as both coffee kiosks on their route were closed.

"It's a conspiracy," Lauren laughed as they pulled into The Steaming Cup.

"You wanted a quality drink," Harriet reminded her.

"Do you think Raven, and therefore Jenny, will have shown up for class when we get back?" Lauren asked when they were back in the car with their large lattes.

Harriet guided her car out of the parking lot and headed back to the stable.

"My money's on yes. I think Raven's determined to fit in with the other girls who ride. And sadly, violence among the adults around her may not be an unusual event in her life."

Lauren sipped her latte and gazed out the window.

"Poor Jenny. She must be torn."

"What do you mean?"

"For Brian's sake, she probably wants them to never go to the stable again, but as you say, Raven would be upset if they pulled her out. Even if they found another stable for her."

Harriet chuckled.

"What?" Lauren asked.

"I was just wondering if they had riding stables at convents."

Lauren smiled.

"You're wicked."

"You should talk."

✂ -- ✂ -- ✂

Jenny was sitting in the bleachers getting an earful from Crystal as they watched their respective daughters circling the ring with three other riders. Simon sat in his ATV in the center, calling out instructions.

"Raven, keep your hands quiet. Molly, you, too."

"I can tell you," Crystal said forcefully, "if there was another option for Paige, I'd yank her and her horse out of here so fast it would make his head spin."

Lauren and Harriet slid into the bleachers, and Crystal paused her tirade briefly. Jenny locked eyes with them and sighed.

Crystal turned to Harriet.

"You know how to ride, right? You can see how much better Paige is than the rest of the girls out there—no offense, Jenny."

Harriet had to admit, she had a point.

"That jerk Simon wants to hold her back so he can be sure someone from his stable will win the first-level class. There's a good chance Paige could win the second-level class. She would at least place."

Harriet watched the girls. As much as Crystal annoyed her, Paige *was* a good rider, and her horse was up to the task.

"I just wish there was some way to get rid of him." Crystal's face colored, and she glanced at Jenny. "I don't mean get rid of him like that. I just mean remove him from his position as teacher. With his wife as the manager there's no chance of that. I've already tried talking to her. I even wrote to the owners of the stable."

Lauren leaned forward. "Did they answer?"

Crystal pursed her lips.

"They said they left all personnel decisions to the manager, and I was welcome to take my business elsewhere."

"Clearly, someone with more money than sense," Lauren observed.

"I know this sounds terrible, but, Jenny, I was glad when your husband punched that twit out," Crystal continued. "He deserved that and more. If it had been me, he wouldn't be out there teaching today. I hope your husband doesn't suffer any consequences."

"He'll be fine," Jenny said quietly.

Harriet stood up.

"Crystal, if you're willing to keep an eye on Raven, maybe Jenny could come while I try the quarter-sheet I'm making on Fable."

Jenny looked up quizzically as Lauren stepped over the seat in front of hers.

"Come on, Jenny, maybe you can give me some ideas for mine, too."

"Sure, if you think I can help."

Lauren smiled. "I'm sure of it."

Harriet led them out of the arena and into the barn. She stopped in front of Major's stall.

Jenny's shoulders slumped. "You don't really have blankets with you, do you?"

Harriet rested her hand on Jenny's arm.

"No, we don't. I couldn't stand listening to that woman, and it was all I could think of."

Jenny gave her a weak smile. "I appreciate it. She's hard to take at the best of times, but she's over the top today."

Lauren sipped her latte.

"She does seem to have a bit of a blood lust where Simon is concerned."

Major tapped the stall door with his hoof. Harriet set her cup on the bench in front of his stall and pulled the baggie of carrot pieces from her pocket.

"Don't get me wrong—I find Crystal Kelley to be very irritating—but she does have a valid point regarding the class placement of her daughter." She opened Major's stall door and offered him a handful of carrot pieces. "Paige is clearly better than any of the other students in her group, and from watching her ride by herself, Crystal's right about how she'd fare at level two. Simon is clearly keeping her behind so she'll be the top score in first level."

Jenny shivered.

"I just find the woman creepy. I don't like the way she encourages her daughter to use her emerging sexuality to appeal to Simon's perversion in hopes he'll advance her to the next level."

Lauren laughed.

"I don't think I'd call it creepy. I think abusive, or maybe illegal, is more like it."

Harriet emptied her carrot bag into her hand and gave Major his last treat.

"Speaking of Crystal's willingness to ignore Simon's bad behavior, we'd better get back to see what he's up to."

Jenny took a deep breath and blew it out slowly and then smiled.

"Robin keeps telling me deep breathing will help me cope with all this, but I don't know."

Harriet chuckled. "It can't hurt, right."

✂-- ✂-- ✂

Stella Bren opened the door to Essy's stall and started to lead him out as Harriet, Jenny, and Lauren passed in front of it. She abruptly stopped.

"Oh, I'm sorry, I didn't realize anyone was out here."

Harriet smiled. "We were giving Major a treat. How's Essy doing?"

Stella brought him out and clipped him to the cross-ties as they talked.

"It's too early to tell. The vet says we shouldn't ride him for at least a year, and even then, it's not certain his foot will heal."

"Oh, Stella, I'm sorry."

"I feel bad. If I'd known how badly his foot was injured, I would never have ridden him in that last show, but I swear, he wasn't limping at all."

"If he wasn't limping, you couldn't have known," Harriet said in an attempt to reassure her.

"Milo is going to kill me if it turns out to be a permanent injury."

✂-- ✂-- ✂

Crystal stood up when Harriet, Jenny, and Lauren returned to the bleachers.

"Raven is really improving," she told Jenny. "Has she ever ridden before?"

Jenny set her purse on the bleacher before sitting.

"Not that she's ever mentioned."

"She seems very comfortable on her horse." Crystal picked up her purse and scarf. "I'm going to go find something warm to drink. I can't stand watching Simon anymore. Paige already has all these skills, so he pretty much ignores her, and it just makes me angry to have to watch it."

She stepped over the empty bleacher rows in front of them and, with a last glance into the arena, left.

Chapter 24

$\mathcal{H}$arriet was working at her long-arm machine when Luke backed through the door from the kitchen, a large cookie in each hand.

"Want one?" he asked, holding one out to her.

"Why, thank you. To what do I owe this incredible act of generosity? Not that you aren't normally generous, but you usually eat like a wild animal when you first get home from school."

"I'm hurt," he said with a grin.

"What is it you want to ask me?"

He ate a bite of his cookie and then laughed.

"How do you always know?"

"I'm learning your habits. Now, what can I help you with?"

"Emily is being trained how to prepare all the feed for the horses, as well as how to distribute it to all of them. They said if I wanted to come watch, I could eventually be a backup to the backup feed person."

"That all sounds good. What's the part that requires a cookie bribe?"

Luke held his hands in front of him and winced as he spoke.

"I have to be there at six-thirty tomorrow morning?" He watched through his fingers for her reaction.

She laughed.

"I was expecting something really awful. Six-thirty is no problem. I can do my run after I get back from dropping you off."

"When I get my license, I can drive myself."

"You need to take drivers-ed first, and it's up to you to fit that into your schedule."

He blew out a breath. "I know. Unless they change the schedule next term, all the driver's ed classes are during the only time they'll let me do my work-study at the stable."

Harriet stood up and patted him on the back.

"Life is complicated, young man. It's all about priorities."

"I need another cookie," he said, and went back through the connecting door and into the kitchen.

✂-- ✂-- ✂

Harriet walked the dogs early the next morning and brought them back into the kitchen for their breakfast. James had left for the restaurant more than an hour earlier. She was dressed in her running clothes so she could head out as soon as she got back from the barn.

Luke came downstairs, rubbing his eyes.

"Hey, sleepyhead. James made oatmeal, it's on the stove."

Luke picked a bowl James had left out for him up from the counter and filled it.

"Thanks for doing this."

"It's not a big deal. I need to try on Major's quarter-sheet for the thousandth time. I put the strip that goes under his tail on it and it looks too small to me, even though I measured it."

Luke sprinkled brown sugar onto his cereal.

"He loves all the attention. Especially if you bring him carrot pieces."

"James has an unending supply of those." She put Fred's dish down on his placemat and picked Scooter up. "You sit here with me so Fred can eat in peace."

Luke finished his oatmeal and stood.

"I just need to brush my teeth and I'll be ready to go."

Harriet tucked Scooter in the crook of her arm while she dug around in the refrigerator looking for the bag of cut-up carrots. She glanced down at Fred, who was licking his bowl clean.

"Okay, dog, you're free." She set him down on the floor. "You little rascals be good until I get back."

✂-- ✂-- ✂

Luke hurried into the barn ahead of Harriet and disappeared into the feed room. Harriet gathered Major's blanket and headed down the aisle. Simon was sitting in his chair in front of Major's stall, his back to her.

Oh, great, she thought. She'd been hoping to slip in, try Major's blanket on, and go home for her morning run. Simon undoubtedly was waiting for Luke, as she couldn't imagine what he'd want to talk to *her* about.

"Simon," she called when she was two stalls away. He didn't reply. She called out again, louder, as she continued closing the distance. He still didn't respond. She slowed her approach.

His head was leaning at an odd angle. She made a wide circle around his chair.

"Oh, Simon," she murmured as she pulled her phone from her purse and dialed 911.

He was slumped against the headrest of his chair, his skin gray-blue. He had an angry-looking red ring around his neck where something had clearly been used to squeeze the life from him.

"Yes, this is Harriet Truman," she said when her phone connected. "I'm at the Miller Hill Equestrian Center, and I've just found a dead man in front of our horse's stall...Yes," she replied when the speaker asked if she was sure he was dead.

She agreed to stay where she was and to not touch the body. She didn't need to be told. This wasn't her first dead body, after all.

The 911 operator hadn't said anything about calling her friends, so she dialed Lauren, keeping her eyes down the aisle on the feed-room door. So far, it was still closed.

"You realize it's not even seven yet," Lauren said by way of greeting.

"Lauren, listen, I just dropped Luke at the stable and was going to try on Major's blanket again, and I found Simon sitting outside the stall, dead."

"Whoa."

"I'm waiting for the police to arrive."

"I'll be right there. Shall I stop for coffees?"

"Yes, I have a feeling we're going to be here for a while. And can I borrow a sweatshirt or something. I'm in my running clothes."

"Sure. See you in a flash."

With that done, Harriet texted James and Aunt Beth. Her aunt would let the remainder of the Loose Threads know what had happened.

She debated finding Luke to warn him. She wasn't sure who was teaching them about feeding. If it was Angela, she didn't want to be the one to tell her about Simon. The police could handle that.

She stared at the feed-room door, ordering it to stay closed, until she heard sirens approaching.

A paramedic ambulance from the fire station arrived first, and two EMTs hustled in carrying their various bags and pieces of equipment. A thin woman with short blond hair stopped in front of Harriet.

"Haven't I seen you before?"

Harriet pressed her lips together.

"Sadly, yes. Here's your guy." She pointed to where Simon sat, still dead in his chair.

She stepped across the aisle so they had room to examine him. They crouched on either side of his chair, but she knew there wasn't going to be anything they could do.

The blonde stood up and came over to her.

"Well, you were right, the man is deceased,"

Harriet bit back a sarcastic retort. Did people often call them out only to discover their dead person was really alive?

"Who is he?" the medic wanted to know.

"His name is Simon Tavarious."

The woman wrote his name in a spiral notebook and looked at her watch, then wrote again. Presumably noting the time and date.

"His wife is the manager of this place," Harriet volunteered. "He's a trainer."

"The police will take care of the notification."

Luke and Emily came out of the feed room with an older woman Harriet had not seen before.

"What's going on?" Luke called to her.

"Stay where you are," she told him. "There's been an accident. You and Emily should go back into the feed room for now."

Luke gave her a questioning look but retreated as ordered. The older woman continued to approach.

"I'm sorry, ma'am, but you can't come down here," the EMT told her.

"We need to feed the horses."

"The police are arriving, and they'll tell you where and when you can come to this end of the barn."

The woman looked like she wanted to argue, but she spun around and went back to the feedroom instead.

Officer Jason Nguyen led the trio of police officers that entered the barn.

"Oh, geez," Harriet said, not realizing she'd spoken out loud.

"What?" the EMT asked.

Harriet shook her head. "Nothing. Nguyen and I have a bit of history."

The EMT smiled as she repacked her unused equipment.

"Good luck with that, then."

I must not be the only one to have history with him, Harriet mused.

✂-- ✂-- ✂

Harriet started to speak when Nguyen reached her, but he held up his hand, cutting her off.

"I don't even care why it's you again. Just tell me what happened."

"I walked up to our horse's stall and found a dead man sitting here."

"Do you know him? Why do I even ask—of course you know him. You always do. So who is he?"

"He's Simon Tavarious. His wife is the manager here, and he teaches riding classes."

He made a note in his notebook.

"I don't suppose you know what he's doing here, or how long he's been here."

"No idea on either count. I brought Luke, my foster son, here so he could learn the feeding routine. He does work-study here. I was going to try a blanket I'm making on his horse, and I found Simon just as you see him. I called nine-one-one immediately."

"Okay, you can go to the other end of the barn while we tape this off. Don't leave, though. I'm sure the detectives are going to want to talk to you."

"The woman who's teaching the kids how to do the feeding is pretty anxious to get the job done, and just so you know, my son's horse will start banging on his door if you make him wait too long."

"Duly noted. Now, leave the area, please."

"Don't say I didn't warn you," Harriet muttered as Major began whinnying and banging on his door as he realized the carrots he had smelled were leaving his vicinity.

Chapter 25

$\mathcal{H}$arriet was standing inside the barn entrance when Lauren arrived carrying two large steaming cups of hot cocoa, a gray sweatsuit over her arm.

"You didn't mention sweatpants," she said as she handed Harriet her drink. "But I figured your legs would be cold if you were wearing tights, which I see you are."

Harriet took a sip of the cocoa to steady her nerves.

"Maybe you should sit down a minute," Lauren said and took the cup from her. "You're looking a little pale. Put your head between your knees."

Harriet did as instructed, and it did help. She'd seen a dead body before, but being that close to Simon, slumped in his chair, had gotten to her.

"Put the warm clothes on, too."

"Thanks, I didn't think I was going to be here long enough to have to worry about warmer clothes."

Lauren waited for her to finish dressing and handed her the cocoa again. "So, what happened?"

"I really don't know. We got here, Luke went into the feed room, and I started down to Major's stall and saw Simon sitting there in his chair, his back to me. I called out to him as I got closer, and he didn't answer. Then, I realized he hadn't moved, either. And, well, it turns out he couldn't move."

"Oh, geez. I wonder who did it?"

"No idea. Although I could think of a few candidates."

Lauren frowned.

"He wasn't a popular guy, that's for sure."

Harriet stared at the floor. "Being unpopular or even being obnoxious isn't a reason to kill him. We better warn Jenny." She pulled her phone from her purse.

Lauren grabbed her arm.

"Didn't you text your aunt after you talked to me?"

"I did."

Lauren let her go.

"Don't you think Beth and probably Mavis or Connie will be talking to Jenny?"

"Okay, you're right, but I'm going to check just to be sure," Harriet said. She shivered even with the extra clothes and hot drink. She pressed her aunt's number on speed dial. Beth picked up on the third ring.

"You're on speaker phone," Beth said before Harriet could say anything. "Mavis and I are on our way to Jenny's house. She needs to know about this. I assume that's why you texted me earlier."

"And this sort of news should be delivered in person," Mavis added.

"You're on speaker phone, too. Lauren's with me at the barn, and Jenny is what we were calling about. We wanted to be sure someone was going to be with her."

"Has something else happened?" Beth asked.

"Not really. I was chased off the immediate area but told not to leave the premises until I'd been interviewed. The forensic people are still working. They haven't moved Simon yet."

"We should go," Mavis said in the background.

"We'll take care of Jenny," Beth said before hanging up. "Let us know if you learn anything else."

The older gray-haired woman came out of the feed room and joined Harriet and Lauren.

"Hi, I'm JoAnne Moore. I'm the assistant manager. Luke told me you know at least one of the police officers and might be able to get his attention long enough to make him understand that we have to start feeding."

Harriet chuckled.

"Luke's being a little optimistic about the nature of my relationship with Officer Nguyen, but I'll give it a try." She handed her cup to Lauren and went to the entrance, where a young officer she'd not met before was stringing additional police tape and turning away people who had come to prepare for the first class of the day.

"No, you can't leave," he informed Harriet when she approached him.

"Fortunately, I don't want to. The assistant manager wants to feed the horses before they stage a fullscale revolt. A lot of the horses here are expensive and are on special diets. People who can afford these horses can also af-

112

ford to sue the Foggy Point Police Department if any harm results because they missed their breakfast."

"Seriously?"

"I'm not kidding. I was thinking you could let them feed the animals in the pony barn. They can go around through the two arenas and avoid this area. They can reach the last six stalls that are beyond your taped-off section that way, too. Maybe by then your forensic people will be finished, and they can go feed the last eight horses. Or maybe she can give you the feed and let you hand it out."

"I'm not going in with that big one that's banging on his door."

"That's my son's horse."

"He's a scary one."

"Can I tell her she can start?"

"As long as she stays out of the taped-off area."

"Thank you, Officer."

"Okay," she told JoAnne when she was back with the other women. "He says you can start in the pony barn, and then do the horses outside of the area they've taped off. I was thinking you could go through the two arenas and then back into the pony barn and the back end of the main aisle."

"I can do it all myself, if you'd prefer, to keep the kids away," JoAnne offered.

"Thanks, but I think it's better if they're busy. Just send them back up by the same route when you're done."

"Thank you for asking for me," JoAnne said, and returned to the feed room.

A minute later, Luke emerged and hurried over to them.

"What's going on?"

"I'm afraid Simon's had an accident, and the police need to investigate."

"Is he dead?"

"Yes, he is, and they don't know how or why. The police are going to let JoAnne feed the horses, but I've told her I don't want you and Emily to go into the back end of the barn where you can see Simon. You can go to the pony barn through the arenas."

"Are you okay?" he asked. "You look kinda pale."

"I'll be fine. It was just a bit of a shock."

Luke put his arm around Harriet and gave her a quick hug, before following JoAnne and Emily to the feed room.

James came up to the stable door where the policeman guarding the barn entrance was trying to send him away.

"He's with us," Harriet told him.

"Officer Nguyen told me to tell people they can't come into the barn."

"And Officer Nguyen told me not to leave. Either let me out to see my husband or let him in. I promise he won't run down and contaminate the crime scene."

He looked at Harriet, and then James, and let out a sigh. "You can explain it to Detective Morse when she gets here."

The officer stepped aside, and James swept her into a hug.

"What are you doing here?" she asked him. "I just texted you in case someone came into the restaurant and was talking about it. I didn't want you to worry."

"What's going on, and where's Luke? Simon's dead?" he asked in a rush as soon as he released her. "Are you okay?"

"I'm fine, Luke's fine, Lauren's fine. We're all fine, except Simon. He's down at Major's stall, dead. Strangled, by the look of it."

Lauren shook her head.

"I offered to put in motion detectors after someone tried to get to Major, but Angela didn't want to spend the money. And from the look of it, she either didn't replace the lights that were out, or someone took them out again. Simon is sitting in a shadow I noticed in front of Major's stall. That's why we couldn't see who tried to go in the other day when he broke his door."

Harriet had to recount what had happened twice before James would let go of her hands.

"I'm okay, really. You don't have to stay if you need to be at the restaurant. I have to wait to talk to Detective Morse, since I was the one to find Simon. I don't have anything to tell her beyond the obvious, but it's procedure."

James rubbed his hands up and down her arms.

"I do have a large private party coming in for lunch, so if you're really okay, I'll go back and help the crew."

"We are *fine*, and Lauren's here with me."

He kissed her and trotted back to his car.

✂-- ✂-- ✂

Harriet and Lauren were still waiting for Jane Morse when a woman Harriet didn't recognize, wearing a colorful knitted hat, joined them at the entrance.

"What's going on?" she asked.

"There's been a death in the barn," Harriet explained.

The color drained from the woman's lined face.

"Who is it?"

Harriet gave her a onceover before answering. There was something vaguely familiar about her.

"It's the horse trainer, Simon Travarious."

The woman put her hand over her heart and breathed a sigh of relief.

"I'm sorry, that's terrible, but my daughter Emily works here." She held up a quilted bag. "She forgot her lunch; I was bringing it to her."

Harriet smiled.

"I'm Harriet Truman, Luke's foster mom."

The woman tossed her waist-length braid over her shoulder. She wore a paisley print skirt over thermal leggings and thick wool socks cuffed over worn work boots.

"I'm Rain Roberts. She's told me about you and your beautiful quilts."

Harriet's cheeks pinked.

"I have a long-arm quilting business, so a lot of what she's seen are customer quilts on my machine. We have a lot of talented quilters in our community."

"What happened to Simon?"

"We don't know," Lauren answered. "I'm close friend and confidante Lauren, by the way."

"Sorry," Harriet told her. Then, she continued, "I came out early this morning to drop Luke off and to try a blanket I'm making on his horse, Major. I found Simon dead in his chair in front of Major's stall."

"Oh, my gosh, how awful for you. Did he have a heart attack or something?"

"Unfortunately, no. It appears someone strangled him."

Rain covered her mouth with a hand.

"Oh, my gosh. Where are the kids? Are they okay?"

"They're fine," Harriet assured her. "They're in the other barn, feeding the ponies. I asked JoAnne, the assistant manager, to not let them at the back end of the barn unless Simon's body has been removed."

"Well, I'm going to wait here until I see Emily for myself."

Harriet looked out the door and down the drive, hoping to see Detective Morse drive up.

"Emily's father isn't going to like this," Rain finally said. "He's not very supportive of her horse obsession."

Harriet didn't know what to say. She and James were happy Luke had found Major and horseback riding.

"Think it's going to snow?" Lauren said. Harriet could see she was fighting a snicker.

The trio was silent for a long moment.

"Rain, my husband James was just saying he'd like to invite you and your husband over for dinner at our house. The kids are spending so much time together, we should probably get to know each other."

Lauren was standing at an angle to Rain and turned her head slightly so when she rolled her eyes, only Harriet could see it.

"Sure, did you have a day in mind?"

They compared calendars and decided the following Wednesday would work for everyone.

Detective Morse finally arrived and with a brisk nod of her head as she went by, strode down the aisle, putting on paper booties and nitrile gloves and signing the crime scene log before ducking under the tape.

✂-- ✂-- ✂

"Ladies," Officer Nguyen said, nodding to Rain and ignoring Harriet and Lauren. "I'm afraid you are going to have to move your coffee klatch elsewhere. We need to move the body out."

"I'm not leaving until I see my daughter," Rain objected. "She's in the pony barn." She gestured down the aisle.

"Ma'am, that's fine, you just can't stand right here. Maybe you could go into the arena."

Rain glared at him, but retreated without another word.

Lauren grinned. "I like her," she said as they followed.

Chapter 26

"Shall we wait until everyone gets here before you tell us anything?" Beth asked Harriet as they sat down at the big table at The Steaming Cup.

Harriet set her cup and bagel down and took her coat off. She'd finally managed a short run when Morse had finished questioning her. She'd taken the dogs out, then run four miles before grabbing a quick shower and joining the Loose Threads for a postmortem of the morning's events.

"That would be easier for me. By the way, Lauren texted me she'll be a few minutes late, but we can start without her."

Robin breezed in and dropped her legal tablet and pen on the table before leaving her purse and coat on her chair.

"I thought I was going to be late," she said, looking around. Connie and Mavis were at the counter ordering their drinks, and Carla was on her way to the table with her food in hand.

"Get your drink," Beth said. "You've got time. DeAnn and Jenny are both on their way, and Lauren is coming late."

✂-- ✂-- ✂

Harriet looked around the table at her friends. She was pretty sure everyone was pondering the same thought—Was anyone going to mention Brian? He was everyone's number-one suspect in Simon's death, but, who was going to say it out loud?

Jenny was returning from the counter with her coffee, so the answer would be imminent. Aunt Beth pulled out the empty chair that had been strategically left between Mavis and herself.

"Here, sit down, and we'll get this gathering underway."

Jenny did as instructed, dropping her purse to the floor beside her chair and letting her coat slip off her shoulders.

"Harriet," Beth instructed, "tell us everything that happened. Don't leave anything out."

As if it had been choreographed, everyone set her cup down and leaned forward slightly.

"There really isn't much to tell," Harriet began. "Luke needed to be at the stable by seven o'clock for training on how to prepare and deliver food for all the horses in the stable. He wanted to be early, so we left our house around six-thirty.

"He went straight to the feed room, and I had brought my latest blanket trial to try on Major. The tail piece looked too small, and I wanted to be sure it was right. Anyway, I went to his stall, and as I approached, I saw Simon sitting in his chair, his back to me and right against the stall door. I called out to him, and he didn't answer. I moved closer and called again, eventually reaching the stall and moving around to the front of his chair, where it became obvious he was dead."

"How could you tell?" Mavis asked.

Harriet smiled briefly and then coughed to cover it.

"His head was leaning back and to the side, exposing an angry red line across his throat. It was deep, almost a cut. And of course, his skin was turning blue-gray. There was no doubt he was dead, and it wasn't from natural causes." Harriet sat back in her chair. "And that's all I can tell you. Police were called, and of course Officer Nguyen came, and the rest you can imagine."

The only sound at the table was the scratching of Robin's pen on her tablet. Mavis sipped her tea and set her mug down with a thump.

"Before we go any further, let's deal with the eight-hundred-pound gorilla in the room. With Simon dead and Brian having given him a thrashing just the day before yesterday, we're all assuming he's going to be suspect number one. Of course, none of us believe he did it." She smiled at Jenny. "And it's possible the police will zero in on the correct perpetrator, and that will be that."

"And if you believe that, I've got a bridge I can sell you," Lauren said as she slid into the last empty chair without stopping at the coffee counter. "Sorry I'm late. I do have to work every once in a while. As I was saying, in spite of Mavis's belief in our local police, they'll at least have to look at Brian. Sorry, Jenny. I'm not sure what you all think we can do about it. As Detective Morse has told us many times, police work is none of our business."

118

Harriet chuckled.

"On that happy note, I guess we can drink our tea and go home and just leave everything to Detective Morse."

Beth glared at her.

"I don't think it can hurt anything for us to jot down a few notes about our collective observations, just in case things go sideways for Brian."

Jenny gasped.

"If they do," Beth continued, "we'll turn over anything we discover to Detective Morse, to help her come to the correct conclusion."

Connie cleared her throat.

"Don't you think you're selling Morse short?"

"Maybe," Mavis said.

"And maybe not," Beth finished for her.

Robin tapped her pen on her tablet.

"Professionally, I'm with Lauren on this one. The police are quite capable of solving this or any murder without a bunch of mostly middle-aged women interfering."

Jenny's cheeks reddened. Robin turned to her.

"But given that this could impact one of our members, and since we've spent more time than most at the stable these last few weeks, it can't hurt for us to put down what we know, and if it seems like it might be helpful, we can pass it on to Morse."

Jenny sighed. "Thank you for that."

Harriet sipped her tea and scanned the faces of the Loose Threads.

"Is everyone good with that?"

One-by-one, the group nodded.

"Okay, Robin, get your pen ready. Group, what do we know?"

✂ -- ✂ -- ✂

A vigorous discussion of Simon's bad behaviors ensued. Finally, Harriet announced

"I'm going to get a refill. Anyone else want anything?"

Lauren stood up.

"I'll come with you. I'm not sure what I want yet."

"So far, it seems like we've got 'Simon was a jerk and probably a pervert' pretty well covered," Harriet continued. "Can we write down what we know that indicates who might have wanted him dead badly enough to take action?"

Jenny held her cup up.

"I think I'm going to need more coffee for this."

Harriet took it and headed to the counter. Lauren waited until they were out of earshot to speak.

"Do we have anyone to put on the list besides Brian?"

"Stan. He seemed to have a problem with Simon."

"We don't know enough about what happened between them to know if Stan would be angry enough to kill over it."

New orders delivered, Harriet handed Jenny her coffee and sat down with her tea.

"Okay, what have we got?" Harriet asked.

Jenny sighed. "Let's get this over with. Put Brian down—he punched out Simon for groping Raven and maybe wasn't done."

Robin held her pen over the page and finally wrote *Brian*, because Simon molested Raven.

"Stan, because he and Simon have bad blood from their army days," Harriet said, and Robin wrote it on their list.

Silence descended until Carla cleared her throat.

"I'm not sure if this belongs..." she started, and then hesitated.

"Go on, honey," Connie prompted her.

She cleared her throat again. "I met a mother at Wendy's pony class, and they have a horse boarded there. They brought it there because the stable where they used to keep it burned down."

"Let me guess," Lauren whispered to Harriet.

"Angela was the manager at that stable," Carla continued, "and Lexi —that's the mom—she said a bunch of horses died, and a lot of those owners were pretty sure Simon was the one who set the fire."

Robin scribbled notes.

"Did she say why they thought that?" she asked.

Carla looked down at her hands.

"No," she said quietly.

Connie patted her arm.

"Honey, that's okay. That's good information." She looked up at Lauren.

"Here it comes," Lauren muttered.

"Maybe Lauren can find something about it on the internet."

"Sure, Lauren would be happy to do more research."

Mavis glared at her.

"No, really," Lauren said. "Can you tell me Lexi's last name and anything else you know about her? That will be my starting point. Also, if you see her and can find out the name of that stable, that would be useful, although there can't be that many stables in the Northwest that burned down in the recent past."

"I'll find out," Carla said without making eye contact with Lauren.

Robin held her pen up.

"Anything else?"

The Threads looked at each other, but no one had anything else.

Harriet sipped her tea.

"I'm not sure you need to write this down, but I'll be taking food from James to the homeless camp tomorrow. I can ask and see if either Stan or one of the others can tell me anything else about the problem Stan had with Simon."

Robin wrote it down.

"And I'll put down Lauren's research. Any other action items?"

No one had any.

A brief discussion of the quarter sheets ensued, and then the group broke up.

Chapter 27

"**I** wish whoever killed Simon would have parked him somewhere else," Luke complained as Harriet pulled her car into the garage. "Major really wanted to go out for a ride today."

Harriet tried not to laugh.

"Did he tell you that?"

"I could tell when I fed him. He kept making little noises and rubbing his nose on my chest."

"He was probably telling you who did it. Too bad we don't speak horse. I would imagine the police will release the place by tomorrow morning. There can't be that much to process."

"Major's really going to be upset if we can't go out tomorrow."

"In the meantime, I know a couple of little clowns who can and would like to go out."

"No problem," he said and went into the kitchen to leash the dogs.

✂-- ✂-- ✂

Harriet was pulling a bowl from the refrigerator when Luke came back, giving each of the dogs a biscuit before hanging the leashes up.

"James left us some chicken salad to make sandwiches with if you're hungry," Harriet told him. "Can I make you one?"

He grinned, and she laughed.

"Silly me. Of course, you want a sandwich." She retrieved a loaf of bread from the tin-lined bread drawer. "Speaking of food, I talked to Emily's mother, and unless James has a problem with it, they're going to come to dinner on Wednesday."

"Does James know they're vegan?"

"He does not. It's a good thing you mentioned it. I'm sure he has a full repertoire of vegan dishes."

"I don't think they're super-hardcore about it. They aren't against leather shoes or that sort of stuff. I think her mom was raised in a commune and just always ate vegan. Emily said her mom never got used to eating meat."

"Has Emily said what sort of commune it was?"

"Is there more than one type? Em says her mom hasn't told her a lot about her childhood, but I guess it was one of those extreme religious deals. And she said they aren't allowed to visit her grandpa."

"How does Emily feel about it?"

"I don't think she thinks about it. It's just her life. Her dad's parents are divorced, and both remarried, so she has four grandparents on that side. Emily says she doesn't think she could deal with any more grandparents."

"Do you know any of *your* grandparents?"

"Not really. My dad used to call his mom when he needed money, which was all the time. His dad would yell and tell him to get lost, and then his mother would come around and drop off an envelope of money. She never stayed long. I think Dad having kids with different women he wasn't married to was hard for her to deal with. I'm not sure she even knew all of us."

"That's too bad. She's missing out, not knowing you."

Luke took the sandwich she'd made him to the table.

"Hey, I hit the grandparent jackpot with Grandpa Will and Grandma Kathy. Em's jealous of them."

"They have to be to make up for my parents' absence."

Luke laughed.

"You can't have everything. You got Aunt Beth and Jorge and the rest of their gang."

"True. The Loose Threads pretty much cover all the bases."

Harriet sat down with her own sandwich.

"Are you okay after today's events? Do you want to talk about it?"

Luke set the second half of his sandwich down on his plate.

"I'm probably awful, but the guy was such a perv with the way he was bugging Emily and Raven and the others, I'm kind of relieved he's not a problem anymore. I mean, it's bad that he's dead, but I don't think any of us are going to miss him."

"That's okay. You get to feel how you feel. You don't have to pretend to be sad that a guy who hurt your friends is no longer here to be a threat. I'm sorry if he suffered, but that doesn't take away the bad things he did."

"I didn't want him to suffer—not much, anyway," he said with a grin. "I just wanted him to leave the girls alone."

"Detective Morse is going to have her hands full figuring this one out. I think Simon had more than one enemy."

"Wouldn't surprise me if Angela did him in."

"Really? Why do you say that?"

"They were always fighting. She didn't like the way he did his classes. She thought he yelled too much and put people down. She thought he should let people move up a class if they wanted to try it, but he never wanted to. He said it would look bad for the stable, and she said people would get frustrated and quit. Then, he said with the other barn gone they didn't have a choice unless they wanted to move out of town."

"Wow, I had no idea."

"I think they didn't do it when adults were around. When us kids were in mucking stalls, it was like we were invisible."

Harriet reached across the table and squeezed his hand.

"You're never invisible to me and James."

His face turned red.

"I know."

Chapter 28

Harriet awoke to the aroma of blueberry pancakes being prepared in the kitchen downstairs. She could hear the quiet murmurs of James and Luke as the master taught the student the nuances of Sunday morning brunch.

She got up and showered, reveling in the fact that this was her day off from running. They usually went to church after breakfast; but this morning they were delivering breakfast to the homeless camp, and James was preparing a more elaborate meal than usual, so it would take additional time to cook and serve.

He would prepare blueberry pancakes for the homeless, too, cooked on a griddle over the fire they kept burning around the clock in the winter in their common area.

When Harriet came downstairs, Luke was cutting oranges into quarters and dropping them into a large plastic container while James finished the pancakes for the three of them to eat before they left for the camp.

Luke cut his last orange and snapped the lid onto the container.

"If you think Stan is the one who killed Simon, is it safe for us to go out there asking questions?" he asked.

Harriet sat down at the kitchen table. "If it is Stan, his problem is with Simon, not the rest of us."

James wiped his hands on a dish towel and brought the plate of pancakes to the table.

"He wouldn't do anything with the rest of us all around. Whoever killed Simon did it at night, when no one was around, and he kept to the shadows. If it was Stan—and remember that's a pretty big if—he wouldn't do anything in the light of day."

Harriet wondered how James could be so sure. People who killed other people were unpredictable, in her experience, in spite of what they always said on television. She assumed he was trying to assure Luke, but still...

"Let's stick together while we're in the camp. No going off on our own, no trips back to the van by ourselves," she said.

"Okay," James agreed. "I have to say, I'll be surprised if Stan turns out to be the killer. I've talked to him when we do the meal after their horse therapy. He's educated, and he's aware of his PTSD and is working through it. He has a plan. It doesn't seem like he'd throw that all away on Simon."

Harriet took two pancakes and spread butter on them.

"I still want to talk to him."

✂ -- ✂ -- ✂

Joyce Elias was smoothing the embers of the large fire when Luke and James carried the large grill and the tub of supplies into the homeless area. Harriet followed with a smaller cooler containing the pancake batter, several dozen eggs, and two pounds of bacon.

"I'm glad you came by last night and told us you were doing this wonderful breakfast for us," Joyce said to James. "I hope I've done the fire right. We've kept the back half of the pit burning hot for our warmth and have been moving coals to this front side."

James set his grill rack and griddle over the area of coals Joyce had prepared.

"This looks perfect. Luke, can you hand me the trays from the box?"

Luke brought the trays while Harriet helped Joyce retrieve the tin plates from the supply box at the back of the clearing. Harriet's architect friend Tom had led a project the previous year to create some permanent structures in the homeless camp. The common area had a large table with benches, a permanent fire pit, and a waterproofed wooden trunk that was lockable and held dishes, extra bedding, towels, and hardware that was useful for hanging tarps, anchoring tents, and whatever else needed doing. He'd also gotten a non-profit to build showers in the nearby restrooms.

As James began cooking bacon and Joyce made coffee in a large blue-speckled coffee pot, residents of the camp began drifting in, drawn by the aroma of breakfast. Harriet handed out coffee cups as they arrived.

"Hey, Tim," she said. "How are you doing with Blue?"

Tim chuckled.

"I think I'm getting the hang of it. It helps that old Blue is really patient."

She smiled at him. "Good, I'm glad it's going well."

Diandra, a stout army vet, joined them.

"Kirby isn't quite as forgiving as Blue. She stepped on my foot last time. It's a good thing they made us wear boots."

"I'm glad you were wearing them. When I was young, I got stepped on while I was wearing tennis shoes, and it broke my toe," Harriet told her as she watched more residents enter the space. She was looking for Stan, but so far, he was a no-show.

James finished cooking bacon, and after scraping his large griddle, he started eggs on one half of it and blueberry pancakes on the other. Harriet set a thermos of maple syrup on the table along with a container of butter. Joyce stacked plates next to James as Luke delivered cutlery to the table.

"Is Stan coming?" Harriet finally asked Joyce.

"His tent is up by Max's, maybe he knows. Max," she called to the older man who was sitting at one end of the table. "Did you see Stan when you came down?"

Max shook his head. "He took off yesterday. He was going to catch the bus to go to the Vets' hospital."

Tim looked up from his food. "He goes to a clinic in Silverdale," he volunteered. "They want to send him to the hospital to do more surgery on his leg, but he's not too keen on that idea. He said he's had enough of army hospitals."

Diandra set her coffee cup down.

"Haven't we all? It's too bad the money end of the army isn't as efficient as the cutting and stitching part."

"Let's not trouble these nice folks with our complaints," Max announced, ending the discussion. "These pancakes are wonderful, James," he added.

✂-- ✂-- ✂

Luke hauled two gallon jugs of water from the restrooms to the fire, where James emptied them into a large stainless-steel vat used to heat water for dishwashing. The diners formed an assembly line washing, rinsing, drying, and stowing everything back in the big box. Harriet repacked their cooking tools and empty food containers, and carried them back to the car. On one of her trips, she paused to text Lauren.

Coffee in an hour?

Steaming Cup? came the answer a moment later.

Yes, she wrote back.

✂-- ✂-- ✂

127

Lauren was waiting when Harriet came into the Cup. Luke had decided to take Major for a ride if the police were done, and over his protests James decided he'd go along to make sure nothing untoward happened at the stable.

"What's up?" Lauren asked as Harriet got settled, removing her coat and putting both hands around her cup of London Fog.

"James got a wild hare to make fresh hot breakfast for the homeless camp this morning, so he took his outdoor griddle setup and made them pancakes and eggs and bacon."

Lauren sipped her coffee.

"Wow, that's elaborate."

"He likes to challenge himself. And they love the meals he makes. Actually, I think he and Jorge are a little competitive about it."

"Whatever works. I'm guessing you learned something interesting, or we wouldn't be here."

Harriet blew out a breath.

"I'm not sure it means anything, but Stan wasn't there. They said he left yesterday to take a bus to a clinic in Silverdale."

"That is interesting. Especially if he doesn't have an alibi for the time of the murder."

"They didn't give any details about his actual departure, so I don't know if they saw him yesterday, or if he'd told them Friday he was going to Silverdale on Saturday, which is a weird time to be going to an appointment, if you ask me."

Lauren stirred another packet of sugar into her coffee.

"I suppose he could have a friend or even family he stays with when he goes to his appointments at the clinic."

"True. But also, interesting that he happened to leave right after his enemy Simon is murdered."

"It could be a coincidence, but for now, he remains firmly on the suspect list."

Harriet picked up Lauren's empty sugar packet and folded it into ever smaller squares.

"I'm really hoping Brian was home with Jenny, Raven, and a few other people, if possible."

"Me, too. Jenny has her hands full with Raven, she doesn't need her husband to be a murder suspect at the same time."

"We also need to figure out where Crystal Kelley was."

Lauren laughed.

"The way that woman likes to overshare, that shouldn't be too hard. All we need to do is cross her path, and I'm sure she'll tell us everything we want to know and more."

Harriet chuckled.

"I think you're right." She pulled her jacket up over her shoulders and sipped her tea.

"I'll be glad when this cold weather is done with us."

Lauren looked out the window to where snowflakes had begun to fall.

"Me, too," she said, "Me, too."

Chapter 29

J ames and Luke were still at the stable when Harriet and Lauren finished their coffee break. She decided to join them, since she'd not gotten to try Major's blanket on him the previous day and it was still in her car.

Luke was riding in the small arena when she arrived. James stood outside the rail, and Harriet slid her arm around his waist when she reached him. He kissed the top of her head.

"I continue to be amazed at how well he controls that giant animal." Harriet smiled.

"He's a natural at riding, and it helps that Major seems to like him."

"I suppose he benefits from having a horse the same way the veterans do with their horse therapy."

"Animals are amazing healers. Too bad they couldn't help Simon with his problems."

"I wonder if he was that way before he lost the use of his legs." Harriet smiled as Luke passed by.

"If Stan is to be believed, he was a jerk back in his army days. And I don't think his liking of young girls is anything recent."

"I guess so."

"On another topic, with all this, I haven't had a chance to tell you—I connected with Emily's mother in the middle of the police and forensics and everything. I've invited them to dinner on Wednesday, pending your approval."

James thought for a moment.

"Wednesday works for me."

"Luke told me the family is vegan."

"That's interesting. Will they disapprove of our leather shoes and belts?"

"He said they aren't hardcore. Emily told him her mom was raised in a commune, and *they* were vegan. It's more a habit than a philosophy."

"Hmmm…" James said, hand on chin and looking to the roof. "Let me review my secret recipe box and see what I can wow them with."

Harriet laughed.

"I'm sure they'll be impressed no matter what you make. By the way, do you know why he's riding in this arena instead of the big one?"

"Some lady is giving a lesson in the big one."

"Angela?"

"No, someone I didn't recognize. I'm sure Angela has family arrangements to make."

"I was going to say, it would be pretty cold if she was back teaching already. I think I'll wander over and see who it is."

"Okay, I'm going to stay here with the kid. I know he thinks he can take care of himself, but I don't want him to be alone out here right now."

"Good idea."

✂-- ✂-- ✂

Harriet slid into the empty bleachers and watched as a dark-haired young woman guided a small gray horse around the ring. She looked over at the platform where the instructors often stood and was surprised to see Stella Bren.

"Keep your hands quiet, Morgan," Stella called out.

Harriet wasn't sure why it surprised her to see Stella teaching a student. She knew Stella wasn't a beginner—Essy wasn't a beginner's horse. She probably rode third level or better. She continued to watch as the girl moved through trotting, walking, and then trotting again, Stella calling out corrections. She was definitely competent to teach this level.

Stella noticed her and waved. Harriet waved back and continued watching. She was so focused on the action in the ring, she didn't notice Crystal had arrived until she spoke.

"Huh," she said. "Angela has Stella teaching now?"

"I've not spoken to Stella, but at least she's teaching this student. Angela probably needed to cover her classes quickly, and Stella was handy. I'd be surprised if Stella wanted to teach on a permanent basis."

"I'm going to see if she'll give Paige a lesson, see what *she* thinks of Paige's ability."

"Has Paige ever had a lesson with Angela?"

131

Crystal looked disgusted.

"I thought I told you before. Simon was the gate. He had to approve a student moving up to the next level, and he would never pass Paige up, so therefore no Angela."

"Well, maybe you can ask Stella to schedule a class before Angela tells her she can't."

"I think I will wait until she's done with this one and ask."

Harriet saw a woman who looked to be about her own age sitting on a bay horse outside the entry gate on the opposite side of the arena. Crystal was going to have to be quick.

"I'm going to go back and see how my son is doing."

"You know, he'll never get out of first level on that monster horse."

"I don't think he cares."

✂-- ✂-- ✂

"Why so glum?" James asked her when she was back at his side and watching Luke canter by.

She smiled.

"Oh, just a pleasant encounter with Crystal Kelley. She told me Luke is never getting out of first level with 'that monster horse'."

"Did she just insult our horse?"

"And our son. I told her I'm not sure he cares about getting out of first level."

"Does he even want *in* to first level?" James asked.

"I don't think so."

Luke pulled Major to a stop in front of them.

"Did I just hear you say 'first level'?"

"I was talking to Paige's mother. You know she's obsessed with getting Paige out of first and into second."

"I'm glad I'm not doing that. Grandpa Will said if I do chores for him this summer, he'll buy Major a western saddle and he'll teach me how to ride that style."

"He did, did he?" James said and smiled.

The smile left Luke's face.

"Is that okay?"

"Of course. Grandpa just needs to remember to tell us what he's committing to, is all."

Luke looked relieved.

"I think Major and I will like western riding. I think it might be a little closer to what he was used to in the police."

"I suspect you're right," Harriet said. "You should walk him for a bit after cantering, so he can cool down."

Luke rode off, and James led her away from the ringside.

"I guess we're going to have to talk to Grandpa Will."

"It's not a bad plan, right?" Harriet asked.

"It's a great plan. He just needs to let us in on any plans he makes. I mean, what if *we* were going to get him a saddle, or have him help in the restaurant for the summer? Dad needs to talk with us."

Harriet smiled.

"He probably thinks since he's your dad, he doesn't need to ask your permission."

"Yeah, my sister's had this kind of trouble, too. Grandpa wants to be sure his grandkids have all the advantages he and his children, who really didn't want for much, didn't have."

Harriet hugged him.

"Hard to argue with that."

✄ -- ✄ -- ✄

James had the car warmed up when Harriet and Luke came out of the barn.

"I called my mom to see if we could stop by," he said when they'd gotten in. "She asked if we could stay for early dinner. I told her I thought it would be okay, but I needed to ask you two first and would call her back if it wasn't."

"We should stop by and pick up the dogs if we're going to be gone for several hours," Harriet said.

James smiled.

"Dad loves the dogs."

Chapter 30

Will was bent over poking at the logs in the living room fireplace when Scooter and Cyrano raced into the house. James' mother had opened the door, and he kissed her on the cheek as he walked past her on his way in.

The dogs raced in a circle around the coffee table, stopping to tussle with Will each time around.

"Settle down," James ordered in a stern voice.

His father straightened.

"Oh, let them have a little fun."

Kathy opened the closet in the entryway.

"Can I take your coats?"

They handed her their outerwear and joined Will at the fire.

"I made some mulled cider," Kathy announced. "Can I bring everyone a cup?"

"Do you need help?" James asked her.

"Maybe Luke could carry the tray for me."

Harriet sensed a setup. Whatever James had said to his mom on the phone, she knew her son well enough to know he had ulterior motives; and clearly, she wanted to get it out of the way immediately so as to not spoil the visit.

"Your mother says you wanted to talk to us about something." Will raised an eyebrow at his son. "Out with it."

James sighed. "Mom is never wrong. We were just out at the stable watching Luke ride—"

"Ah," Will interrupted. "He told you about our arrangement concerning the saddle."

James started to speak, but his dad held a hand up.

"The boy needs a proper saddle. The one they sent with the horse doesn't fit Major and doesn't fit Luke. And it's been modified to hold police equipment. I've been on Major, and he's trained to neck rein; and I think Luke might like to ride Western."

"You mean because that's how you ride?"

"Is there something wrong with that?"

Harriet came to the fire, holding her hands out to warm them.

"There's nothing wrong with Luke learning to ride Western, and I agree —I think he'd be happier riding that style. Look, James and I are trying to figure out this whole parenting thing, and maybe we're wrong, but we were thinking we should know about any arrangements being made on Luke's behalf. What if we'd been planning on buying him a Western saddle for graduation?"

Will rubbed a hand across his mouth.

"I hadn't really thought of that."

Harriet put her hand on James's arm to stop the retort she could see forming on his lips.

"It turns out we aren't, and I think your plan sounds fine. I'm hoping in the future, though, you'll let us in on your plans when it concerns Luke."

Will smiled at James.

"This one's a keeper. She's managed to scold me without inciting World War Three, which is what you would have done."

Harriet was afraid all her diplomacy was going to be wasted, but Kathy reappeared, followed by Luke carrying the tray of cider mugs.

"Here we are," she said, smiling brightly. "Now, tell us, what have you been up to this fine cold day?"

Luke told his grandparents about James cooking breakfast at the homeless camp. His admiration for James was apparent in his embellished description of the meal.

Harriet sipped her cider.

"Mmmm, this is delicious."

"It's my mother's recipe," Kathy said and looked into her cup. "I think the dash of nutmeg is what sets it apart from the ordinary."

Harriet took another sip.

"It really hits the spot after being at the camp and then at the stables."

Kathy set her mug on the coffee table.

"Speaking of the stable, have you met a woman named Stella Bren?"

135

"Yes. In fact, I just saw her teaching a student while Luke was riding."

"She's in my Master Gardener's group. I didn't know she taught riding. She's always complaining about needing more time to work on her garden."

"I don't think it's a regular thing. One of the teachers died yesterday, so I'm guessing they asked Stella to fill in until they can find someone to take over his students."

"I think she's been surprised by how much time that horse of theirs is taking up. I should say, rather, that it's her husband expecting her to vie for the top prize at every show, and the time it takes that caught her by surprise. She was imagining horseback riding as more of a leisure activity."

Luke set his empty cup back on the tray.

"She has a pretty fancy horse for leisure riding."

Kathy smiled at him.

"There's more cider in the pot if you want a refill."

He grabbed his mug and headed to the kitchen.

"Milo Bren only buys the best of everything—Stella should have seen it coming. He bought her a teacup chihuahua a couple of years ago, and then had the breeder take it to shows until it got the highest championship level it could qualify for. All *she* wanted was a lap warmer."

Scooter, as if hearing his cue, jumped into Kathy's lap, startling her. Everyone laughed.

"Speaking of lap warmers," James chuckled.

Will reached over and stroked Scooter's head.

"My dear, have *you* longed for a pedigreed rat?"

Kathy rearranged Scooter in her lap and smiled at her husband.

"Granddogs are just fine for me. I get to spoil them. and then send them home."

"Gee, thanks, Mom," James said.

✄ -- ✄ -- ✄

Kathy had made a big pot of chili and set out bowls of shredded cheese, sour cream, chopped green onions, and sliced black olives. She'd also baked cornbread and set it out with whipped honey butter.

"This looks great, Mom," James complimented her.

"It's been so cold I wanted something that would stick to our ribs."

"It's great, Grandma Kathy," Luke said. "I love chili, and I didn't know regular people could make it without opening a can."

Kathy laughed.

"Regular people can make lots of stuff without cans being involved."

"While we're gathered here, and in the interest of not stepping on anyone's toes," Will began, "I was thinking about Luke's saddle. Or rather, Major's saddle. Kathy's going to need some work done in her garden beds and in the greenhouse before spring planting. Luke really needs his saddle now. What if we go ahead and get the saddle now, and let him work it off."

Luke's eyes got big.

"I can wait. I don't have to have it now." He sounded panicked.

"What do you think, Mom?" James asked Kathy.

Kathy leaned back in her chair.

"I don't think it's fair to have this discussion with Luke sitting here, is what I think. But now you've opened the topic for discussion, you owe it to Luke to settle this in the least stressful way for him. And, Luke, if having this discussion with the whole family here is too hard, we can drop it altogether and you three can talk about it at home."

Luke looked down at the table.

"I don't want people mad at me."

Harriet reached over and took his hand.

"No one is mad at you. We're learning how to be parents and how to work together with your grandparents. This is the first time for James and I."

"I don't want to be a problem."

"Luke," James said. "Look at me," Luke obeyed. "No matter what we do about the saddle, or how much my dad and I disagree about how to do things—and by the way, we've been disagreeing since long before you were born—we aren't going to let you leave us. Unless you want to, of course.

"We're together for the long haul. Good families are like this. They laugh, they cry, they argue, but none of that changes how everyone feels about each other. Now, having said all that, do you have an opinion about the saddle?"

Luke's cheeks turned pink.

"If the choice is saddle now or saddle later, I'd like it now. I promise I'll do all the work to pay you back, but the saddle Major has doesn't fit me very well. I think his last rider was short and heavy. And I'm not really sure they gave us the saddle anyone used on Major, anyway."

Will put his palms on the table and stood up.

"Okay, that's settled. Now, who wants ice cream?"

Chapter 31

A cold drizzle was falling during Harriet's run the next morning. She ran five miles, going through the woods that started at the end of her street to help blunt the rainfall. She had just gotten out of her post-run shower when her phone rang.

"Did I give you enough time to finish your run?" Lauren asked.

"Perfect timing. I just got dressed. What's up?"

"Well, you know how you all asked me to do a bunch of research on a bunch of things. I was doing that and getting nowhere when I decided to go back and look at the security footage at the stable. I still have access from when I set it up. No one ever changed the passwords, even though I suggested they do that on a regular basis.

"Anyway, I found some interesting footage. Do you have time to meet me at Annie's for a hot drink so I can show you? I need to pick up some fabric when we're done. You're welcome to join me for that, too."

"That sounds great. Hopefully, Annie has been baking this morning. I could use one of her cinnamon twists. And I'm always up for a trip to the fabric store."

"See you in thirty?"

"Perfect."

✂-- ✂-- ✂

Harriet was more than a little curious as to what Lauren had found. They'd already established Simon had been in a shadow, obscuring whatever happened to him.

Lauren was already in Annie's, sipping a latte, a plate with two cinnamon twists in front of her, when she arrived.

"I got your twist in case there was a rush on them before you got here." Harriet laughed.

"Thanks for that." She went to the counter to order hot chocolate.

They ate their warm cinnamon twists in silence for a few minutes. Finally, Harriet set hers down, licked the sugar off her fingers then wiped them with a napkin.

"So, what have you got?"

Lauren opened her iPad and turned it toward Harriet before pushing the go arrow. It took Harriet a moment to orient herself to what she was seeing.

The grainy gray video was one of the cameras Lauren had installed outside, showing the driveway.

"Angela said they'd disconnected all the outside cameras to reduce costs. Apparently, she missed this one."

Harriet watched a car move down the driveway from the gate to the manager's house.

"What am I seeing?"

"If you look at the time stamp, this car is there during the window when Simon was killed. Could have been before or could have been after. The interesting feature is, I believe it's Angela's car, returning from somewhere. Keep watching."

Harriet did as she was instructed. Lauren sped up the video then slowed it again.

"Now, notice this car coming in."

"Is that Crystal Kelley?"

"Sure looks like it to me. Again, in the same window of time when Simon might have been killed. That barn is a very busy place at o-dark-thirty in the morning." She flipped to another camera. "And someone was being mindful of the cameras."

"What's wrong with this one?"

"Someone has cleverly smeared dirt over the lens on the camera that shows the view from the opposite end of the barn. If you watch in the center of the screen...now..." She pointed. "...you can see shadowy motion."

Harriet leaned closer to the screen.

"I guess, but it could just be screen anomalies."

"I can try to filter it more on my computer, but someone's done a good job of masking the camera."

Harriet leaned back.

"Aren't the cameras mounted pretty high?"

"There's a glitch in the image, probably a disconnection of the camera. Someone had about sixty seconds, and when it came back, it was obscured. If I were going to do it, I would unplug the system, spray the lens with a dirt mixture, and then reconnect it."

"Wouldn't you be able to see the person unplugging it on another camera?"

"Remember—Angela disabled some of the cameras to save money, so the system is downgraded to a couple of basic cameras. And here's the kicker—they're wired in through the attic dormitory. Only part of the attic is floored and has living space; the rest of it is open. A person could go up there and unhook the camera wire, and you'd never see it."

"Why isn't it more secure?"

Lauren shook her head.

"It all comes down to money. They quit having the system monitored, so no alarm went off when the camera was disconnected. Angela and Simon could monitor it from the house, but otherwise, no one would know. He was in the barn, and she was either in the attic disabling the camera, or someone else knew she was going to be gone in the middle of the night."

"Have you showed this to Detective Morse?"

"Not yet. Technically, I don't have permission to access this footage anymore. Although no one officially said I didn't."

"Could you at least suggest she check their footage? Or show it to her off the record and let her figure out how to 'discover' it?"

Lauren sighed. "I'll figure something out." She picked up her latte and took a long sip.

"*We* could try to talk to Angela," Harriet suggested. "If we think about it, we could come up with a reason."

"Let's ponder it for a while and see if any ideas come to us. I thought someone besides me should know about it, anyway."

They sipped their drinks, and when they were finished, Harriet carried their cups back to the counter.

"Let's go look at fabric," she said when she returned to their table. "That will help, I'm sure."

✂ -- ✂ -- ✂

Harriet moved to the end of a row of fabric bolts and stopped in front of a rack that held pre-cut squares of coordinated fabrics.

"Look at these layer cakes," she called to Lauren. "I'm thinking I could make a quarter-sheet background by sewing these together. What do you think?"

"It's worth trying. It might help it drape better. I've put double darts in mine to do the same. Today, I'm shopping for something else. Glynnis and Beryl are scheming on a fundraiser for the local wild bird 'tweetment' center. You know there are going to be a bunch of people coming to town in April to do bird counts. I didn't commit to a quilt, but I said I could do a couple of quilted throw pillows."

"That sounds good."

"They asked if they could come to our next Threads meeting, and I told her to ask your aunt."

"Geez, we're not even done with our horse blankets, yet."

"I know, in this town it never ends. Heaven forbid we should want to do a quilt for ourselves."

Harriet held up two of the fabric stacks.

"Which one do you like best?"

Chapter 32

𝓗arriet decided to make a quick stop at the grocery store on her way home. Even after months, she and James weren't completely tuned into how much food they needed to buy during their weekly shopping trip to keep a growing boy fed.

Her intention was to dash in, grab bread and milk, and be on her way. It was going well until she turned into the bread aisle. Crystal Kelley was at the other end, comparing the labels of two peanut butter jars.

"Hey, Harriet," she called.

"Hi, Crystal."

Crystal wheeled her cart to where Harriet stood.

"Have you heard anything about Simon?"

"You probably know more than I do."

Crystal gave her a knowing glance.

"I think we both know you have sources normal people don't."

"Crystal, I don't know what you think I know, but I'm like everyone else. I read the newspaper and the internet and watch the evening news."

"I've read about how you've caught murderers, right here in Foggy Point."

"I don't know what to tell you, Crystal. I don't have any idea who killed Simon. I do have a question for you, though. "What time do lessons start at the equestrian center?"

"Why are you asking me? You know they start at seven-thirty. You and your quilter friends have been out there observing."

"I was curious because my husband James has a restaurant here in town," Harriet started.

"Oh, we're well aware. We've eaten there a few times."

"Well, you probably know that when you own a restaurant, your day starts quite early." She silently apologized to James for the whopper she was about to tell.

"I don't see what that has to do with me." Crystal started unconsciously tapping her foot on the bottom rack of her cart.

"Saturday morning, James was on his way to that new artisan cheese-maker. It's beyond the equestrian center on Miller Hill Road. It was very early, five-thirty or so. He said he was surprised to see you turn into the driveway. I thought maybe they were doing make-up classes early or something."

Her foot stopped, and she looked away before answering.

"I lost my wallet, and the last time I remembered having it was at the stable on Friday when I got out my credit card to pay our fee."

"And you went to look for it at five-thirty in the morning?"

"I'm an early bird, so sue me."

"Did you find it?"

"What?"

"Did you find your wallet?"

"Yes, it was at home the whole time. It had fallen out of my coat pocket in my dressing room."

"I'm glad you found it. Redoing all your ID is a real hassle."

Crystal started pushing her cart past Harriet.

"So, you really don't know anything about who killed Simon?"

Harriet shook her head. "I really don't."

✄ -- ✄ -- ✄

Harriet turned her car back toward Miller Hill Road. Now that she'd involved James in the story she'd told Crystal, she needed to buy some of the cheese for him in case the Kelley family decided to eat at the restaurant in the next few days. She wasn't sure how much cheese was enough, but she bought ten pounds of their grass-fed cow cheddar for the restaurant and a round of aged gouda for home.

James kissed her cheek when she entered the kitchen at the restaurant.

"It's always delightful to see you, but to what do I owe the pleasure of today's visit?"

Harriet held up the bag of cheese blocks.

"This is my attempt to cover the tracks of a fib." She recounted her meeting with Lauren followed by her chance encounter with Crystal.

143

James laughed. "I got your back; and I've been wanting to try this cheese. I've got a nice little appetizer in mind."

"I bought a round of their aged gouda for us to have at home."

James put his arm around her waist and pulled her to him.

"Well done, my sweet." He kissed her. "What are you up to now?"

"I need to do some client quilting."

One of the restaurant servers came to the kitchen door and gestured to James. He kissed her again.

"I've got to go back to work. Thanks for the cheese."

"Thanks for covering for me."

✂-- ✂-- ✂

A familiar vintage Bronco was sitting in her driveway when Harriet pulled in. Aiden wasn't in the car. *He must be inside with Luke.* She hoped his new maturity was still in play, and she wasn't going to have to deal with emotional drama.

Luke and Aiden were at the kitchen table eating gingersnaps when she came in.

"Aren't you supposed to be in school?" she asked Luke.

"Today's a half-day. Teacher training or something."

She lifted the teakettle and, finding it full, turned the stove on.

"To what do we owe a vet visit? Are the boys okay?"

She knew the answer; Scooter was in Aiden's lap, and Cyrano was begging beside Luke's chair. Fred supervised from the counter.

Aiden leaned back in his chair and let out a breath.

"It's possible I'm imagining things, or maybe it's just having hung out with you and your buddies enough that I'm seeing crime everywhere, but I wanted to run something by you."

"Go on," she prompted.

"I was out at the stable a little while ago seeing to a horse with a bruised hoof. As I've pointed out before, I'm not a large animal specialist and especially not a horse doctor." He paused.

"But…" Harriet said.

"But it sure seems like Miller Hill has a lot of foot problems. In school, we had a few hot nails, or random cuts, but mainly horses that were outside more. We saw colic, or horses choking on their food, or random bellyaches. I was curious, so I called a buddy of mine from vet school who specializes in horses, and he agrees with me. It could be coincidental, but according to him, it's pretty unusual."

"What do you think is going on?"

"I'm not sure, but what with the manager's husband being killed, I wondered if someone is sabotaging the horse's feet and he caught them in the act."

"*Could* someone purposely cause the injuries you've seen?"

"They could. Especially if they know what sort of injuries horses get at a stable. They could figure out how to make them look natural. The cut foot bulb could have been done with a box cutter or scalpel, the bruised hoof I just saw could have been done with a hammer. Likewise, the nail. The horse could have stepped on it, or someone could have purposely driven it into the hoof."

Harriet got up and went to the stove to fill her mug.

"Anyone else want tea?"

Aiden and Luke shook their heads.

"I guess with the upcoming show in a couple of weeks, a rival might be trying to improve their chances," Aiden suggested.

Harriet brought her tea to the table and grabbed a couple of gingersnaps before sitting down.

"The various horses that have been injured wouldn't necessarily be in the same class, so they wouldn't all be direct competition. At least, I wouldn't think so."

Luke took another cookie.

"Maybe there's a rival stable that wanted to have a show, but Miller Hill beat them out."

Harriet sipped her tea.

"Maybe. I don't know all the stables within driving distance of here, but somebody said the closest one burned down sometime in the recent past."

"I can ask Dr. Billings when I talk to him again. He should know." Aiden got up and carried his empty water glass to the sink. "I have to get back, but I wanted you to know I'd seen another foot injury, since you have a horse there."

Luke stood up.

"I'll bet that's why Major broke his door. Someone he didn't know tried to get in, and he pitched a fit."

Harriet smiled.

"He does seem to have a pretty strong sense of self-preservation, but thanks for warning us, Aiden. If what you think is true, all the owners should be warned."

"I don't have any real evidence," he cautioned. "It just seemed weird to me."

"Well, thanks for letting us know. If what you suspect is true, someone dangerous could be lurking around the stable," Harriet said.

"It never hurts to be careful."

Luke stood up.

"Yeah, thanks for letting us know, Dr. Jalbert. I'm going to go call Emily and warn her."

Aiden looked like he wanted to say something else when Luke had gone upstairs, but he turned and left without speaking.

Chapter 33

Another cold drizzle was falling from gray skies when Harriet arrived at the Loose Threads weekly meeting. It was being held earlier than usual so the members who were volunteering with the Tuesday veterans' therapy session would get there on time.

Lauren, Aunt Beth, Connie, and Mavis were already around the table in the meeting room when she sat down and pulled her latest try at her horse blanket from her tote bag.

"Is anyone done with their blanket yet?" she asked.

Mavis shook her head.

"I decided I was trying to make mine too big. My newest attempt will cover the critical areas but isn't going to hang down the sides as far. I think that will make it easier to fit over the hips."

Beth made her a cup of tea from the carafe in the middle of the table.

"Wait until you see Jenny's. Here she is now. Jenny, we were just talking about how hard it is to fit these blankets over the horses' hips and how you solved the problem."

Jenny set her tote on an empty chair and pulled her blanket out. Lauren set her travel mug down with a thump.

"Whoa."

Jenny's blanket had a deep scalloped edge that started longer under the rider's leg area and ended in a neat half-circle at the tail.

Harriet stuffed her blanket back in her bag.

"I hope you don't mind, Jenny, but I'm going to try that."

Beth looked pointedly at her niece.

"You do have to finish before the show, you know."

"I will. I haven't liked my trials so far, and they haven't fit well enough to use," Harriet said.

Robin and DeAnn arrived in time to see Jenny's blanket before she put it back in her bag. Robin pulled hers out.

"I didn't do scallops, but I did stair-step the edge. It looked messy when I left it the same length from the side to the tail. I hope they approve."

DeAnn sat down and pumped hot water from the carafe into her cup and selected a teabag.

"That was a question I had. Does someone need to approve these? I wondered if there's some official rule about how they look or how big they are."

Connie stood and removed the plastic wrap from a tray of cookies she'd brought.

"I made cookies for Wendy's preschool class at the church, so we have lemon drops, sugar cookies, and ginger cookies. I made a batch of chocolate chip cookies just for us. They don't let the littles have chocolate because it's too messy."

Lauren reached for a chocolate chip cookie.

"I promise I won't make a mess, and my guess is Angela will be the final word on our blankets, since she's the one who asked us to make them."

Aunt Beth sipped her tea.

"We should probably try to finish them up by the end of this week, so we have time to try them on the horses and make corrections." She eyed Harriet. "Or make them over."

Harriet grinned at her.

"I'm going to have a spectacular quarter-sheet that will fit Major like a glove."

Lauren laughed.

"Is Major even going to be in the show?"

Harriet glared at her friend.

"No, but that's beside the point."

Beth shook her head.

Glynnis Wilson and Frieda Conn from the Small Stitches quilt group arrived, ending the discussion.

"I heard you ladies had some excitement out at the equestrian center," Glynnis said.

Beth rolled her eyes. "Don't ask."

Frieda was less inclined to gossip and got down to business.

"If you haven't heard, there's going to be a birdwatching and counting event in April, and we were asked by the local Audubon chapter to do a fundraiser for the 'tweetment' center they'd like to build. Of course, we said yes, because how could we not?"

Glynnis took the cup of coffee Mavis offered her.

"Now, we all appreciate the fact that you bailed us out on quilts at Christmas," Glynnis said, "so we were thinking if you wanted, you could make table runners or sofa pillows or something small like that."

Lauren sat back in her chair.

"I can handle making a table runner."

Frieda smiled at her.

"Anything you want to do would be helpful."

"Before you ask," Lauren continued, "if anyone gets the idea that we should take in roommates, count me out. Once was enough. My guest was nice, but no thanks."

Glynnis sipped her coffee and set it down.

"No one has suggested we do that, and we haven't volunteered. I don't know how it was for you ladies, but we had a couple of real doozies. We agreed right from the start that we would not be participating in any lodging schemes."

Frieda stood up.

"Come on, Glynnis, we've taken enough time from their meeting. I'll send an email to Beth, and she can forward it to the rest of you, with dates we need to collect items. Thank you for helping us."

Glynnis thanked them as well, and took a few cookies for the road before they left.

"Now that we have that out of the way, can we get on with business?" Beth asked.

Harriet raised her eyebrow.

"Business?"

"We need to know what's going on with the investigation of Simon's death," Beth said.

Mavis took a cookie and put it on her napkin.

"First of all, Jenny, how are things with you and Brian?"

Jenny put her face in her hands. Harriet was afraid she wasn't going to speak, but finally, she dropped her hands.

"The police have taken him in for questioning three times. He was out jogging by himself when Simon was killed, and even though he told them that several cars passed him on his route, no one has come forward to say they saw him."

Lauren got her tablet from her bag and set it on the table.

"How are they searching for people who might have seen him?"

Jenny shook her head.

"I'm not sure, but I think they said something about canvassing the neighborhood closest to the stable."

Connie slapped her hands on the table.

"That's not going to help. They need to ask people along his route."

Robin pulled out her yellow pad and pen.

"Jenny, can you tell us what his route is?"

Jenny took the pen and wrote out a list of roads and trails.

"I can't be certain, but this is his usual route. I've gone with him a few times."

Robin took the list back.

"If anyone wants to help, look at this list and see if you know anyone on it. If you do, call and see if they might have been up that early, or know someone who was, and ask them to check and see if anyone saw him."

When Robin was done, Lauren held her iPad up, facing out.

"These people weren't on Brian's running route, but they were in the driveway of the equestrian center." She played the grainy footage of first Angela coming home, and then Crystal a few moments later.

"I can't see the timestamp," Mavis said, leaning forward and straining to make out the numbers.

Lauren turned the pad back around and turned it off.

"Crystal drove in at exactly five-thirty. Angela was five minutes before her. I heard Detective Morse talking to the medical examiner, and five-thirty is right in the middle of what they were guessing was Simon's time of death. They've probably refined that time by now, but until we hear anything different, Angela and Crystal both need to stay on our list of suspects."

Harriet wiped her hands on her napkin and crumpled it up.

"This may be neither here nor there, but I ran into Crystal at the grocery store yesterday, and I asked her what she was doing at the stable at five-thirty in the morning."

"Wait," Lauren interrupted. "You didn't tell her about the security footage, did you?"

"Of course not. I told her James saw her turning in there while he was on his way to the cheese place up the road from there."

"And she believed you?" DeAnn asked.

"Everyone knows a chef's day starts early. She didn't question it. Anyway, what I was going to say was Crystal told me she'd lost her wallet and had gone out there to look for it."

"Well, that's a big coincidence," Aunt Beth muttered.

Harriet picked up her cup, but it was empty, and she set it back down.

"I questioned her as to why she was looking for it so early, but she brushed me off, saying she's an early bird."

Robin made a note on the yellow pad.

"I'm not sure that helps us, other than it says she was going into the barn, as opposed to Angela, who might have gone straight into the house without seeing what was happening with Simon."

Harriet stood, picked up her mug and napkin, and carried them to the kitchen before returning for her tote bag and coat.

"I thought you should know about Crystal, even though I'm not sure how it helps at this point."

Aunt Beth got ready to leave as well.

"We'll see you at the stable," she said. "Or next week, for those of you who aren't volunteering today."

Chapter 34

*L*uke came into Harriet's studio Wednesday afternoon after school, sandwich in hand as usual.

"Should I start setting the table?"

Harriet looked at her watch and smiled.

"Sweetie, I know you're anxious, but James said he'll be home early. He should be here any time now. I'm sure he'll have a plan about the table. He may bring a tablecloth from the restaurant, or a centerpiece or something. Finish your snack, and then if you want you can take the dogs out for a long walk so they can burn off a little energy."

"What if you guys don't like her parents? Will you make me stop seeing Emily?"

"Do you have a reason to believe we wouldn't like them?"

"No, but you never know."

"What aren't you telling me?"

"Well, they *were* born in a religious commune," he reminded her.

"I'm not sure where they were born matters. Anyway, relax, I met Rain at the stable the other day when I invited her to dinner. She seemed like a normal parent." She got up from her machine and put her hands on his shoulders. "Don't worry. It's going to be fine. We'll have dinner, they'll go home, and life will go on as usual."

"But..."

"No buts. Let's go leash up the beasts."

✂-- ✂-- ✂

Harriet watched Luke out of the kitchen window until he reached the end of the driveway and turned toward the forest trail. When he was out of sight, she dialed James.

"Are you on your way home?" she asked when he answered. "Luke is a nervous wreck."

"As well he should be. And yes, I'm on my way home. I'm picking up a centerpiece at the florist on the way."

"I can see you're not taking dinner too seriously."

"It's important. We don't want to embarrass Luke. And we need to make a good first impression. If they don't like us, they might not let Emily see Luke anymore."

"That's hardly likely. They have horses at the same barn we do. Still, it would be great if you could help calm him down when you get home."

"Okay, deep breaths, deep breaths."

"See you when you get here."

✂-- ✂-- ✂

"Hi, I'm Drew Roberts, and this is my wife Rain," Emily's dad said when Harriet opened the front door.

"Come in," she said. "Can I take your coats?"

They shrugged out of their coats, and Harriet hung them on the ornate Victorian coat tree that stood in her entryway. Rain's waist-length hair was held back with a silver clasp. Her husband had a full russet beard and shoulder-length brown hair.

She led them all into the parlor, where James took their drink requests, and they sat down.

"Have you heard anything about the man who was killed at the stable?" Rain asked.

Harriet picked up her cup of tea, then set it down again.

"Not really."

Drew sat on the edge of the Victorian settee.

"Do you think it's dangerous for the kids to be out at the stable?"

"Luke," James said, "why don't you take Emily to the TV room to try your new video game."

He got up quickly, and Emily hustled after him. James blew out a breath.

"I'm not wild about Luke being out at the stable, but his horse is there, and we don't have a better place to move him to right now."

Drew sat back.

"We're in the same boat. And the horse means a lot to Emily. She was bullied when she was younger, and getting involved with horses saved her."

Harriet sipped her tea.

"My friends and I have been volunteering at the stable, so we're often out there. Hopefully, that's a deterrent to anything happening when the kids are there."

"I feel a little better," Rain said, and picked up her glass of water. "James, Emily tells me you own a restaurant."

James described his journey from baseball prospect to chef training to Smugglers Cove owner.

Drew revealed he was a cabinetmaker. Rain was a custom jeweler who had a home studio. Emily had already told her parents about Harriet's quilt-making and long-arm business.

This exchange of information took them until dinnertime.

James had outdone himself. His main course was butternut squash with rice pilaf, pecans, dried cranberries, and chopped parsley. The salad was mixed baby greens with diced pears and vegan blue cheese dressed with balsamic vinaigrette. To the side, he served corn pudding.

When the meal had finished with James's signature "death by chocolate" dessert, Emily and Luke excused themselves to go finish their game. Harriet brought after-dinner coffee to the table.

"Has Emily decided what she's going to do when she finishes high school?" she asked as she sat down. "Is she going to college around here so she can be near Fable?"

Rain looked at Drew and then back to Harriet.

"I guess Emily hasn't been talking about her plans yet."

Harriet and James shook their heads.

Rain took a deep breath.

"I don't know if Emily has mentioned this before, but Drew and I both grew up in a religious commune. I'm third generation, Drew is second. We both chose not to remain in the commune, but we didn't leave until after we'd graduated college."

Drew continued.

"Our commune has service as one of its core values, and even though we're no longer living onsite, we still share that value. We both did two years of international service before college, and it affected us profoundly. We'd like Emily to have that experience as well."

James picked up the coffee press and topped off Drew's cup.

"Where did you do your service?"

"Our group is affiliated with the Missionaries of Charity, Mother Teresa's organization, so we go where the poorest of the poor are. In my case, it was the slums of India," Drew said.

"I worked with prostitutes in Thailand," Rain said.

Harriet sipped her coffee.

"That sounds intense. Is that what Emily wants?"

Drew shrugged.

"She's getting there. She didn't grow up with the commune's constant indoctrination."

"We didn't want that for her," Rain interrupted. "We wanted her to make her own choice. Until the horse thing came along, she would have chosen service."

Everyone sipped their coffee in unison, putting their cups down with embarrassed chuckles.

"We're not sure what Luke's plans are," Harriet said, taking the attention off the Robertses.

"We've offered to take him to visit colleges, but he hasn't taken us up on that yet," James added.

Harriet sighed.

"He's had such a tough life. He's worked really hard to get all the credits he needs to graduate. He often wasn't able to attend school, through no fault of his own."

Rain smiled.

"He's lucky he has you. So many children get lost in the system. I do some volunteer work with the junior high school, trying to find students who aren't attending and help them solve the problems that keep them from doing so."

"What's the predominant issue?" James asked.

"That's part of the problem—there isn't a single issue. Poverty is often involved, but some kids are taking care of disabled parents. A fair number have drug addicts for parents. Some have emotional and physical problems due to long-term abuse," Rain explained.

"I wish we could help them all," James said.

"We all do," Drew said. "For now, do you know anything about the woman who took over Simon's classes? Emily will be taking lessons with her when Fable's foot is better."

Harriet finished her coffee and set her mug down.

"I've talked to her a few times. She has a really expensive horse, and assuming she can ride up to his level, she's probably pretty good."

Rain smiled again. "I shouldn't be sexist, but after Simon, I'm relieved Emily has a female trainer."

Harriet grinned. "I hear you."

James stood up and picked up the empty coffee press.

"Can I get anyone anything else? I can make more coffee."

Drew shook his head.

"If we drink any more coffee, we'll be up all night."

"We should probably be going, anyway." Rain added. "Thank you so much for the wonderful dinner."

"You're very welcome." James beamed.

Harriet stood up.

"I'll go get the kids."

Chapter 35

"Are they gone?" Luke asked after Harriet and James had seen them out and began clearing the dinner dishes.

Harriet looked out the kitchen window.

"Their taillights are headed out, so unless one of them jumped out and is hiding in the bushes, they're out of here."

"What's up?" James asked.

Luke's face turned red.

"Did Drew and Rain tell you what they're making Emily do?"

"If you mean their encouraging her to go volunteer in poor areas internationally, they did mention it," Harriet said.

James opened the dishwasher, and Luke started handing him dirty dishes.

"It's not exactly encouraging her. They're pressuring her pretty hard."

Harriet went to the sink and started filling it with hot water for the hand washables.

"They told us it was her choice."

"That's a joke. They slip it into every conversation they have with her. Why does it have to be so far away? At least you guys aren't making me go that far. I'll—"

James dropped a plate into the dishwasher with a bang.

"Hold on a minute. We aren't 'making' you go anywhere."

Harriet turned away from the sink.

"We're only giving you options. You don't have to take them."

Luke slumped into a chair. Harriet and James followed. He hung his head.

"I don't want to be ungrateful. I should do whatever you think is best for me."

Harriet reached for his hand.

"We don't want you to do what we want. We want you to do whatever *you* want to do."

"So far, everything you've wanted has worked out pretty well, so it doesn't seem like I should do something else."

"Luke, sweetie, we just want you to be happy," Harriet assured him.

James leaned back in his chair.

"Okay, for just a minute, let's pretend you can do whatever you want, wherever you want, with no strings attached. What would you do, and where would you do it?"

Luke closed his eyes and tilted his head back. Harriet and James watched him.

A minute passed, and then another. Finally, he opened his eyes.

"I want to stay here," he said.

"O-kaa-y," Harriet said, drawing the word out. "As in, stay a high school senior forever?"

Luke barked a laugh. "Of course not. I mean, I like you guys, and I like it here; high school, not so much. I've been thinking about this for a while, but I didn't know how to bring it up."

"Just tell us," Harriet encouraged him.

"What if I went to Peninsula College and lived here? I could still ride Major, and if Emily gets to stay around..."

Harriet relaxed and smiled.

"I think that is a fine idea. I know Major will agree with me."

"Do they have a degree program you're interested in?" James asked.

"They have a couple I'm interested in. I thought I could take general studies the first year, and then narrow things down."

"Do you want to live near campus?" Harriet asked.

"No!" he said loudly, then repeated "no," in a normal voice. "I mean, if it's okay with you guys, I'd like to stay *here*. That's why I want to go to Peninsula. I'm still getting used to living in a normal family. I don't want to give it all up this soon. I know that sounds selfish."

"No, Luke," Harriet said. "It doesn't, not at all. You've had to look after yourself your whole life. No one can blame you for wanting to be a kid while you still can."

James went back to loading the dishwasher.

"Will it change your plans if Emily goes off to India or somewhere while you stay here?"

Luke's cheeks flamed again.

"I like Emily…a lot. But…" He looked down at his hands. "I want to be the 'kid', as you said, for a while longer, and even though it feels selfish, I think I need to spend some more time learning how to belong to a family before I move on to the next stage in my life."

James came over and put an arm around his shoulders in an awkward hug.

"It's not selfish, and you are very wise not to rush things." He looked at Harriet, and she nodded slightly. "And we would love to have you stay with us as long as you want to. Going to Peninsula is a good plan."

"And, Luke," Harriet said, "Emily is going to have to figure out how to talk to her own parents regarding her situation. I don't know them well enough to judge if they're being honest, but they said they are encouraging her but not making her do a service project. I think there's room for negotiation. And they are well aware that having Fable has changed things for her. They didn't seem to have plans to take Fable away from her, either."

"Maybe she can convince them that doing therapy-horse work is a good service. Before Simon died, he said we were going to begin working with disabled children," Luke said with enthusiasm.

"Sounds good," James said. "Help me with these dishes, and we'll have time for a gaming rematch upstairs."

Harriet smiled to herself. James and Luke had a competition that had been going on since Christmas. It was hard to tell which one of them was enjoying it more.

Luke grinned. "You're on."

Chapter 36

I t was dark when Harriet pulled out of the garage the next morning. It was cold, too, but thankfully neither raining nor snowing. She had realized the night before that she still hadn't measured the tailpiece on Major's blanket, and she experienced a sense of déjà vu as she drove to the barn once again dressed in her running clothes. She had agreed to meet her aunt and Mavis for coffee after her run to report on last night's dinner, but she needed to take care of Major's tailpiece fitting first.

She was deep in thought about how she was going to describe Emily's parents to her aunt when she pulled into the stable parking area and realized that, in spite of the early hour, she wasn't the first to arrive. Crystal Kelly's unmistakable lavender car was already there.

Major nickered softly as she approached.

"Hey, big guy. Let me set my things down, and I'll be right there." She put her purse on the bench and pulled the requisite bag of carrot bits from the interior, dropping her phone in at the same time. She draped the horse blanket over her purse, but as she turned to unlatch the stall door, it fell to the floor. As she turned back to pick it up, she noticed a stall door farther down was open a few inches. It was in the area where Paige's horse's stall was.

She picked up Major's blanket and set the bag of carrots on top of it.

"I'll be right back," she told the horse, and walked down the aisle. She heard the horse inside the stall snorting and stomping as she approached.

"Crystal?" she called.

160

The horse whinnied, but there was no other reply.

"Crystal?" she tried again. She reached the door and pulled it farther open. Paige's horse was crowded against the back wall, her eyes wild. Crystal lay at her feet.

Harriet started to kneel at Crystal's side when something hit her back and an electric jolt coursed through her body, making her muscles spasm and lights flash in the periphery of her vision. She fell to the floor in incredible pain, landing across Crystal's inert form. She lay helpless as the stall door was slammed shut.

It felt like an hour but was actually only a few minutes before she was able to control herself and rise to her knees. She reached out and felt for a pulse in Crystal's neck, sagging back on her heels when she found none.

"Oh, Crystal," she said quietly. "I didn't really like you, but you didn't deserve this."

After a few minutes, she got up and staggered to the door. She tried unsuccessfully to open it, confirming her worst fear—she was locked in. She patted her hip, where her cell phone normally resided, before remembering she was in her running tights, and her phone was in her purse in front of Major's stall.

She knew she shouldn't disturb a crime scene, meaning she definitely shouldn't move anything, but Crystal's body was in the middle of the stall, and if it wasn't moved, the agitated horse was likely to trample it. The stall's feed trough, hay net, and water bucket were all suspended from the front wall, so the area underneath seemed like it would be the safest place to stash the body.

Harriet surveyed the stall and finally studied the horse. She didn't remember, if she'd ever known, the mare's name, but the horse was wearing a blue stable blanket. Given nothing else to work with, she approached the agitated animal.

"Easy, girl, easy. I need to borrow your blanket for a little while."

Thankfully, the horse was wearing a halter, and when she was close enough, Harriet grabbed it with one hand and patted the mare's neck with the other, then slid her hand down to the blanket buckles. The mare calmed, and Harriet was able to push the blanket to the floor.

Slowly and carefully, so as to not spook the horse, she spread the blanket beside Crystal's body, then rolled her onto it. As the dead woman flipped over, Harriet could see an angry red line around her neck. Definitely not an accident.

She rolled Crystal up and dragged her to the front stall wall, tucking her under the feed trough. With the body secured, Harriet started looking for a way out. The lower part of the walls was made from wood planks that extended high enough the horses couldn't see each other. The upper part was made of metal bars to allow for circulation. The bars were too close together for a person to squeeze through. Some stalls had space midway up the door to allow the horse to stick its head out; unfortunately, this wasn't one of them.

Not seeing a way out, she went to the door and started calling for help.

"Hello? Is anyone there?"

Major nickered at her, but no one else answered.

Harriet rubbed her arms. She needed to start wearing a heavier jacket over her long-sleeved running shirt until she was actually running. She stepped over to the mare and stroked her neck, tucking herself as close to the horse's shoulder as she could get to share her warmth.

It seemed like an eternity, but she finally heard noise at the far end of the aisle.

"Hello?" she called out.

"Harriet?" answered JoAnne.

"I'm down here locked in Paige's horse's stall. Call nine-one-one, and then see if you can get me out of here."

"What am I calling them about?"

"Crystal's dead."

"Oh, my gosh," she heard JoAnne say, and then silence, which she hoped meant the woman was dialing.

Moments later, she heard rattling at the stall door.

"Police are on their way, and there's a padlock on your door. I'm going to need to find some bolt cutters to get you out of there."

Harriet was torn between asking JoAnne to stay with her until the police arrived and telling her to hurry up and get those bolt cutters. Then she heard the crunch of gravel as someone else arrived.

"Oh, Stella, I'm glad you're here," JoAnne said.

"I brought those herbal supplements for Essy we talked about. I wanted to bring them in time for his breakfast."

"I haven't started feeding yet. Harriet accidentally got locked in Paige Kelley's horse stall. Could you stay with her while I find a pair of bolt cutters?"

"Sure,"

The footsteps moved nearer.

"Harriet?" Stella called. "How on earth did you get locked in there?"

"I came to try Major's quarter-sheet on, and when I got here, I noticed this stall door was open."

The sound of multiple vehicles interrupted her story. She heard more footsteps approaching.

"Where's the victim?" a male voice asked.

"I don't know what you're talking about," Stella told him.

"In here," Harriet yelled through the door.

"She's locked in the stall," Stella explained. "I'm not sure that qualifies as being a victim, but she's in there."

"Go get the bolt cutters." The man came close enough to the stall Harriet could see it was a fireman. The fire station was closer to the stable than the police were, and the dispatcher would have sent EMTs.

A second fireman returned the same time that JoAnne did, both holding bolt cutters. The fireman quickly cut the lock and let Harriet out. Two paramedics were striding down the aisle; Mary Pierce, the blond woman Harriet knew from before, was carrying two boxes of equipment, a muscular dark-haired man she hadn't seen before pulling the gurney.

"What do we have?" Mary asked Harriet.

"I found Crystal Kelley dead in the stall when I came to see why the stall door was open. I stepped inside, and was hit with what I assume was a Taser, and while I was incapacitated, the stall door was shut and locked behind me."

Harriet saw Stella's eyes widen and the color drain from her face.

"Crystal is…dead?" Stella stammered.

The second paramedic let go of the gurney and took Stella's arm, guiding her to a bench across the aisle.

"Why don't you sit here for a minute," he said, and took her wrist in a practiced move, measuring her pulse. "If you start to feel faint, put your head between your knees."

She looked up at him gratefully. "Thanks, I'll be okay. It's just a bit of a shock."

Mary looked over Harriet's shoulder and into the stall.

"Where's the body?"

Harriet grimaced.

"The detectives aren't going to like this, but she was lying in the middle of the stall, and the horse was getting more and more agitated. The mare had a blanket on, so I removed it, rolled Crystal onto it, and put her under the feed box against the front wall."

"Anything else?" Mary asked.

"That's about it. The horse and I waited for someone to arrive."

"Are you okay?"

"I'm not sure I'll ever be okay after the Taser, but otherwise, I'm fine."

"Have Randy check your vitals just to be sure." Mary indicated her partner standing beside Stella. "Could someone take the horse out so I can get in here?"

JoAnne took a lead rope from a hook beside the door and led the mare down the aisle and around the corner toward the pony barn. As she left, the police arrived.

Harriet did feel fine, but she went across the aisle and sat beside Stella anyway.

"Mary said I should have you check my vitals, since I was Tased," she told Randy, more to avoid a likely encounter with the newly arrived Officer Nguyen than anything else.

Randy performed the standard tests while Harriet watched Mary go into the stall, returning a moment later to speak to Nguyen, undoubtedly letting him know Crystal was, in fact, dead.

Major whinnied and banged his foot on his stall door. Randy finished determining Harriet was fit, and she stood up, calling to the big horse as she started down the aisle.

"Don't go anywhere until I talk to you," Nguyen called to her.

"I'll just be down here," she answered. She dug out the bag of carrot bits along with her phone and went into Major's stall. She called her aunt, cradling her phone against her shoulder as she fed Major his treat and quickly brought her up to speed.

"We'll be there as soon as I let everyone know what's going on."

Harriet hung up and speed dialed Lauren.

"I hope you don't have any appointments this morning," she said as soon as Lauren answered. "We have another situation."

Chapter 37

Detective Morse arrived at the barn nearly an hour later. Lauren had gotten there ahead of her, and once again delivered the sweatsuit and a cup of hot cocoa to Harriet. They sat on the bench outside Major's stall.

"Thank you so much for this," Harriet said as she sipped her drink.

"Let's not make it a habit. I barely had the suit back in the drawer when you called."

"Geez, I washed it before I returned it."

"I wasn't sure, so I threw it into the laundry, which I just did last night."

Harriet let out a sigh. "I promise, I will put some warm clothes in the back of my car when I get home. And I do appreciate your support."

"Hey, it's the least I can do. You're the one who got Tasered and had to wrestle a dead woman around."

"I suppose."

Detective Morse walked up and stood in front of them, notebook in hand. Her jaw was clenched, and her lips pressed together.

"Would you like to tell me what happened here?"

"Take it easy there, Sarge, this woman was Tasered an hour ago. She's a little shaky," Lauren said.

Morse glared at Harriet.

"She looks fine to me."

"Why are you mad at me?" Harriet asked. "I came here this morning early so I could try the horse blanket I'm making on Luke's horse before I went running. I saw an open stall door across the aisle and down two doors.

When I opened the door further to check why the door wasn't shut, since a horse was in there, I was jolted with the worst pain I've ever felt, and I fell onto what turned out to be Crystal's body.

"When I could stand, I discovered the door had been locked. The horse was panicking, and I was afraid it would trample her, so I removed its blanket, rolled Crystal into it, and pushed it under the feed box. I used the blanket to maneuver her and did not touch her with my hands or any other part of my body."

"Then what? How did you get out?"

"I waited until I heard JoAnne arrive, called to her, and she called the cavalry and went to look for her bolt cutters. The fireman arrived with their cutters first and let me out. Oh, and Stella Bren arrived somewhere in there, too. She'd brought a supplement she wanted JoAnne to add to her horse's feed."

"Did the paramedics check you out? Tasering isn't generally harmful, but still."

"Yeah, they said I was fine."

"Did you see any cars in the parking lot when you arrived?"

"Only Crystal's. Otherwise, none."

"Were there lights on at the manager's house?"

Harriet thought for a moment.

"I didn't really pay attention. I think the porch light was on, but I don't know if there were lights in any of the windows."

"Did you hear anyone else in the barn before JoAnne arrived?"

"No, but I was pretty focused on trying to keep the horse calm and wondering what happened to Crystal."

"Is there anything else you can tell me?"

Harriet sipped her hot chocolate while she thought. Finally, she shook her head.

"I can't think of anything else."

Detective Morse let out a breath.

"I'm sorry for coming on so strong. I'm just frustrated. My boss is pressuring us to clear Simon's murder. After the murders a month ago, the public is pressuring the mayor about safety and he in turn is pressuring the brass. And for them it's all about the upcoming elections."

She looked up and down the aisle. "You didn't hear this from me, but we have nothing on Simon's death, and so far, this isn't looking to be any easier. You have a horse boarded here, which means you're out here and know the people. If you hear anything, let me know. No matter how insignificant or unrelated."

"I'm not very connected, but I have been volunteering with the veteran's horse-therapy program, so I'm around a couple of times a week."

"I'd appreciate anything."

They all looked down the aisle as the medical examiner came out of the stall and headed for the door.

"She's good to transport," the ME said as she passed them.

"Are you willing to say anything yet?"

The ME turned around.

"The victim is dead. You want anything else, you'll have to wait until I have her on the table."

"Thanks for nothing," Morse muttered.

"If it helps, when I fell on her, she was still warm," Harriet volunteered.

"About what time did you get here?" Morse asked. The ME paused for her answer.

"A little before six. I had planned to run and shower after, and then meet my aunt and friends for early coffee."

"That does help," Morse said. "Can you come by the station and sign your statement? I'll get it typed up."

"Sure."

"Can we leave?" Lauren asked.

"Yes, as long as Harriet signs her statement later."

Lauren stood up.

"Let's go. I talked to your aunt on my way here, and she called everyone, and we're supposed to call them to meet us at the Steaming Cup when we're done."

"Works for me."

Aunt Beth met Harriet at the door when she arrived at the Steaming Cup and pulled her into a bear hug.

"Are you okay? We were all so worried when Lauren told me you'd been Tasered."

Harriet stepped back when her aunt finally released her.

"I'm fine. It's not anything I'd ever want to experience again, but I survived."

"Come in and sit down. Let's get you something to drink."

Harriet held up her half-finished hot chocolate.

"Lauren took care of me."

Aunt Beth put her arm around Harriet's waist and guided her to the group table.

"Something to eat, then. How about an apple fritter? The sugar and fat combo should help put things right."

"Sure," Harriet knew arguing with her aunt when she was in mother-hen mode would be useless. She sat down next to Mavis while Beth went to order her food.

"Are you okay?" Mavis asked.

"I'm fine. Not something I'd like to repeat anytime soon, but no lasting damage."

"I suppose you'd better wait to tell us any more until everyone's here," Mavis said.

Beth set Harriet's pastry in front of her and sat down with her own drink and a blueberry scone. In the next few minutes, the rest of the Loose Threads came in and, after a stop at the food counter, joined them at the big table.

Robin pulled her yellow tablet and pen from her bag.

"Beth didn't tell us what happened this morning, Harriet, so why don't you start by filling us in, then we can figure out where to go from here."

Harriet recounted her unpleasant morning, finishing with Detective Morse's statement about the lack of any progress in the investigation of Simon's death and her fear that Crystal's would be the same.

"Seems sort of early for her to be giving up," Lauren added.

Harriet wiped her hands on her napkin.

"I don't think she's giving up. She's just frustrated."

Robin wrote headings on a fresh page of her tablet. *Suspects* was the first.

"Okay," she said. "Who are our suspects in Crystal's death?"

Beth, Connie, and Mavis all turned to Harriet.

"Don't look at me. Crystal was obnoxious, but that's no reason to kill the woman."

Lauren set her cup down.

"Let's think about this. It would be way too much of a coincidence for the murder of Simon and today's murder to be unrelated events. I'm thinking we need to look at the suspects we have in Simon's murder and try to figure out how Crystal fits in with them."

Robin wrote *Stanley* in the Suspects column.

"How do we think Crystal relates to Stanley?"

"She was knocked off her feet when Stanley's horse ran away during therapy," Carla offered.

Robin made a note.

"It's more a reason for Crystal to dislike Stanley than the other way round, but you never know."

Jenny sipped her coffee.

"Before anyone asks, unless she's a client of Brian's business, he doesn't know her." She hung her head. "He was out running early this morning, so once again, he doesn't have an alibi for what I assume was the critical time."

Mavis reached out and patted her hand.

"Oh, honey, no one thinks Brian killed anyone."

Jenny shook her head.

"I just wish he had an alibi."

Beth looked around the table.

"Has anyone had any luck with the neighbors on Brian's running route?"

"None of our immediate neighbors saw him," Jenny said.

"My client near the stable," Lauren said, "didn't see anything. I asked her to check with her neighbors, and she did, but no one saw him. People don't tend to look out their windows when it's still dark."

Robin wrote Brian's name down and made a note of his lack of alibi.

"Moving on," she said. "How about Stanley? Does anyone know if he's back in town?"

Harriet shook her head.

"I haven't heard, but I can go out to the camp and ask. I'm sure James has food that needs to be delivered."

Robin noted that Harriet would check next to Stanley's name.

"What about Angela?"

Connie brushed muffin crumbs from her hands.

"The better question is, do any of us know the woman well enough to know if she had any reason to want Crystal dead?"

"Has anyone else read the Miss Marple mysteries?" Harriet asked. "Miss Marple liked to point out that there could be an X on the list. Someone we don't know about yet."

Lauren chuckled.

"That's not helpful. That's like saying it could be the tooth fairy or the Easter Bunny. Possible, yes. Probable, not likely."

Harriet sat back in her chair.

"The other possibility is Crystal saw something or someone, and someone killed her before she could tell."

"She had plenty of time to share what she knew," Robin said as she made a note on her paper under the heading of *Motive*. "But it's as good a motive as any."

Lauren sat up straight.

"What about JoAnne? I mean, she was the one who found you. Maybe she was there the whole time."

"I didn't see any other cars," Harriet reminded her.

"Maybe they have an employee parking area," Lauren countered.

Harriet sipped her now-cold chocolate.

"If there *is* a parking area behind the arena, then anyone could have been there. I can walk around the back the next time I'm out there to check."

Robin made a note.

"So far, we've got Harriet checking on the homeless camp—"

"I'll go with her," Aunt Beth interrupted.

"Okay," Robin said and noted it. "And Harriet is going around the arena to look for other parking."

Mavis held her hand up briefly.

"I'll do that with her when we have our next volunteer session."

"Good," Connie said. "I don't think any of us should go to that place by ourselves until this is over."

DeAnn crumpled her napkin and put it on the table.

"I feel like I'm not doing much to help the cause."

"I know it's not very glamorous, but if you could continue the search for someone who saw Brian when he was jogging, it would help," Robin suggested.

"I can do that. My daughter is selling candy bars to raise money for her soccer team. I'll make up a reason to ask about a man jogging in the neighborhood where he runs."

"Have we forgotten anything?" Robin asked.

Lauren drained her cup and set it on the table.

"I can poke around the internet and see if Crystal had anything else going on that could have resulted in her death. I don't believe in coincidence, but just to be thorough, we should make sure she didn't have her own problems."

Harriet sighed.

"If it wasn't related to Simon's death, why would someone choose to kill her at the stable in the predawn hours?"

"To make us believe it was related to Simon's death," Mavis suggested. "Maybe they just took the opportunity that presented itself."

Beth looked at her like she'd grown a second head.

"You don't really believe that."

Mavis smiled. "Not really, but we need to consider every possibility."

Harriet picked up her empty cup and the remains of her apple fritter.

"I think I've considered as many possibilities as I can. I need to go home."

Aunt Beth patted her hand.

"I think you should, and I'm coming with you. You need a nice bath and a nap after the morning you've had."

"Works for me," Harriet said, and headed for the door.

Chapter 38

$\mathcal{H}$arriet took the dogs out as soon as she returned home, and was still in the yard with them when Aunt Beth pulled into her drive, accompanied by Mavis and Connie.

"I know I promised you a bath and a nap," Beth began as soon as she was out of her car. "I promise we won't stay too long."

Mavis headed for the door without stopping.

"I'll get the tea started."

Connie stooped and picked up Scooter, who was yipping and licking and generally making a nuisance of himself. She laughed.

"I've missed you, too, little man."

Harriet handed Connie the leash and bent to pet Cyrano.

"Don't worry," she reassured him, "you're cute, too."

Mavis and Beth had the tea made and a plate of gingersnaps on the kitchen table by the time Connie and Harriet brought the dogs inside. Harriet sat down, and Mavis handed her a mug of tea while Aunt Beth slid the plate of gingersnaps to her. All three women watched her.

"What? You three clearly have something on your minds."

Connie picked up her mug.

"Oh, honey, we're just worried about you."

Harriet raised her left eyebrow. "Why?"

Aunt Beth picked up a cookie.

"You've found two bodies in as many weeks."

"Yes, but they're not my first bodies," Harriet pointed out.

Mavis stirred honey into her tea.

"We know that. It's just that we were talking on our way here, and we're worried that whoever is killing people is going to notice that you've been close behind them when they've done their killing."

"What if they decide you've seen something or know something?" Aunt Beth finished for Mavis.

Harriet sipped her tea and considered this.

"They could decide that about any of us."

"But Crystal wasn't there when Simon was killed, was she?" Connie asked.

Harriet thought for a moment and finally shook her head.

"I don't remember, but Simon had been dead for a while when I found him. Whoever did him in was long gone before I got there."

Mavis tasted her tea.

"We don't think you should go to the stable alone until this business is all settled," she announced.

"I don't think that's necessary," Harriet protested.

"We've already discussed it," Aunt Beth said firmly.

Harriet took a bite of her gingersnap.

"What if I promise not to go when it's dark out? No early morning or late nights?"

Beth crossed her arms and glared at her.

"Okay, fine. You asked for it, though. I still haven't tried my blanket on Major, and I need to do that so I can figure the tail piece out."

Connie took a second cookie.

"That's fine. Maybe you can do your measuring when we're all at the stable for the therapy session tomorrow."

"Good, that's settled," Beth said. "Now, tell us how dinner with Emily's parents went."

Harriet spent the next half-hour describing dinner and Luke's first major relationship crisis.

"They want her to go off by herself to who-knows-where with everything that's going on in the world today?" Connie exclaimed.

Harriet finished her tea.

"They aren't abandoning her in the wilderness by herself. I'm sure they'll send her to a place where their religious group is already doing work."

Mavis wiped her mouth on her napkin.

"She's a little young, if you ask me. After college would be a different thing."

Harriet carried her mug to the sink.

"It's not clear she's bought into their plan, in any case. They can't force her if she really doesn't want to go. Look, I'm not ready to take a bath and nap right now, so would you guys be offended if I go out for a short run?"

Aunt Beth pressed her lips together.

"Will you stay away from the woods?"

Harriet smiled.

"Yes, ma'am."

"Would you mind if we stayed here and then went to the homeless camp with you when you've finished your run and whatever else you need to do?" Mavis asked.

Harriet sat down and started peeling Lauren's sweatpants off.

"That would be fine with me. I'll need a shower when I finish running, and we'll have to go by the restaurant to pick up the food. You're always welcome to stay here and stitch, or go up and watch shows, or whatever you want."

"Perfect," Aunt Beth said.

✂-- ✂-- ✂

Harriet loved her aunt and the rest of the Threads, but it felt good to get out by herself—Beth could be a little suffocating when she thought her niece was in danger. However, she needed time to think. She felt like there was something she was missing, that there was a connection between the two murders if she could just see it.

She jogged down the hill below her house, zigzagging through the neighborhood until she reached the road into downtown Foggy Point before starting back up the hill, taking a more direct path on the way home. The house smelled heavenly when she opened the door—someone had baked blueberry muffins, and they were cooling on racks on the kitchen island and counters. Mavis, Connie, and Beth sat at the kitchen table stitching on the emergency handwork projects they always carried in their bags.

Mavis appliquéd Civil War-era flowers onto an off-white background while Connie and Aunt Beth both worked on wool appliqué pieces for a block-of-the-month they were both doing.

"Who's been baking?" Harriet asked.

Connie looked up from the leaf she was whipstitching.

"Beth thought we could take some muffins to the homeless camp. They smelled so good she made a second batch so we could each have a few for our breakfasts."

Harriet inhaled deeply. "They smell heavenly."

Beth smiled.

"I hope you don't mind I used some of the blueberries from your freezer. Go take your shower, and you can have one on the drive over to the restaurant."

Harriet grinned. "You've got a deal."

✂-- ✂-- ✂

James was always happy to have Harriet drop by the restaurant, but he was especially happy when she told him she and the Threads were there for food to take to the homeless camp.

"As it happens, we've got chicken running out our ears. Last night, everyone wanted beef in every way shape and form; we couldn't give chicken away. I've got some lemon caper chicken breasts, and some Korean barbecue thighs you can take.

"We're grilling more of the breasts and running a chicken Caesar salad special for the lunch crowd, but you're not here to hear about how I'm going to solve my food balance problems." He signaled to one of his workers who was setting up tables. "Go tell Marko to package up a dozen of the lemon caper breasts and a similar amount of the thighs for the homeless camp."

The young man headed for the kitchen.

"We're not usually this far off in our planning, but this cold spell has everyone off their normal diets."

Harriet kissed him on the cheek.

"We're glad you have something to keep the homeless people fed."

"Lots of times Jorge and I cook just for them, but today, they're helping me as much as we're helping them. I've got to get back in the kitchen. Marco should be out in a minute. Do you ladies need anything else?"

"We're good," Harriet said before her friends could ask for anything.

Chapter 39

Joyce was poking at the campfire in the main meeting area when Harriet and her friends arrived at the homeless camp. Harriet held up the thermal bag she was carrying.

"We brought your lunch, compliments of James."

Mavis set a platter of plastic wrap-covered muffins on the table.

"We made some blueberry muffins for snacking, too."

Joyce smiled. "You are all too kind. We're going to get fat and lazy if you all keep this up."

Max came into the clearing and set about removing the cover from the muffins, taking one when he finished.

"Speak for yourself, woman."

Beth looked at the older man's skinny frame and chuckled.

"He's got a point."

A few more people drifted in, empty coffee cups in hand. They filled their cups from the pot on the fire and then took muffins. Harriet waited until everyone was settled with their snack.

"Has anyone seen Stan?" She tried to sound casual, but wasn't sure she'd succeeded.

Joyce stood up and went to one of their storage bins.

"As a matter of fact…" She reached into the bin, retrieving a folded piece of paper. "Stan came back last night."

Harriet gave her aunt a meaningful glance as Joyce handed the paper to her.

"He isn't here right now, but he asked me to give you this note if I saw you before the therapy session tomorrow."

Harriet glanced at the note and put it in her pocket.

"Thank you. We'd better be on our way—we've got a few more errands to run."

"We do?" Connie murmured.

"Okay, what's the note say?" Beth demanded as soon as they were all back in Harriet's car with the doors closed.

Harriet pulled the paper from her pocket and handed it to her. Beth read it aloud.

"'Could you please meet me at the corner of Second Street and Alley after horse therapy?'"

"You're not going to go, are you?" Connie asked.

"What's on that corner?" Mavis asked at the same time.

Harriet let out a breath and gazed into the distance, reviewing her mental map of downtown Foggy Point.

"Isn't that where Carla's friend went for mental health services?"

Beth turned to face her two friends in the middle seats.

"That service moved to a bigger space on the other side of Blood Moon, but I think someone else is in there."

Harriet started the car.

"I'll let you know."

"You can't possibly be thinking of going," Aunt Beth said.

Harriet smiled.

"I am not only thinking of it, I'm going. And don't worry, I'll get Lauren to go with me. It's across the alley from Annie's coffee shop, for crying out loud. I'm not driving out to a deserted house in the middle of a forest."

Beth settled back in her seat, arms crossed across her chest.

"I don't like it."

Connie opened the plastic box of muffins.

"Here, this'll help."

Beth shook her head and laughed.

"I think we're going to need a stop at the drive-through coffee window. I still don't like it, though."

✂-- ✂-- ✂

It was afternoon by the time Harriet pulled into her driveway and later than that before Aunt Beth, Mavis and Connie left. She watched as they drove off, then dialed Lauren.

"Want to go on an adventure tomorrow after horse therapy?" she asked without preamble.

"Am I the bodyguard?"

Harriet laughed.

"Not exactly." She explained about the note from Stan.

"Hmmm, that does sound interesting. And you're right, someone would have to be pretty bold to try anything in the middle of town."

"I don't think Stan is a danger. He could be a suspect in Simon's death, but I can't think of a motive for him to harm Crystal."

Lauren chuckled.

"Other than her charming personality?"

"There is that."

"I agree he's probably not her killer, and I am curious as to what he wants."

"Thanks. I would have gone anyway, but I'll feel better with company."

"It's a date. Tomorrow after horse therapy."

"Perfect."

✂-- ✂-- ✂

James came into the kitchen from the garage that evening carrying a Dutch oven with quilted mitts.

"I hope you guys are in the mood for a new chicken recipe I'm trying."

Luke was setting the table as Harriet twirled lettuce dry in the salad spinner.

"You know we love anything you make," she said, and kissed his cheek as he grabbed a trivet and set the pot on the counter.

Luke came over and inhaled. James tilted the lid away from him and waved his hand through the released steam, moving the aroma toward the boy.

"That smells amazing. How soon can we eat?"

"As soon as you go to my van and bring in the thermal bag that has the rice and rolls in it."

Luke had hustled out for the garage before he'd finished speaking.

James wrapped his arms around Harriet and nuzzled her neck as she poured lettuce into the salad bowl.

"How are you doing after your ordeal this morning? And by the way, you should have called me sooner."

Harriet smiled to herself.

"There wasn't anything you could have done. And Aunt Beth and some of the Threads were all over me."

"Still, I was worried when you finally told me."

"My friends and I have agreed that none of us are going to go to the stable alone until all this is sorted."

Luke brought the thermal bag in and set it down on the counter directly in front of James.

James laughed.

"Okay, I get the hint. Bring me soup bowls, and I'll serve it here."

Harriet put a cup of chopped tomatoes and carrots in the lettuce and tossed it.

"What do you call tonight's creation?"

"This is a Low Country dish called country captain, a chicken stewed with peppers, onions, curry, currants and RO-TEL tomatoes. I'm trying the variation made with black-eyed peas."

"It sounds very Southern," Harriet said.

Luke carried the full bowls to the table.

"I don't care what it's called. It smells amazing."

James laughed again.

"Don't let me slow you down—dig in."

✂-- ✂-- ✂

James pushed back from the table when he'd finished his second bowl and, after feedback from Luke and Harriet, proclaimed his experiment a success.

"I'm not sure I should suggest this, given what happened today, but a buddy of mine is an assistant coach for the Vancouver Canucks hockey team, and he called and offered Luke and me VIP tickets for this weekend's home games."

Harriet glanced at Luke, who was beaming with excitement.

"I think you should go. I'll be fine here. And if it would make you feel better, I can ask Lauren or Mavis or someone if they want to come stay. We can binge one of our mystery shows. And we do have a state-of-the-art security system." She tilted her head at the two dogs and the cat, who were lined up begging for scraps.

"A lot of help they'd be," James said with a smirk. "What do you think, Luke?"

"Do you think Harriet will be safe?"

"You may have noticed Harriet's pretty good at taking care of herself. Besides, as long as she has someone staying with her, she'll be fine."

"Then, yes, I'd love it." Luke's grin returned, but then his face got serious. "Harriet, could you take Major out for exercise? He'll expect to go for a ride outside on the weekend."

"I would love to take Major out." She glanced at James. "And I'll take Lauren with me. I'm sure we can borrow a school horse."

James stood up.

"Great. I'll call my friend and make us a hotel reservation."

Harriet went to the house phone to call Lauren and begin the process of convincing her friend it was time for a riding session.

Chapter 40

Weak sunlight shone in through Harriet's bedroom window the next morning. All three of her pets were unconscious, lying on their sides in a row on the foot of the bed, where the light made a rectangle of warmth. Fred looked up briefly when she crawled out of bed, then flopped back down.

"You guys are pathetic."

At the sound of her voice, there was a soft knock on the door. She opened it to find Luke, a sweatshirt in each hand.

"Which one of these should I pack?"

"Definitely the blue one. The Canucks colors are blue, green, and white, so that'll be perfect. I'm pretty sure James will take you shopping in the team store at the first game, so you'll be set."

He smiled and returned to his room to finish packing.

"Is James picking you up after school?" she asked as she passed his room. He was sitting on his bed looking at his hands.

"He really is taking me to a hockey game, right?"

"Of course, he is." She went in and sat beside him. "What's bothering you?"

"Nothing in my life works out like this. I don't deserve it. I keep thinking that any minute it's all going to fall apart. I'll be back in foster care, and all of this will have never happened."

Harriet put her arm around his shoulders.

"Sweetie, you do deserve it, and more. James and I are not going anywhere. Has something happened that's made you worry?"

He took a deep breath and blew it out.

"I've been thinking about Emily, and her parents sending her away when she graduates. Do *I* have to leave when I turn eighteen?"

Harriet thought she and James had made it clear to Luke they would be here for him no matter what and forever, but apparently, he'd been battered enough by life he still didn't truly believe it.

"You do not have to leave when you turn eighteen. And after high school, it's up to you what to do about college. We're able to send you wherever you want to go, but it's up to you."

He turned to look at her.

"I've been thinking more about the plan we talked about," he started.

"Yes?" she encouraged him.

"I think I *would* like to stay here and do the community college thing. That way, I can still see Major and everything."

Harriet smiled. She assumed she and James were the "and everything"

"I think that's a perfect solution. We can deal with what comes after that when the time arrives, but file this away—when and if you decide to go to school elsewhere, Major can go with you. Some colleges even have places to board horses on campus."

"Whoa."

"Now, finish packing and come down and eat. I'll drive you to school. I need to go to town and pick up some thread for my machine, so I'll be going right by there."

Luke gave her a quick hug.

"You're the best."

The long-arm quilting thread was on a rack at the back of Pins and Needles, but it was impossible to visit the store without checking out the new-arrivals shelf. Harriet was immediately drawn to a new birds-and-flowers collection. Its bright blues and reds and purples were a cheerful contrast to the gray skies outside the shop windows.

Marjorie, the shop owner, joined her.

"Are you making a quilt for the fundraiser for when the birdwatchers come to town?"

"Not sure about a quilt. I was thinking a set of quilted throw pillows this time. Just to mix things up."

"That sounds like a good idea. People who aren't willing to spend big dollars on a quilt might be tempted by a pillow; and it would be easier to pack on a plane for those who are coming from farther away."

"I'm still thinking about it, but it's an option. I like how bright this fabric is."

The bell on the shop door tinkled, and Harriet looked up as Glynnis Wilson entered.

"You must be thinking about the fundraiser for the upcoming bird-watcher's event," she said

"I'm actually here to buy thread," Harriet told her.

"I'm picking out backing fabric for a quilt I just made for my grand-daughter, but I do need to make something for the fundraiser. Actually, when I saw you, I was hoping your group was meeting."

Harriet dropped the edge of the fabric she'd been holding.

"Why's that?"

"I wanted to thank Jenny for her husband helping me when I had car trouble yesterday morning."

"Yesterday morning? What time yesterday morning?"

Glynnis thought for a moment.

"It was early. Does it matter?"

"It might to Jenny."

"I was going to my son's house to babysit, so it would have been six or so. He has to be at work at seven-thirty, but I needed to fix breakfast for the kids so he could get ready. My daughter-in-law is staying at her moth-er's while she recovers from gallbladder surgery, and their regular babysit-ter got sick."

"Where were you when you had your car trouble?"

"I was driving along the waterfront right before you get to downtown. My car just quit. Brian was running by and recognized my car. He was so sweet. He called the tow truck and then waited until they came. I was so up-set about letting my son down, Brian volunteered to take me to my son's house. He really went above and beyond."

"I'll be seeing Jenny later today. I can pass on your appreciation, if you want."

"Yes, please do. I'll call her tonight, too."

Harriet left Glynnis and bought three cones of gray thread and one of beige before leaving the store and returning to her car. If Glynnis's story checked out, she'd just provided Brian an airtight alibi. It didn't cover the time Simon was killed, but given it was likely whoever killed Crystal also killed Simon, it left Brian in the clear.

She pulled out her phone and dialed Jenny, and then Aunt Beth, telling them both what she'd learned.

"I'll let everyone else know," Beth said. She sighed. "I really hoped Bri-an wasn't involved."

Harriet started her car.

"Me, too. I'm going to go home and work—I've got a quilt I need to have done by Monday. I assume I'll see you at horse therapy in a couple of hours?"

"That you will."

Chapter 41

Harriet arrived at the stable before the rest of her friends. She'd brought a couple of whole carrots for Major—with her guys out of town, they would never know she'd passed over the bag of restaurant carrot sticks.

Major whinnied as she approached, and when he saw what was in her hand, he started banging his foot on the door.

Stella stepped out of the tack room.

"Oh, Harriet, I'm glad it's you. When I heard Major, I was afraid someone he didn't know was trying to get in his stall."

Harriet held the carrots up.

"He spotted these." She broke a carrot in half and handed it to him through the bars of his stall.

"When you're done there, could you come to the tack room? There's something I'd like to show you."

Harriet handed Major another half-carrot.

"Sure, this will just take a minute."

The tack room near Major's stall was one of two such rooms in the barn. The back wall had a double row of saddle racks while the side wall was made up of storage lockers, labeled with each owner's name. Stella was standing in front of the locker belonging to Paige; she'd set several whips, both long and short, on a nearby bench, along with a spare stall blanket.

"Paige's father called Angela and told her they're moving back east. Apparently, his family has a horse farm in Virginia, and he'd been trying to talk Crystal into moving there for some time. He has a van coming to-morrow to pick up their horse and asked to have their equipment packed up and ready.

"Angela asked me to take care of it, since Simon's family is in town for his memorial service. Anyway, that's all to explain why I'm digging around in their locker. What I wanted you to see is this."

She pulled a caddy out and set it down in front of Harriet, then point-ed to a gallon-sized plastic zipper bag decorated with snowmen.

"This bag has a farrier's nail hammer, a bag of nails, and a box cutter in it. I don't know about you, but I can't think of a good reason a horse own-er would have those."

"You're thinking Crystal is the one who's been injuring the horses' feet?"

"I don't want to speak ill of the dead, but if you wanted to create the foot injuries we've been seeing, these tools would do the trick."

Harriet crouched down to get a better look in the caddy.

"It looks like there's a coil of wire under that brush."

Stella started to reach for it, but Harriet stopped her.

"Don't touch anything. I'm going to call the police. They might want to check this out."

Stella stepped away from the locker.

"What I can't figure out is who would kill Crystal. It makes sense that she would kill Simon if he caught her injuring horses, but who would kill *her*?"

"Her being the one injuring the horses does confuse the issue. I would have said the same person killed both her and Simon, but now I'm not so sure. It's possible there's another player we're not aware of.

"I can imagine Crystal having an enemy or two, given her charming personality, and Simon certainly could have people unhappy about his be-havior with the young ladies. It isn't likely they would have the *same* enemy, but you never know."

She pulled her phone from her pocket and called Jane Morse, explain-ing what Stella had found.

"Detective Morse will be over in about thirty minutes. She said for us to close the tack room door and not to let anyone else go in until she checks it out."

"Hopefully, she won't keep us out of here too long. We've got to have Paige's stuff packed before the van gets here."

"Unless Detective Morse finds something besides what's in the caddy, I can't imagine her keeping us out for long."

Stella let out a sigh.

"I hope your detective friend can figure things out quickly. Since Essy is likely to be out of commission for most of the year, my husband decided I need another horse. He's anxious for us to go to Germany to horse-shop, but I don't feel like I can leave until Angela hires a trainer to take Simon's classes."

"Detective Morse is pretty sharp," Harriet assured her. "I'm sure she'll figure it out." She hoped it was true. Morse hadn't sounded very optimistic last time they'd talked.

Major banged his door again.

"I better get back to the big guy."

"You're here for the veterans, aren't you?"

Harriet nodded.

"I'll let you know what the detective says."

"Thanks."

✂ -- ✂ -- ✂

Lauren was sitting in the bleachers with Aunt Beth and Mavis when Harriet entered the arena.

"I just saw something interesting in the barn." She described the bag of tools Stella had discovered in Paige's grooming caddy.

"You don't think that girl was injuring horses, do you?" Aunt Beth asked.

Harriet sat back on the bleacher.

"Huh—I didn't even consider Paige. Stella and I assumed it belonged to Crystal. But it's a thought. If Crystal was the one hurting horses, you'd think she'd keep her tools somewhere her daughter wouldn't find them."

Lauren brushed dirt from her pant leg.

"We have no real way of knowing, but Crystal may have brought the tools with her yesterday morning with the idea to injure another horse, but went to check their horse first. Someone saw her, killed her, and took the tool bag back to her locker, which was open because she was doing something with their horse."

Beth shook her head.

"That's a stretch. Why would Crystal's killer put her tools away? Why not leave them at her side, so everyone would know she was the one doing the damage?"

Lauren chuckled.

"Hey, I'm just trying to put the puzzle pieces together."

Angela came in and joined the group on the bleachers. Her face was pale and drawn; she clearly hadn't gotten much sleep lately. Beth stepped down to the floor and gave her a hug.

"How are you holding up, honey? Is there anything we can do?"

Tears threatened to spill from Angela's eyes.

"It's so hard. I know Simon had his faults, but he didn't deserve this. His parents arrived and are understandably hysterical."

"What can we do?" Mavis repeated.

Angela looked at Harriet.

"Do you think you can handle the veteran's session? I know it's a lot to ask, but I can't leave Simon's family alone."

Harriet came down the bleachers.

"No problem. There are only a few of them who need a lot of attention, and it turns out Stan has a lot of horse experience, so he can help. Lauren has ridden some, too."

Angela gave her a weak smile.

"Thank you so much." Angela looked around the group. "All of you."

Beth patted her arm.

"You just let us know if there's anything else we can do."

"I'm not thinking very far ahead at this point. If you can handle today, that will help." She turned and walked away.

Mavis shook her head.

"I feel for her. She's right, Simon may have been a jerk, but he was her jerk. And she's left with this business to run by herself."

Harriet sat down on the lower row of the bleachers and pulled a notepad and pencil from her purse.

"Okay, let's figure out who's going to do what."

Chapter 42

By the time the veterans arrived, Harriet and Lauren had all the horses tied to the side rail. Connie, Mavis, and Aunt Beth had managed to roll the mounting ramp out, and DeAnn and Robin, who hadn't been scheduled to help but came when called, had collected the saddles and bridles in the four-wheel vehicle and driven them out to the aisle outside the arena.

"Stanley," Harriet called as soon as the veteran's group entered the arena.

"Hi," he said and walked over to where Harriet was reviewing assignments. "Did you get my note?"

"I did, but that's not what I wanted to talk to you about." She explained the situation.

"Sure. What would you like me to do?"

Harriet showed him her notepad, and he read what she had planned.

"The only change I would make would be to swap Mateo and Diandra. He actually has experience with horses—his family had a sheep ranch. He's not used to English-style riding, so he could go with the independent group. Diandra's been putting up a brave front, but back at camp, she's talked a lot about how terrified she is. She apparently had a bad experience in Afghanistan that involved a horse. She'll do better in the intense-attention group. If you don't mind, I'd like to help her."

"That sounds great," Harriet said. She looked at the other volunteers. "That okay with all of you?"

They nodded, and everyone headed into the arena to start organizing people.

Lauren worked with Gus and Mateo, both of whom, it turned out, had previous experience. She hadn't ridden in years, but as a child, she and her twin Les had spent summers with their grandparents riding all over the family's two-hundred-fifty-acre ranch.

Her group started with grooming and saddling their horses, with Lauren mostly observing and only speaking to correct minor points. Connie and DeAnn helped Joyce, while Harriet and Mavis worked with Tim. At Stan's suggestion, Diandra went back to having three helpers—Robin and Aunt Beth at the sides and him leading the horse.

Mavis had very little experience, but after raising five boys, much of it by herself, she was good at helping young men navigate difficult situations. Harriet let her take the lead, which gave *her* time to observe Stan as he helped Diandra and directed Beth and Robin as his helpers.

Diandra seemed more relaxed by the time the groups had all completed at least thirty minutes of riding time. At that point, Detective Morse came into the arena with her partner Detective Jason Martinez. She made eye contact with Harriet before climbing the bleachers and sitting down.

Harriet waited until Tim had the saddle off and was grooming Blue before she left him with Mavis and joined the detectives.

"Thanks for getting Stella to call me about the farrier's hammer and nails."

"It seemed like you should know about it. And before you ask, I have no idea what it means."

Morse smiled.

"That was going to be my next question."

Stan climbed the bleachers and interrupted them.

"What's up?" Harriet asked.

"Is it okay if I take Lily out for a little exercise while everyone is eating? Diandra is finished, and I'll put her horse away first."

"I'm sure that's fine. And thank you for helping Diandra. It looked like she was doing better."

Stan looked down at his dusty boots.

"I think she'll get over her fear of the horse, but she'd really do better if she'd make use of some of the counseling the VA has."

"She has to be ready to accept help," Harriet said.

"That's the truth," he said, but instead of leaving, he continued standing in front of her.

"Is there something else?" she asked him.

"I heard you mentioning a farrier's hammer and nails. If it's connected to the number of hoof injuries the horses around here have been having, you can bet Simon was involved somehow.

"I'm sure you're aware there was no love lost between me and Simon, but I can tell you he was a con man to his very core. He always had multiple scams going on, everything from black market goods to prostitutes. If you could make a dollar on it, he was involved. If there was something going on with the horses, my money is on Simon."

Harriet tilted her head to the side as she thought.

"I believe you. I just don't see how injuring the animals could help him."

"I don't know, either," he said. "Maybe he was going to come up with some snake-oil remedy for their feet. That would be his sort of con. He'd wait until the horses were mostly healed, and then spring his potion on the owners for a pretty penny."

Martinez cleared his throat.

"Is there any proof he or anyone was doing something like that?"

"Not that I know of," Harriet said. "But then, we haven't really looked for anything like that. And there's still the issue that the hammer and nails showed up in Paige's grooming caddy days after Simon passed away.

"I suppose Angela could have discovered what he'd done and planted the evidence to save his reputation, but again, no evidence to support that theory."

Stan turned to leave.

"I'm going to go get Lily."

"Thanks, Stan," Harriet called after him as he descended the bleachers.

He waved without turning back.

Morse got out her notepad and scratched a few lines.

"Do you believe him?"

"He has reason not to like Simon—apparently, Simon did something in Afghanistan that resulted in Stan being injured and a number of other Marines being killed. On the other hand, that doesn't mean Simon wasn't a con man.

"For the life of me, I can't see how Simon's death and Crystal's demise are connected. The only thing I can see they had in common, besides the obvious horse connection, is that they both had obnoxious personalities. Simon preyed on young girls, and Crystal was apparently willing to offer hers up if he was willing to promote Paige to the next riding level."

"And he wasn't willing to do that?" Morse asked.

"It seemed like that was the case. What I saw of the girl riding indicated she should be in the higher level. Simon might have been entering her in the lower level so he could ensure his stable won the class."

Martinez made a note.

"Seems like that would be a reason for Crystal to kill Simon, assuming that would result in her daughter being moved up. But it doesn't explain why she's dead."

Harriet stood up.

"I don't know what to tell you. I can't figure it out."

Morse rose.

"Thanks again for getting Stella to call. It may not help now, but the more puzzle pieces we have, the sooner we can solve this case."

"I better get back to the veterans," Harriet said, and went down to join her aunt and the rest of the Threads in the eating area.

Jorge had prepared a taco bar for the group, and had a hot tray with pans of pulled pork and spicy shredded beef and chicken, along with another hot tray containing seasoned rice and both black and pinto beans. He also had guacamole, sour cream, shredded cheese, pickled jalapeños, and radishes.

Aunt Beth handed Harriet a plate with a taco on it when she joined the others.

"I'm guessing your sidekick here is staying with you, since you haven't asked me or Mavis to come over." She gestured to Lauren, who was stuffing her mouth with her own taco.

She looked at Harriet with a raised eyebrow and then nodded.

"Yes, I am," she said when she'd finished chewing. "We're going riding tomorrow," she added.

Beth shook her head.

"You two are terrible liars. James called me on his way out of town and asked me to be sure someone stayed with you while he's gone," she told Harriet. "I'm glad now you've been caught you'll honor his wishes."

"I was going to ask Lauren," Harriet protested.

Aunt Beth scowled at her.

"I don't know how many times you're going to have to be hit on the head, Tasered, or otherwise injured before you'll take your own personal safety seriously."

"I really was going to ask Lauren. I just hadn't had a chance yet."

Chapter 43

𝓗arriet and Lauren waited until Stanley left before following him to the address he'd given Harriet.

"Do we have time to dash into Anne's and get a cup of coffee before we meet whoever we're meeting?" Lauren asked as she slid into the passenger seat.

"We'll take the time, since he didn't specify exactly when we were supposed to be there."

"Alrighty then," Lauren said with a chuckle.

✄-- ✄-- ✄

Harriet pulled her gloves off as she approached the counter at Annie's.

"Ladies," the man in front of her said. Stan turned around. "May I buy your drinks?"

"Uh, sure," Harriet stammered. She wasn't sure what the etiquette was when a homeless person made such an offer. Would he be insulted if she declined or, worse, offered to buy his?

"We'd like coffees," Lauren told him.

He turned around and ordered, and Lauren shrugged when Harriet gave her a questioning look. He handed them their drinks and picked his up, following them to the condiment bar.

"You're probably wondering why I asked you to meet me next door."

"We are," Harriet replied.

He stirred a packet of sugar into his cup.

"I'm not being mysterious on purpose, but I haven't told the camp group yet. I don't want to tell people until it's a done deal, but I'm moving into a house."

Harriet took a sip of her coffee.

"Wow, that's big."

"I've been thinking on it for a while, but when I saw Simon again and then he died…"

"You took it as a sign?" Lauren suggested.

Stan gave her a half-smile.

"I guess." He snapped a lid on his cup. "If you two are ready, we need to go."

The sign on the glass door read *Helping Hand*, and it opened onto a small waiting room. A large bearded man wearing a brightly colored dashiki entered from the opposite side.

"Stanley," he said in a booming voice.

"Milton," Stan answered. "This is Harriet Truman and Lauren Sawyer."

Milton smiled.

"I've had the pleasure of making Miss Lauren's acquaintance."

"Is your software still working?" Lauren asked.

"Purrs like a kitten," he said with a grin. "I see you already have coffee, so shall we get down to business."

He led them down a short hallway and into a small conference room. When everyone was seated—Stan, Harriet, and Lauren on one side and Milton ("Call me Milt.") on the other, he picked up a file folder and opened it.

"I assume Stan has explained why you're here," he started.

Harriet sipped her coffee, stalling.

"I started to at the coffee shop, but then it was time to come here," Stan stammered.

Milt looked from Harriet to Lauren and then back to Stan.

"Well, it says something right there that these two are willing to come see me with you, without knowing."

Harriet squirmed in her seat.

"Maybe one of you should tell us what we've agreed to."

Milt grinned.

"Not to worry. Stan here has applied to our housing project. It is open to veterans and first responders who have been permanently disabled. We are particularly interested in candidates like Stan, who has been houseless for a period of time. We have somewhat limited resources, so we like to be sure the people we choose for our homes are likely to succeed in our community.

"To that end, we asked Stan to produce proof that he is involved in the community and not just passing through. We realize this is more difficult, given his living situation, but during his interview he said he was participating in a horse-therapy program. I understand the man teaching the class has recently passed and is therefore unable to speak to Stan's involvement, but Stan said he could ask you—particularly Miss Harriet, to provide a reference.

"It is a bit unusual, but our architect was in the office at the time we were discussing this matter, and he assured me if Miss Harriet said Stan was okay, I could take it to the bank."

"I'm guessing your architect is Tom Bainbridge?" Harriet asked. She and Tom had dated briefly while she was trying to sort out her relationship with Aiden. In the end, Tom had felt more like a brother than a boyfriend. She respected his dedication to helping the homeless in Foggy Point.

"One and the same," Milt replied.

Lauren tapped her stir stick on the side of her cup.

"Now that we've established our bona fides, can we get on with this?"

Milt looked over the first page from his file.

"Looks like your military references are in order," he said and plucked another page from the file. "Here we are. Miss Harriet, can you verify that Stanley has participated more than once in the therapy-horse program at the Miller Hill Equestrian Center?"

Harriet straightened in her chair.

"Stan has not only participated as one of the veterans, tonight he taught one of the groups, as the manager of the stable is busy with the memorial service for her husband. He's quite good with both the horses and the other veterans."

Milton made a note on the page and slipped it back into the file, closing the cover. He sat in silence for a moment before speaking.

"Stan, I have to ask you—this won't go in your file—but I'm curious. What happened?"

"What do you mean?"

"You've been living wild for three years, if your application is right, but when I look at your financial statement, it's not for lack of resources. I understand your desire to have a home outfitted to accommodate your particular physical needs, but you could live in an apartment or rental house while you wait for your name to come up."

"It's hard to explain," Stan began. "After my incident, I just wanted to be somewhere quiet. I've been in therapy for my PTSD, and I was in and out of the hospital for the first two years. I didn't want to have to keep talking about the war to everyone I met. Living in the woods is peaceful."

"I ask again," Milton pressed. "Not that it's my business, but I'm curious. What changed?"

Stanley hung his head.

"I've had a hard time accepting the fact that things happen that are beyond our control. Even though Simon Tavarious played a role in my injury, being angry about it doesn't change anything. I need to move forward and deal with how things are now.

"I guess when Simon died, I realized he would never take responsibility for what he did. I was mad at him for the guys that died because of him, but those soldiers knew the dangers we all faced when we signed up. Whether it was the enemy or a jerk like Simon, we all knew we might not come back, and if we did, our lives might not be the same.

"Anyway, when Simon died, I left for a week and spent the time with my counselor at the VA center in Lakewood. I finally get it. Make no mistake, I was already most of the way there. As you know, I'd put in my application months ago. But now I know I'm really ready to move forward."

Milt stood up and put his hand out. Stan took it.

"I shouldn't tell you this, but Tom was so sure you would fulfill all our requirements, he's already started on the modifications to your home."

Stan's face lit up.

"When do I get to see it?"

Milt grinned.

"Not until we're ready to hand you the keys. We like our little bit of drama when we present a house."

✂-- ✂-- ✂

"Can we give you a ride back to the camp?" Harriet asked Stan when they were back outside.

"I hate to trouble you any further," he said.

Lauren led the way to Harriet's car.

"Oh, stop it. It's freezing, and your limp is getting worse. Just get in."

Harriet held her breath, waiting to see what his reaction would be. Stan looked at her and grinned.

"I like her," he said, and got in the car.

Chapter 44

𝓗arriet and Lauren found themselves at the stable earlier than they had planned the following day, owing to the shenanigans of their respective dogs. Cyrano and Scooter were delighted to have Lauren's dog Carter spend the night, but Fred was not amused. The cat showed his displeasure by poking each of the three dogs, then running until he had all of them chasing him up and down the stairs, all this at the crack of dawn. The third time Fred jumped on Harriet's pillow and slithered down under her covers to evade his pursuers, she surrendered and got up.

"Come on, you little scoundrels. Let's go out, and then you can all eat your breakfast. Maybe that will settle you down."

Lauren stumbled out of the guestroom pulling a sweatshirt on over her pajama top.

"What is that racket all about?"

"It would seem the dogs and cat are enjoying their sleepover."

"Couldn't they enjoy it a little more quietly? And a little later in the day?"

Scooter jumped up against Harriet's leg.

"I'll take the clowns out if you'll put the kettle on."

When Harriet returned, Lauren not only had the tea water heating but she'd dished up the animal food and had toast in the toaster. She carried mugs to the table while Harriet got her basket of teabags and the sugar bowl.

"I called Tom Bainbridge last night."

Harriet stopped midway to the table.

"I didn't know you'd kept in touch."

Lauren smiled. "You don't know all my secrets."

Harriet set the plate of toast on the table and sat down.

"Do tell."

"Nothing to tell, really. I had some business in Angel Harbor last year, and I ran into Tom in the coffee shop. He asked me to join him, I did, and it became sort of a thing. When I'm there, I call him, and we have lunch or coffee and the same when he comes to Foggy Point. No big deal."

"Sounds like a big deal to me. We went to bed after eleven last night."

"He's a night owl, what can I say? The important thing is, I did call him last night, and he filled me in on Stanley Oliver."

Harriet took a bite of her toast.

"What did you learn?"

"You know how we were wondering last night about why Stan needed a house with accommodations? I asked Tom about it. It turns out Stan's leg is more damaged than he's let us see.

"He told Tom his lower leg needs to be amputated. The doctors bolted it together with plates and screws, but apparently, it hasn't healed properly. I guess Stan has a pair of collapsible crutches in that backpack he wears. Tom says he's waited as long as he can. That's why they're trying to get him in the house so quickly."

"Wow. That was worth a midnight call," Harriet said and sipped her tea.

"Tom says he was quite the hero in the war. He carried several of his fellow Marines to safety even though he was seriously injured himself."

"Well, if he was at the VA hospital for the last week or ten days, it takes him out of the picture as our murderer."

Lauren took another piece of toast.

"Brian is eliminated, and now Stan. Crystal could still be Simon's killer, but of course, not her own."

"We're running out of suspects. Angela is still in the frame, I guess. Although, why she'd kill Crystal, I don't know." She shook her head. "We're missing something. Something big that would make all this make sense."

They drank their tea in silence, giving the crusts of their toast to the dogs when they finished.

"Shall we go ride?" Harriet finally said.

"Just give me a few minutes to get dressed."

✂-- ✂-- ✂

Major whinnied when he heard Harriet enter the barn.

"Okay, big guy, I'm coming," she called to him. Then, to Lauren, she added, "I asked Angela about you riding one of the school horses, and she

197

suggested Fargo. He and Major go out together in a paddock and get along well. His stall is one down from Major's, too."

Lauren had downplayed her riding skills whenever the subject came up, but she proved to be quite competent. She cross-tied Fargo at the other end of the aisle from Major and proceeded to saddle him and put his bridle on without assistance.

"I'm taking Major into the small arena to use the mounting block. It's taller than the one in the outdoor ring, and I need all the help I can get with this guy."

"Whatever," Lauren replied and followed her into the arena.

Harriet stopped and looked around once she and Lauren were both mounted and left the training ring.

"I didn't realize how much property the stable owned when we first started coming here." She pointed to the left. "They own the forest property all the way to the top of that rise, and Angela said it goes down to Miller Hill Road to the right."

Lauren surveyed the area indicated.

"Question number one has been answered. There isn't an obvious driveway or parking area back here."

"I think we should take that trail." Harriet pointed in the direction of Miller Hill Road. "There might be a gate with a drive from that way. If that doesn't tell us anything, we can go up the rise and see what we can see."

Lauren rode up beside her.

"Sounds good to me. Lead the way."

✂-- ✂-- ✂

Harriet stopped in a small clearing after they'd been riding for a quarter-hour. A small sign stood to one side. It showed a map of the trails and gave a history of the woods.

"They've planned the trails well. According to this, you can ride for five miles if you make the right loops and turns, or we can zigzag across the middle to the Miller Hill boundary pretty much as the crow flies if we want to. Let's memorize that route."

Lauren guided Fargo close to the sign and pulled her phone from her pocket, snapping a picture.

"Done," she said.

"I'll follow you," Harriet said.

✂-- ✂-- ✂

"The local crow didn't fly very straight," Harriet commented after they'd taken their third detour around steep drop-offs and rockpiles.

"It isn't much further. According to the map, we'll be leaving the woods and crossing a meadow pretty soon."

Harriet stopped Major when they reached the edge of the wood. Lauren came up beside her.

"Gosh, I didn't realize there was a neighborhood back here."

"That's because we're above the road. When we drive by, all we see is the stone wall." She pointed to the right. "Look, there's a gate. It's one of those private communities."

Harriet moved Major forward.

"Let's get a little closer."

"Isn't that Crystal's lavender car?" Lauren asked when they'd stopped again.

"It is, and there's a moving van in front of the house. This could explain how she showed up at the stable without her car being in the driveway. It would be a bit of a hike, but probably less than a mile if she took the most direct route."

"Look who's coming out of the house next door," Lauren said and pointed to the left. "Isn't that Angela?"

"Sure looks like it."

Lauren pulled out her phone out and took a picture of the house.

"I can blow this up and get the house numbers, and then look them up on FoggyPointMaps-dot-com."

"What will that tell you?"

"It's a website that gives all the tax information on a property as well as the sales history and the current owner's name. We can find out who Angela is visiting. I'll just bet this is where she was coming from in the middle of the night when she was caught on the security camera."

"I'm not sure that helps us with our problem. If Angela was visiting whoever lives there, then she wasn't killing Simon at the same time."

"Unless she came here after," Lauren pointed out.

"Let's ride on down to the fence. I'm sure there's a gate along there somewhere, but let's verify it."

Lauren turned Fargo to the left.

"I want to get a picture of that big place at the end of the street. I'm curious who lives in a walled compound within a gated community. Maybe it's the people who own the stable or something else big in Foggy Point."

"Shall we head back?" Harriet suggested when they'd located the gate that would allow a person access to the equestrian center grounds. "I'd like to ride up the hill. Major could use the workout."

"Works for me," Lauren replied, and followed her back into the woods.

Chapter 45

It was just past noon when Harriet and Lauren rode back into the small arena and dismounted before leading the horses back into the barn.

"You ladies look like you've been out for a ride," Stella said as they led their horses to the crosstie areas for unsaddling.

Harriet smiled at her.

"I've never been out on the property here, so we decided to go for a trail ride. I hadn't realized how big this place is."

"I've not taken Essy out there, and now…" She shrugged. "But we're getting another horse, so maybe I'll take the new one out after he's settled in."

Harriet busied herself with taking Major's tack off while Stella watched.

"Crystal told me there's a gate at the back of the property so she could walk over here when the weather was good."

"Did she do that often?" Harriet asked as she brushed Major.

"I saw her here a time or two when that lavender abomination she drives wasn't here. I assumed her husband dropped her."

"She didn't really strike me as a person who did a lot of aerobic exercise, but maybe she did." Harriet wasn't sure why Stella was so interested now that Crystal was dead, but she was about to find out.

"I was thinking," Stella began. "What if Crystal's husband was upset about the way Simon…" She paused. "…'handled' Paige, and he walked through the woods and came and killed Simon."

Harriet brushed Major's front legs and took the opportunity to look under his belly at Stella, who was staring at the ceiling, finger on her chin.

"I suppose that's possible, but why would he kill Crystal? Assuming the same person killed both of the victims."

"I was thinking maybe Crystal followed him and saw what he did. He killed her so she couldn't tell anyone. We both know she couldn't have kept a secret like that. And now he's fleeing."

"I guess it could have happened like that. Why would he kill her at the stable?"

"He wants the police to think someone at the stable killed both of them."

Harriet stood up and looked Stella in the eye.

"I think we both know someone at the stable *did* kill both of them. And I doubt it was Crystal's husband."

"We just don't know who," Stella said softly. "Do we?"

Harriet held her gaze until the other woman looked away.

Lauren joined them in front of Major's stall when she had finished grooming Fargo and given him a couple of carrots she'd brought. Harriet's phone buzzed in her pocket, and she retrieved it and read the text message.

"Aunt Beth said Jorge is making Birria tacos and wants to try them out on the Loose Threads tonight," she told Lauren. "Are you available?"

"Since I'm pretty sure I'm staying at your house again tonight, if you're available, I'm available."

"We'll be there," Harriet said aloud as she typed the response and sent the response to her aunt.

She put Major back in his stall and gave him a carrot. Stella was still standing beside Lauren.

"Maybe you could call Detective Morse and run your idea by her," Harriet suggested. "She probably would want to know before Mr. Kelley leaves town."

"I'll try that," Stella said and turned to go back to Essy's stall. "Thanks."

"What was that all about?" Lauren asked when Stella was out of earshot.

"It was kind of weird," Harriet said and recounted the conversation.

"I'm not sure why she felt the need to tell me about it. She's met Morse. She could have just called her."

"She probably wanted to see if you thought her idea was crazy, which by the way, it is. Or at least a nice piece of fiction. She didn't have any evidence that Crystal's husband has ever been here, did she?"

"No. And now that I think about it, she must have been thinking about it for a while. I wonder if she's worried about her safety."

"Do we know what Birria tacos are?" Lauren asked, changing the subject.

"They're tacos filled with the meat from a spicy stew then dipped in the fat from the stew and fried. To eat it, you dip it in a small bowl of the stew."

"It sounds messy. And how do you know what they are? James?"

Harriet smiled.

"I overheard James and Jorge talking about it when they were feeding the therapy group last week."

"They sound…interesting."

"According to Jorge the original is made with goat meat, but lucky for us, he's using beef."

Lauren smiled.

"Yeah, lucky."

"I'm going to go home, clean up, and do a little stitching before dinner."

"I think I'll go back to my place and change and do a little work on my computer. I'll come back to your house and drop Carter off, then we can go together."

"Works for me."

✂-- ✂-- ✂

Harriet sat down beside Mavis at the big table in the back room at Tico's Tacos.

"What did you do today with your men out of town?" Mavis asked. "Spa? Lunch out?"

Harriet smiled.

"Lauren and I went for a horse ride. I promised Luke I'd exercise Major while he was gone."

Mavis looked surprised.

"You went, too? I didn't know you rode."

"It's not the sort of thing that comes up in everyday conversation," Lauren said, "but as a matter of fact, I do ride. And it was illuminating." She sat down opposite her. "We explored that wooded area behind the stable."

Harriet took a sip from her water glass.

"We discovered Crystal Kelley lived in that neighborhood."

"And we saw Angela Tavarious coming out of the house next door to hers," Lauren added. "And I discovered something else, while we were doing our own stuff," she said to Harriet.

"Do tell."

"I found out who lives in the big house behind the wall at the end of the street."

"That's Milo Bren's mansion," Mavis told them.

"Way to steal my thunder," Lauren muttered.

202

Mavis patted her hand.

"Everyone knows that, honey."

Harriet laughed.

"Everyone but Lauren and I, apparently."

Aunt Beth joined them at the table.

"Mavis is showing off. The Brens are very private people. He's a bit of a recluse. Mavis was the docent at their house during a tour-of-homes Christmas fundraiser a few years ago."

"It's interesting to find so many stable people clustered there," Mavis said thoughtfully.

Harriet unfolded her napkin and put it in her lap.

"Not really. There's a gate in the fence, and if they choose the right path, they can walk to the stable pretty easily if the weather isn't bad."

"I suppose." Beth said.

"It's weird," Harriet said.

"What is?"

"When I was talking to Stella, I didn't know she lived behind the stable property, so it didn't seem odd that she only knew about the gate because Crystal told her. She said she'd never gone for a ride back there. Living at the end of the road, she'd drive by the gate every time she went in and out. And it isn't subtle."

Beth sipped her water.

"Like I told you, they're very private people. She probably didn't want to tell you she lived there if you didn't know."

"Clearly not that private, if they let half the town tour their house at Christmas," Lauren pointed out.

Mavis leaned forward and lowered her voice.

"We weren't allowed to say who lived at the house. It was listed as being owned by a holding company. We all had to sign a paper saying we wouldn't reveal anything about the actual owners. In fact, they didn't tell us who lived there. I only know because I saw a picture of Stella and her husband they must have forgotten to remove. Don't tell anyone I told you."

"Here's something you might not know," Lauren said. "I found out who Angela is visiting next door to the Kelleys. I looked up the name and realized it's one of my clients."

"And?" Harriet prompted.

Lauren grinned. "I called him."

Mavis gasped. "You didn't."

"I did."

"You just called up a business associate and asked him about Angela visiting him?" Beth asked.

Lauren leaned back in her chair.

"We went to college together. He was a business major, and I tutored him in his computer classes. He owes me."

"So, what did you find out?" Harriet asked her.

"I asked him what the deal was between him and Angela, and he said Simon was an abusive lout to her, and she suspected he was abusing her students. They're friends from childhood, so she turned to him to figure out how to stop Simon without tarnishing the reputation of the stable.

"She was aware of us keeping an eye on Simon, by the way.

"While they were figuring things out, they rekindled their childhood romance. She was going over there in the middle of the night. She and Simon slept in separate rooms, and he took drugs to sleep, so they were able to keep their relationship secret."

"We don't know if that has anything to do with anything," Harriet reminded her.

"I didn't ask if he helped her kill Simon, and he didn't volunteer anything," Lauren said. "But if we're entertaining crazy theories, here's one. What if Angela and Ian—that's my college friend—bumped off Simon, and Crystal saw them, so they killed her, too?"

"That seems like a stretch," Harriet said. "Could your friend do that?"

"I wouldn't say so, but love does funny things to people."

Robin and her husband arrived. He joined the other men at the far end of the table, and Robin sat down beside Mavis.

"I only heard the end of this conversation, but let me remind you, any of these theories are just that unless there's some evidence to back it up."

Harriet picked up her fork and twirled it on her plate.

"Basically, we all have the same theory. Someone associated with Simon killed him, Crystal saw it, and then she was killed to silence her. We still don't have a motive that would suggest one person over the other."

Jorge came out of the kitchen carrying large platters of tacos in each hand and followed by one of his kitchen helpers carrying two more.

"Take several each, and we'll be right back with the bowls of stew to dip them in. And feel free to add salsa or hot sauce."

Lauren picked up a bottle of green hot sauce.

"I tried this one once, and my mouth burned for two days afterward." She set it back down. "User beware."

The tacos were delicious, and the group ate their fill and then finished it off with dishes of flan. When they were finished, Jorge sat down beside Beth.

"Well, what did you all think?"

"They were amazing," Robin said, and the rest of the group agreed.

Beth picked up the pile of used napkins beside her plate.

"You'll need to give the people a few extra napkins, right from the get-go."

Jorge smile at her. "I will make a note of that."

Harriet stood up.

"We better get home to the animals. They've been alone much of the day, and we usually pay a price for that."

Mavis reached out and took her hand.

"We'll see you at church tomorrow. You want to go for coffee after?"

Harriet looked at Lauren, who nodded.

"Sure. We'll see you then."

Chapter 46

James called early the following morning. Harriet had just finished getting dressed and was looking for one of her shoes in the bedroom closet.

"How's everything going at home?"

"Fine," Harriet replied. "I thought you'd be sleeping in."

"I did, for me. I wanted to catch you before church. Luke is having a fabulous time. I hope it's okay, but I bought him a jersey and a sweatshirt. He wasn't sure I should spend so much money on him, but I insisted. Since we had VIP passes, we got to go in the locker room, and he got his jersey signed by a couple of the players."

"That sounds fantastic."

"We've got an afternoon game today and will be back late-ish tonight."

"That sounds great. Lauren is here with me. We went riding yesterday, but I'm not sure what we'll do today. Maybe I'll try to finish Major's blanket."

"Luke will be happy you took the horse out. He's been a little worried Major would be missing him."

Harriet smiled to herself.

"I'm sure Major misses him terribly."

"Okay, I'll let you get going. See you tonight. Love you."

"Love you, too. Bye."

Harriet held her phone to her chest. She missed her men, but knew it was important for them to have father-son bonding time. She didn't have experience with that sort of thing herself, and because of that, she was determined Luke's life was going to be different.

"Are you about ready?" Lauren called from across the hall, breaking her from her reverie.

"Let me take the dogs out, and I'll be good to go.

✂-- ✂-- ✂

Aunt Beth and Mavis were standing in the entryway waiting for Jorge to park the car and join them when Harriet and Lauren arrived.

"Did you hear from James?" Beth asked.

Harriet smiled.

"I did, and he says they're having a fantastic time. James is buying as much fan gear as Luke will allow, and they were able to meet some of the players."

"That sounds great," Beth said. "Which makes me wonder why your smile seems so sad."

"I'm happy they're having a great time. I really am."

"But you wish you were included," Beth finished for her.

"No. Well…yes. Once again I'm on the outside looking in."

Beth put her hand on Harriet's arm.

"Honey, this has nothing to do with how your parents treated you. Yes, they didn't take you out of boarding school when other kids went home for the holidays, but you did get to come here sometimes. I hope you had fun with me and your uncle Hank."

"I did, and I know I'm being silly. Luke needs time to bond with a father figure. We do plenty of family stuff I'm included in. I understand in my head this is a good thing. I guess that damaged little girl just rears her ugly head every once in a while."

"It's okay, sweetie. Everyone has their moments."

"I'm okay, really I am," Harriet assured her aunt. "And what you and Uncle Hank did for me made all the difference in my life. Things have just been a bit stressful with all this stuff going on at the stable. I keep thinking I missed something, and maybe if my life had been more normal, I'd have a different perspective and I'd be able to see it."

"Honey, you're not responsible for everything and everyone. You're not responsible for figuring out what's happening at the stable. That's Detective Morse's job. You just take care of your little family and let her worry about the other stuff."

Harriet blew out a breath.

"Thank you."

Beth rubbed her back and guided her into church.

✂-- ✂-- ✂

"What was that all about?" Lauren asked as she and Harriet followed Aunt Beth, Mavis, and Jorge into a pew.

"I was just feeling sorry for myself because the guys are having fun without me."

Lauren looked injured.

"Aren't we having fun?"

"I appreciate you staying with me. I really do. And thank you for going riding yesterday."

"So, why the long face?"

"To tell you the truth, I can't get Stella Bren out of my mind. Our conversation was weird, and the way she stared at me at the end was creepy."

"Maybe some of the weird from being married to a reclusive millionaire or billionaire or whatever he is has rubbed off."

"Or maybe you have to be weird to marry a recluse in the first place."

"Whatever."

✂ -- ✂ -- ✂

Harriet felt her phone buzz in her pocket. She ignored it until everyone had their heads bowed in prayer. She was sitting at the end of the pew, so it was easy to slip the phone out and glance at the screen. It was a text from Stella.

Major is in trouble, come quick, it read. She slid from the pew, walked quietly down the side aisle, and out the door.

"Hey, Siri," Harriet yelled at her phone once she was in her car. She pulled out of the church parking lot as she spoke.

"Text Lauren," she commanded when Siri spoke through the car speaker, asking what she wanted.

"I'm sorry, I don't understand," Siri answered.

Harriet tried again, driving as quickly as she dared.

"Try again in a little while," Siri responded this time.

Harriet gave up and gripped the steering wheel until her fingers hurt. *What could possibly be wrong with Major? He was fine last night.* She was relatively certain he wouldn't let anyone strange into his stall. The shattered stall door was evidence of that.

Her car slid as she took the turn into the driveway at speed. She undid her seatbelt as she stopped then grabbed her phone, typing a message to Lauren as she ran to the barn.

Stella was standing in front of Major's stall.

"What's wrong," Harriet said, trying to catch her breath.

Stella unlatched his stall door and opened it.

"I don't know what's wrong. I came in to check on Essy. When I didn't see Major through the bars in his stall, I went closer to see if he was lying down, and I found him like this."

Major was flat on his side on the floor of the stall. Harriet went in and knelt beside the big horse, putting her hand on his chest to feel for a heartbeat. Before she could register anything, a powerful and all-too-familiar electric shock coursed through her body. The shock prevented her from feeling the needle that slid into her arm—and everything went black.

✂ -- ✂ -- ✂

Harriet woke and tried to move her arms, but they were bound at her sides. She lost consciousness again. The next time she woke, she could tell the temperature had dropped. She tried to move her legs. Her feet weren't tied together, or if they were, wherever she was, it was a narrow enough space that she couldn't move her legs enough to tell.

Her eyes were open, but there was a total absence of light. She tried to push her elbows out to see if she could identify where she was. Pain shot up her right arm. She stopped moving it and continued pushing with her left. She did the same with her feet and lower legs. Wherever she was, it was narrow. She sucked in a breath of air. It smelled strongly of mold.

She lay still and assessed what she'd learned. The sides of her tomb were not hard. They weren't yielding, but they didn't feel like wood or metal. Her best guess was heavy fabric. She thought hard about what she knew. Her head felt foggy. She clearly remembered going to church with Lauren, but things were a little unclear after that.

She tried to relax her body and her head. She stayed still for what she imagined could have been thirty minutes. Slowly, she reviewed in her mind the steps she knew she'd taken since she'd gotten up this morning—assuming it was still the same day, which wasn't a foregone conclusion.

She'd gotten up, talked to James, taken the dogs out, had toast and tea with Lauren, went to church and then….

It was still fuzzy. She had a feeling she'd left church and gone to the stable—but why? And how did she end up wherever she was now.

She closed her eyes and fell asleep again.

Chapter 47

𝓗 arriet had no sense of how much time had passed while she was sleeping. She was starting to feel thirsty, and she knew if she didn't find a way out of her current situation, it wasn't going to end well for her. That she knew for sure.

Whatever was around her didn't leave her room to move, but she had plenty of air, which must mean either the top or bottom or both were open. She imagined she was in some sort of tube. An air duct maybe? But it was softer. Was she rolled up in something?

She tried scooting forward toward the head end of her prison, but it sent waves of pain into her arm and shoulder. She lay still for a moment waiting for the pain to subside. When she was ready, she took a deep breath and tried using her toes to scoot herself downward.

This maneuver moved her an inch or two. She tried again and was rewarded with another few inches. Progress was slow, but when she had to rest again, she could feel cold air on her ankles. She didn't know if it was day or night, and she didn't know how much time was passing. All she knew was she was making slow but steady progress.

Eventually, her feet met resistance. Unlike the tube containing her, this was hard. She didn't have enough room to bend her knee to enable a kick, but she bent her ankles as far as they would go and tapped. She was pretty sure she was pushing against a wall made of wood.

She rotated her foot to feel the wall with her toes, and felt something that was either insulated wire or thin plastic pipe. She hooked her foot under it and pulled as much as the space allowed, and was rewarded with her body moving six more inches toward the wall. Her feet were now flat against it. The movement had also allowed her knees to escape the confines of the tube.

She bent them and pushed forward, moving whatever was holding her away from the wall and giving her space to use the wire on it to pull her body out of the tube. With one excruciating lurch, she was free.

She lay on the floor panting, like a newborn foal just expelled from its mother. The room she was in was only marginally lighter than the dark confines she'd just escaped. Her hands were still bound behind her back. The pain in her right arm made finding something to free her hands her first priority.

Thankfully, her captor had used duct tape and not the much harder to remove cable ties. She struggled to her feet, resting with her back to the wall a moment to let a wave of dizziness pass. She began sliding to her left, feeling with her bound hands for a nail or other sharp object. A few paces later, she found something hard sticking out from the wall.

She took a deep breath and began the process of working her bound wrists up and down, tears filling her eyes when she moved her right arm. By the time she ripped the tape and was able to pull her hands free, she was sobbing.

She crawled back to what she could now see was a rolled-up carpet and sat down. She had no sense of how much time had passed since she had been injected in the neck. She looked around the dark room. She could have been driven anywhere while she was unconscious—but had she been?

It would make more sense for whoever it was to stow her somewhere in the barn to minimize the amount of time they could be seen with an unconscious woman. The area over the main barn was finished off as a dormitory for visitors during horse shows, but who knew what was above the pony barn or in some of the outbuildings.

It was too much to hope they would have left her cell phone in her pocket, but she checked her pants pockets and then her coat pockets anyway. Everything had been removed. No keys, no phone, no scarf or gloves.

Harriet stood up again and began making her way carefully around the perimeter of her prison. She almost fell when her foot encountered a coil of rope. That could be useful if she was in an attic space. She continued her search, not finding a door anywhere.

The hard wall suddenly became soft. If she didn't know better, she'd have said it was a quilt. But what would a quilt be doing nailed to a storeroom wall?

Harriet tugged gently at the edge, and it came free, letting in a blast of cold air. She pulled harder, and the whole quilt fell down onto her head. Duct tape clung to the binding—someone had covered a broken window by duct-taping a quilt over it. She hoped it wasn't a valuable quilt, but then shook herself. Clearly, her thinking had been affected by whatever she'd been drugged with. If it came down to her or a quilt, no matter how valuable, she won every time.

She sank to the floor, the weight of the quilt too much to bear. Still, it was warm. *The maker must have used wool batting*, she thought, her mind again wandering. She wrapped it around her shoulders and felt her eyes begin to close again; she forced them back open.

She now had a rope and a quilt to work with. She needed to get out of this room and find James and Luke, assuming she'd been unconscious long enough for them to have returned home and discovered her absence. They would be worried.

Oh, Luke, she thought. He must be shattered with his big horse dead. All the more reason she needed to get home. He would need her now more than ever.

She struggled to her feet and, covering her hand with the quilt, she carefully pushed the broken window pieces out of the way, then leaned out to see where she was. She sucked her breath in. She was at least two stories above ground on a piece of land that dropped sharply away a few feet from the building wall. The moonless night revealed little. It was possible she was on the stable property, but she equally could be anywhere else on Miller Hill or, really, anywhere. She just couldn't tell.

She looked back into the dark room. There had to be another way out. If there wasn't a door in any of the walls, there must be a trapdoor and stairs somewhere in the floor.

She was about to drop to her knees to begin the painstaking search when she heard a familiar but impossible whinny. She leaned back through the window and tried to call out.

No sound came out of her dry throat.

Harriet collapsed onto the floor, no longer able to even cry.

Chapter 48

Harriet could hear the whinny getting louder and shriller, but she no longer had the strength to stand up. There was a loud scraping noise from somewhere below her and then voices.

"This looks like it's full of hay," James said.

James, I'm up here!

She sat up and tried to stomp her foot on the floor, but she only succeeded in sending a jolt of pain up her right side and into her injured arm.

"We have to look behind the hay or in the loft," she heard Luke argue.

Yes! Look in the loft. That must be where I am. In the loft.

She heard the horse that couldn't be Major snort and stomp. Everyone was quiet for what felt like an hour but was probably a minute or less.

"We need help to go through this place, and permission," James explained to Luke.

No, you don't! You need to come get me now.

"What if she's hurt?" Luke said, his voice louder and higher.

Yes, Luke, she is hurt. She needs you now.

"He knows she's in there," he added.

Harriet took a deep breath and crawled over to the rope she'd found, dragging it back to her spot in front of the window. After a moment's rest, she struggled to pull her socks off, using only her uninjured left hand. With the intense pain in her shoulder and arm, she hadn't noticed she had lost her shoes somewhere and had been stomping around sock footed.

When she finally wrestled them free, her feet registered the fact it was very cold. She tugged on the quilt she was wrapped in and freed a corner to wrap them in.

She leaned back against the wall and struggled to wind the rope around her socks and tie them together. That accomplished, she used one last burst of energy to toss the socks and rope out the window, they dangled halfway down the wall, and prayed someone would walk around the barn and notice them.

"Whoa, boy!" Luke exclaimed. "James, I don't think I can hold him back. He wants to go around the side of the barn."

"Let him go if you need to. That pathway is pretty narrow, and we don't want you toppling down that rockfall."

Harriet heard stomping and shuffling for what seemed like an eternity. She felt the wall behind her vibrate and heard the sound of a horse kicking. She sagged with relief. She'd been found.

The rope tightened. Someone was pulling on it. With her left hand, she tugged back on the rope.

"Harriet?" Luke called, but she had no voice to answer with.

Finally, she banged on the wall behind her with her left hand.

"James!" Luke yelled. "I think we found her."

It was the last thing Harriet heard as she slipped back into unconsciousness.

✂ -- ✂ -- ✂

Afterward, she had little memory of what happened. She remembered opening her eyes and hearing Luke say, "She's alive," before slipping back into darkness.

It was light outside, and Harriet was in an unfamiliar bed when she woke up again.

"Well, hello, Rip van Winkle," Aunt Beth said from a chair beside her bed. Her hands held a piece of black wool with a red flower halfway stitched onto its surface. "I was wondering when you'd decide to join the living again."

Harriet attempted to sit up. Aunt Beth reached over and pressed a button on the bed's control, raising it.

As she settled into her new position, Harriet examined her arms. The left one had an IV needle and tubing taped to it, while the right one was wrapped from midway up her forearm all the way to her shoulder.

"What happened?" she croaked.

Aunt Beth blew out a breath and pressed her lips together, clearly struggling with her answer.

"We were hoping you would be able to tell us. We were all sitting in church Sunday morning, and during the prayer, you disappeared. No one could find you for most of three days. Finally, Luke and James located you in a hay storage barn at the stable."

"How…?"

"Don't try to talk now. You apparently injured your throat and are supposed to rest. James had to go to the restaurant to sign checks, and Luke is home sleeping. The doctor told everyone not to come back until this evening. Your men, and Lauren, and pretty much all the Threads at one time or another have been camping out here for the past three days. The doctor kept you sedated for the first two after they did the surgery on your arm."

"Surgery?" Harriet whispered, looking at her bandaged arm again.

"He'll explain it all when he comes by later. You just try to rest."

Harriet assumed drugs were contributing to the fact she had little to no memory of the last week.

"I'm going to let your nurse know you woke up," Beth said, and left the room. She returned moments later with a cheerful woman in green scrubs.

"I'm Caroline, and I'm your day-shift nurse," she said. "I hope you're feeling a little better. I just need to do a couple of tests. You should let your throat rest, so try not to speak, okay?"

Harriet nodded, assuming the woman didn't really want her to answer. A blood-pressure cuff she hadn't realized was around her left arm began tightening as Caroline pushed buttons on the box it was connected to. When her blood-pressure measurement was finished, Caroline efficiently took her pulse, listened to her chest, and fiddled with the dials on the IV unit.

"Using your fingers, can you tell me how your pain level is on a scale of one to ten?"

Harriet thought for a minute. Her throat hurt, and her arm and shoulder had a dull ache, but she was pretty sure she was on drugs for that, so she held up five fingers.

"Okay." Caroline glanced at her watch. "I'll be back in a minute with more medication."

She was true to her word, and within moments, Harriet slipped back into unconsciousness.

Chapter 49

$\mathcal{W}$ hen Harriet woke the next time, James was sitting in her bedside chair, and Luke was in the window seat beside Lauren. Beth and Mavis were in chairs against the wall and Harriet was pretty sure she saw Detective Morse just outside the doorway.

Beth went out, apparently signaling that she was awake again. Nurse Caroline arrived and adjusted Harriet's bed into a sitting position, then set a small whiteboard and a marker on her lap.

"You guys all know the rules—fifteen minutes, and if she starts trying to talk, you have to stop."

"Of course," James assured her.

The nurse left, and was replaced by Detective Morse.

"I'd prefer to conduct this interview alone," she said, "But given the circumstances, I'll make an exception this time."

Harriet looked from James to Morse and back again. Morse turned on the record function on her phone and set it on Harriet's table. She identified herself and everyone in the room, and then noted that Harriet would be writing her answers on an erasable board, which she—Morse—would read aloud.

"To spare Harriet, I'd like to start with the rest of you telling what you know. I've interviewed you all, but it might help her to know what was going on while she was missing. Let's start with Lauren." Morse looked at her. "You said you spent the night at Harriet's because James and Luke were out of town. The two of you got up and went to church, correct?"

Lauren straightened in her seat.

"Yes. We went to church and were sitting in a pew halfway down the aisle. Harriet was in the end spot. We all bowed our heads, and I heard Harriet's phone vibrate. When the prayer was over, I opened my eyes, and she was gone."

"What did you do?"

"I signaled to Beth and Mavis, and we went outside, but none of us had any idea where she'd gone. She'd left a text, but it only said there was an emergency."

"What did you do then?" Morse asked.

Lauren smiled.

"We wasted about five minutes debating whether we should finish church first."

This made Harriet smile. She could imagine her aunt championing this idea.

"Then, we decided someone must have called to say the house was on fire or something equally dire, so we went to Harriet's house."

"Everything was fine there," Mavis interjected.

"While we were driving, Beth called James to make sure nothing was happening with him or Luke, but they were fine; and she made up some excuse as to why she was calling so they wouldn't worry until they needed to."

Mavis leaned forward and took over the conversation.

"We went to the Miller Hill barn next. We figured if the men were okay, and the house wasn't on fire, then something must have happened with the horse."

Lauren stood up and paced in front of the windowseat.

"We took some carrots with us, because we knew Major liked them. He was in his stall, and other than being somewhat subdued, he was fine. We couldn't think of anywhere else to look, so we went back to the church to see if Harriet had returned there. We thought maybe she'd had a personal emergency of the female sort and we'd missed her coming and going somehow."

"But she wasn't at the church," Mavis said.

"We called her phone," Beth added, "but she didn't answer."

Lauren sat back down.

"That was when we called you," she said, indicating Morse.

"Anything else you three can think of?" Morse asked.

Beth, Mavis, and Lauren looked at each other, then shook their heads.

"Okay, James and Luke," Morse went on. "When did you find out something was wrong, and what did you do?"

"Well, you called us around ten or ten-thirty, so we packed up, cancelled our visit with my friend, and came home."

Harriet frowned at this and wrote *sorry* with a sad face on her whiteboard. James gently patted her left hand.

"It wasn't your fault. We can make it up another time."

"It took us hours to get home, and we didn't even stop for food," Luke added, more for dramatic effect than information.

"To be fair, we did have car snacks," James corrected. "We came home, and let the dogs out, and then started calling people to find out if they knew anything. No one did. I guess the quilters had called everyone they could think of already."

Morse cleared her throat.

"During this time, I sent several patrol officers out to the Equestrian Center to search for Ms. Truman. We had no evidence she'd gone there, but given what had happened recently, we thought it would be prudent. We didn't find anything. We tried to ping her phone, but it had gone dead. We didn't know if the battery had died or been removed.

"I got a warrant for Ms. Truman's phone records but that takes a little time, especially since we were starting on a Sunday. When we finally got them, two days later, all we found was that a burner phone had been used to send a text that 'Major is in trouble,' which was a lie, since the horse is obviously fine.

"That focused our attention on the Equestrian Center, but we still had no evidence of what had happened or where."

"Meanwhile," Beth said, "We Threads printed posters with a picture of Harriet and plastered the town with them, but we didn't get so much as a prank call in response."

"We were getting very worried," Mavis added.

Harriet, who had grown increasingly confused by the references to Major, took the marker awkwardly in her right hand and wrote *Major dead*.

James read it and showed it to the others.

"Sweetie, Major isn't dead. He's the one who found you."

Harriet shook her head once and began writing again.

I saw, she wrote.

The machine hooked up to the leads on Harriet's chest began beeping. Nurse Caroline came in.

"That's enough for now. You all need to leave." She left briefly and returned with a syringe she expertly emptied into Harriet's IV tube.

"She's going to sleep for a while now. Detective, I know you need to question her more, but I think it would be better if you didn't have such a big group."

Morse put her phone and notepad away.

"I'll be back in the morning."

James stood up, but kept his hand on Harriet's.

"I'd like to be here."

"If it works for Harriet, I would like to have you and Luke here," Morse said. "Since the next part of the story involves you two."

"That will be okay, as long as you don't upset her," Caroline said. "With what she's been through, her memory might be scrambled for a while. Don't argue with what she tells you."

"We can do that," Morse said. "Does ten a.m. work?"

"Luke and I can be here," James said.

"That should be fine, but call the nurse's station in the morning to make sure."

James sighed.

"We can do that." He turned to Morse. "I'll call at nine-thirty, then I'll let you know if we can't meet. Otherwise, we'll see you here." He put his arm around Luke's shoulders. "Come on, let's go feed you and the beasts, and try to get some rest."

Chapter 50

𝓗 arriet learned later that when James and Luke reached home there was a plate of foil-wrapped tamales on the table with a bowl of beans and another of rice beside them. A note was propped up against the tamales.

'*Let us know if we can do anything to help. Love, Connie and Rod. PS - we fed the dogs and cat and took the dogs out.*'

"Wow," Luke exclaimed when he saw the pile of food. "Why are the quilters so nice to us?"

"It's the way people are in a small town. When someone has trouble, everyone pitches in."

He told her he'd done his best to explain to Luke how to be a good citizen of the community. He also told her how upset Luke had been when she'd said Major was dead. Even though he knew it wasn't true, it had worried him.

✂-- ✂-- ✂

It was crisp and clear the next morning as James and Luke made their way to the Jefferson County Hospital. A phone call had confirmed that Harriet would be able to receive visitors. He took the chair beside her bed, with Morse and Luke in two chairs near the foot.

"How are you feeling," he asked when everyone was seated.

Harriet drew a smiley face on the whiteboard.

Morse started her phone recording and opened her notepad.

"If everyone's ready, I'd like to start with Luke and James telling their part of the story."

Harriet nodded.

Luke let out a breath and watched her face as he began.

"I guess Major finding Harriet's phone was the next thing. I went out to ride him for a little while, since he hadn't been out in a couple of days because we were all searching and hanging up posters. I went to take him out of his stall, and he wouldn't move. He kept stomping his foot. When I looked at the foot, he was stepping on a broken cellphone. I picked it up and realized it was Harriet's."

"What did you do then?" Morse asked.

"I picked it up by the edges and set it on the bench outside the stall. Then, I called James."

"And I called the police," James continued. "I met Luke at the barn, and we waited until Officer Nguyen showed up and bagged the phone."

"Did you really?" Morse said. It was clear no one at the PD had told her the phone had been recovered. She made a note in her little book. "Go on."

"Then, I went riding, but I was thinking, too," Luke continued. "After we bought Major, the Seattle police sent us a file with his pedigree and all his certificates for training he'd completed. He had to be certified to be a police horse, but his former rider took him through a lot of other stuff. One was tracking."

Harriet drew a large question mark on her white board and held it up. Luke smiled.

"It turns out horses can be trained to track scent if they're willing. It's a natural skill they retained from the days of wild horses. They're used to sniffing their environment for information, so it's easy to teach them how to signal different scents they smell. And because they're a lot taller than dogs, they can pick up airborne as well as ground-level scents.

"Anyway, after I got back home, I talked to James about it, and he said we could try it the next day. It turned out neither of us could sleep, so he said maybe we could see if Major could try to track Harriet—if he wasn't too sleepy, that was."

James looked down at his hands.

"I felt bad dragging Luke out at two in the morning, but once he told me about it, I couldn't get it out of my mind."

"Harriet had done all the laundry, so all we could find to use was her pajamas," Luke continued. "We put a lead rope on Major and let him take a good sniff of the pajamas and told him to find her."

"I have to admit, I was a little skeptical when he immediately headed down the aisle and then outside," James said. "He followed a track toward what turned out to be a hay storage barn. About halfway there, he stopped where there were a couple of largish rocks in the trail. He stomped around there for a moment or two and then went on to the barn.

"That barn is maybe a quarter-mile from the main stable. They must use ATVs to move hay back and forth, judging by the width of the track. It sits on a slope, with a ledge that drops off into a rockfall.

"We stopped at the front of the barn because the path around the barn is narrow, and Major is a big horse. He wouldn't stay stopped, though, and Luke couldn't keep him from going around the barn. I told him to let him go, and we'd follow him.

"When we caught up, he'd stopped halfway along the wall under a second-story window. A rope was hanging out the window, and at the end of the rope was a pair of socks."

"I tugged on the rope," Luke said. "And Harriet tugged back."

Harriet started writing on her board.

Socks all I could remove.

James laughed.

"I wondered about that. Black kneesocks aren't real uncommon."

Morse wrote notes on this last bit. Finally, she flipped to a new page.

"I know this will be hard, but in your own words, can you write out what happened?"

Harriet swiped at her board, and James took it from her and wiped it completely clean with a tissue.

I woke rolled up in a rug. Hands bound. Got free, found window, found rope, heard horse, tied socks like flag, sent out window.'

"Did you see anyone at either barn?" Morse asked.

Harriet shook her head.

"The doctor said her memory may improve with time if she doesn't push it too hard," James advised.

Morse sighed and closed her notebook.

"Okay, I hear you. If the rest of you think of anything, let me know." With that she stood up. "I hope you feel better," she said and left the room.

Harriet attempted a weak smile.

"Don't worry," James said in a soft voice. "She'll figure it out."

Harriet hoped he was right.

Chapter 51

Harriet spent another two days in the hospital. According to her doctor, it was to insure he could keep her quiet, but finally he gave in to her ever more insistent notes on her whiteboard swearing she would sleep, and therefore heal, much better if she could do so in her own bed.

She felt ridiculous when the nurse's aide rolled her out to the curb in a wheelchair, her arm strapped to a big black foam block and a plastic collar around her neck. She sighed once she was safely belted into James's car. At least she was free.

Aunt Beth, Mavis, and Connie were waiting in her kitchen when they got home. Connie slid out a chair.

"*Diós mio!* Come sit down."

James gave her a questioning look as he pushed her seat closer to the table.

"I'd love a cup of tepid tea," she whispered, and he repeated it. Mavis immediately jumped up, grabbed the kettle, and filled it, handing it across to Beth, who had also stood and gone to the stove, ready to heat it. James sat down beside Harriet and took her coat from around her shoulders.

"Harriet has to be on a semi-soft diet until her throat heals," he advised them.

Beth walked over to the refrigerator and pulled out a bowl of tapioca pudding.

"Honey, if you'd like some of this, I can warm you up a bowl."

Harriet gave her a thumb's-up.

When everyone was settled with tea, pudding, and, for everyone except Harriet, gingersnaps, she held her hand up.

"What is it, honey?" Mavis asked.

"What's been going on since I disappeared?" she whispered.

Mavis took a swallow from her mug.

"Everyone is making progress on their horse quilts. Connie has been helping Carla—she was having trouble with the hip shaping. Lauren finished hers and said she could work on yours, since you aren't going to be able to stitch for a while."

"Sorry," Harriet whispered.

Aunt Beth reached over and patted her hand.

"Jorge and I have been taking food out to the homeless camp so James could take care of Luke and be at the hospital. We haven't seen Stanley out there lately."

The crunch of gravel in the driveway announced a new arrival, and a few minutes later, Lauren came in through the studio door.

"What did I miss?"

Mavis got up and poured her a mug of tea.

"Here, sit down," she said and handed her the mug. Connie moved over a chair so Lauren didn't have to squeeze past her.

"We're catching her up on what's happened while she was indisposed."

"Did they tell you I volunteered to finish your blanket?" Lauren asked her.

Harriet nodded the slight amount the neck brace allowed.

"Stanley's been MIA at the stable," Lauren reported. "I can call Tom and ask if he's working on little houses, if anyone thinks it matters."

"We all went out to the riding center on therapy night," Beth said. "As near as we can tell, the horse show is still happening. Angela is back to giving lessons. She's brought in a young man none of us have been introduced to."

"He's teaching Simon's classes," Mavis finished.

"We watched him teach the little ones and the teens, and he doesn't seem to have an inappropriate interest in either group," Connie added.

"So far, anyway," Lauren said, and sipped her tea. "And by the way, I've been going out to watch Luke and Emily ride." She put her mug down. "We don't have any reason to believe they're in danger, but we didn't think you were in danger, either."

"What's Morse say?" Harriet asked.

Aunt Beth sighed.

"I've never seen her quite so discouraged. Whoever is killing people has been very careful to leave no forensic evidence."

"And they defeated the security system, so they have some skill in electronics," Mavis added.

Connie chuckled.

"These days, that could be anyone over the age of ten."

Harriet sipped her tea.

"Who was at the barn when you came to look for me?"

Lauren thought for a moment.

"JoAnne was in the feed room, Angela was teaching a lesson, Stanley was riding Lily in the small arena…"

"There were a few young people riding in the small arena with Stanley," Beth added.

" Stella?" Harriet asked.

"I asked," Lauren said, "But JoAnne said she was in Germany picking up her new horse."

"Do you know what she bought?" Harriet whispered.

"JoAnne didn't know. She just said Stella and her husband were going to be gone for two weeks, and she'd told them to call the vet if anything happened with Essy. Apparently, she signed a release for them to treat the horse in her absence."

Connie crunched on a gingersnap.

"Was Emily there?"

"Hmm," Lauren said as she thought. "I think she was. Why?"

"Just thinking outside the box. If we need to think of a tech-savvy person who knows the stable property well enough to know about the hay barn, Emily does fit the bill."

Harriet shook her head slightly.

"Can't imagine it."

"Can't? Or don't want to?" Lauren asked her.

"Doesn't feel right."

"But you're the first to admit you can't remember anything," Lauren pressed.

Connie put her hand on Lauren's arm and shook her head slightly. Lauren sighed and picked up her tea again, leaning back in her chair as she sipped.

"Shall we meet in Harriet's studio tomorrow to work on our horse quilts?" Beth asked. "Harriet can come down and visit with us if she's up to it, or just stay in bed and rest if she's not."

"I'll be there," Harriet whispered.

✂ -- ✂ -- ✂

Under Aunt Beth's watchful eye, Luke carried an upholstered slipper chair with its matching ottoman down from the attic and placed it near the big worktable in the studio. When the Loose Threads arrived, Harriet was in it with a fleece throw, two dogs and a cat in her lap, and a TV tray with a cup of tea and a bowl of oatmeal next to it.

Lauren came in first and set a cup of hot chocolate on the tray. She'd asked the barista to make it the temperature they used for children.

"I thought I'd come early and be your door person. I know most people have keys, but they probably won't use them, since they know you're in here."

Robin arrived, got out the flip chart from a shelf behind Harriet's desk, and set it up opposite Harriet. When the pens were in the bottom tray and the roll of transparent tape was on the cutting table, Lauren took a folded sheet of paper from her shoulder bag, unfolded it, and taped it to the flip chart. When she moved out of the way, Harriet got a look at it.

Lauren had drawn a detailed map of the Equestrian Center property and the surrounding roads and neighborhood. She once again reached into her bag and pulled out a zipper bag that contained small paper dolls representing all the relevant people. She even had dolls of some of the horses. With Robin's help, she placed the people and horses in the locations they'd been on Sunday morning. She'd attached a gob of artist's adhesive to each doll to keep it in place.

"Is this pretty much how things looked Sunday morning?" s he asked Harriet when she and Robin were finished.

Harriet scanned the map, studying each area.

"As near as I can remember. I understand that what I remember can't be true, but I can't stop thinking that I left church, went to the stable, and saw Major lying dead in his stall...and then, nothing."

"I don't know what to tell you," Lauren said.

There was a light tapping on the studio door, followed by Detective Morse entering.

"I saw Lauren at the stable yesterday, and she said you were all meeting this morning." She slid her coat off and hung it on the rack by the door. I wanted to let you know we've gotten the report back from your cell provider. It confirmed you did get a message indicating something was wrong with Major. It came, as I told you earlier, from a burner phone, so we don't know who sent the text, but at least we know you were right about why you left church so quickly."

Harriet grabbed Lauren's hand.

"Call Aiden and ask him to come by," she whispered.

Lauren looked at her.

"Are you sure?"

Harriet nodded.

Lauren dialed and spoke briefly, then hung up and turned back to her.

"He'll be here in thirty minutes."

Morse walked over and studied the flip chart.

"Maybe you can explain what you have here while we wait."

Robin smiled.

"We'd be happy to."

Chapter 52

The rest of the Loose Threads arrived while they waited for Aiden. DeAnn went to the flip chart and, using Lauren's temporary glue stick, attached several rock formations between the arena and the hay storage barn.

"I'm not sure how this helps, but I went out to the stable and measured so my paper rocks are to scale. I did this because I have a theory about how Harriet got hurt."

"Do tell," Lauren said.

"I'd like to hear, too," Morse said, moving close to the chart again.

"The Equestrian Center has a tractor and an all-terrain vehicle that's like a very small flatbed truck—there's a platform on the back they use to move heavy things like bales of hay or bags of feed from one place to another.

"I think whoever knocked Harriet out put her on the back of the ATV in the horse barn and took off for the hay barn. From the tracks in the dirt, it looks like the path makes a turn at this pile of rock." DeAnn tapped on one of the images she'd stuck on the diagram. "If the driver was going too fast, I think it's possible Harriet jounced off the flatbed and onto the rockpile, with one point of rock hitting her throat and the other her arm." She looked at Morse. "I didn't touch the rock, but I think there's blood on it."

"Interesting," Morse said. "I'll send a forensic team over to see what they think." She took her phone from her pocket, tapped in a text and hit send.

"Anyone ready for cookies with their tea and coffee?" Connie asked. "Carla and I made chocolate chip cookie bars."

The group was ready, and took a break to eat and mull over DeAnn's theory.

✂-- ✂-- ✂

The Loose Threads got their horse blankets out and were showing them to Morse when her phone rang. She stepped into Harriet's kitchen to take the call, returning a few minutes later sliding her phone back into her pocket.

"Good call, DeAnn. The forensic tech said there *is* human blood on and around that rock formation. It will take a while to see if it's Harriet's, but being relatively fresh, it's likely it will be. None of the surfaces are conducive to fingerprinting, but the techs are going back to the stable and checking the ATV. Given that it's been a week or more, and the vehicle's been used, we may not get anything, but you never know."

The group had just folded up their horse blankets when Aiden knocked on the studio door. Beth opened it, and he immediately crossed to where Harriet sat.

"Are you okay? What am I saying? Of course you're not okay." His jaw tightened, and the muscle jumped. "Who did this to you?" He paced the floor in front of her chair. "I helped with the search for you, and I knew you'd been found, but no one said how badly injured you are."

Harriet reached out with her good hand when he went past her again.

"Stop," she whispered. He did, and she took his hand in hers. "It's not as bad as it looks. I need to ask you something, and I need you to be calm."

Mavis slid a wheeled chair over for him to sit on. He took a deep breath.

"I'm sorry. It just pains me to see you like this."

"Detective Morse is taking care of things, it's not your problem. As you can see, I'm being very well taken care of."

He looked up to see the Loose Threads gathered in a semicircle a discreet distance away and smiled.

"You do have quite a team here."

"When I was found, I had been unconscious for a while. They think I was drugged. Because of that, my memory is spotty. We now know that the text message I received is real. The message said something was wrong with Major and to come quickly. I was in church and left immediately to see what the problem was.

"Now, here's where you come into this. The last thing I remember is arriving at the stable and seeing Major lying in his stall dead.

"Clearly, he *wasn't* dead, and apparently is fine. The problem is, it's such a strong memory. I can't get it out of my head. What I'm wondering is, could someone have done something to make it seem like he was dead? I know I sound crazy, but it's the only thing I can think of."

Aiden leaned back in his chair.

"There's a medication, acepromazine, that when administered properly is a mild sedative. If, however, you shoot it into an artery, the horse will drop immediately. It's very dramatic, but the horse comes to in about fifteen minutes and, other than being a little wonky for a few hours after that, they're perfectly fine."

"Would that be hard to do?" Detective Morse asked.

"Not at all. You shoot it into the carotid artery in the neck. Given that it was Major, I'd guess they gave him some sort of oral sedative so they could get near him with a needle. Either that, or it was someone he trusted. If I remember right, he's reacted badly when strangers have tried to get in his stall to mess with him."

Harriet smiled.

"A trashed stall door comes to mind."

Aunt Beth handed her a fresh cup of tea.

"So, maybe you *are* remembering things correctly. You saw Major lying down and thought he was dead. How does that help us?" Morse asked.

"We don't think I'm nuts for one thing," Harriet said, "which does move things forward a little. Clearly, if I saw Major flat in his stall, I would crouch down to check him for signs of life. That's where my memory ends, so someone must have knocked me out at that point."

Morse sipped tea.

"If that's what happened, it tells us whoever did this knew enough about horses to locate the carotid artery and inject a sedative into it. They also had to have knowledge and access to the drug."

"How easy is it to obtain?" Harriet asked.

"Anyone with a computer can order it online," Aiden said. "You need to know what it is to go looking for it, but it's commonly used before surgery in dogs and cats and for general anxiety in animals."

Connie brought the plate of cookie bars around to the group again. She stopped in front of Morse.

"Do you think one person could have done all this, or would it take two people to sedate a horse, knock Harriet out, then take her to the loft of the hay barn and roll her up in a carpet?"

Morse hesitated before answering.

"A single person could do it if they were strong. It would be easier with two people. But we have to consider that the person who attacked Harriet probably also killed Simon and Crystal. I suppose it's possible it could be two people—or more."

"But you don't think so?" Harriet asked.

"I'd never say never, but it doesn't fit the evidence we have. We only saw one person on the tape when Simon was killed, for instance." She put her cup down. "I need to go, thanks for the tea."

Aiden stood up as well.

"I've got to get back, too. Call me if you need anything else."

Harriet smiled at him.

"Thanks."

"Ladies," he said, nodding to the rest of the group.

Chapter 53

"Okay, everyone, let's gather around our diagram and see what we can figure out," Mavis said.

Robin added a paper doll that represented Harriet.

"Stan was riding Lily in the arena with several other people. Angela was teaching in the big arena." She moved the doll that represented JoAnne into the feed room. "We're not sure where JoAnne was. She was either in the hay barn with Harriet, if she's the culprit, or she was in the feed room if she wasn't."

Harriet smiled.

"She's so small. Do you really think she could have overpowered me, and then lugged me onto the ATV and got me up to the hayloft?"

Robin left her paper-JoAnne in the feed room.

"Let's not eliminate anyone until we get them all on the board. Where do we think Emily was?"

Mavis took a bite of her cookie.

"Don't you think she'd be in the small arena riding? Otherwise, why would she be there on a Sunday?"

Robin stuck Emily's doll on a paper horse and put her in the arena with Stan and Lily.

"What about Stella?" Lauren asked.

"She's in Germany, or at least she was on her way there," Robin pointed ed out.

Lauren took a paper doll of Stella and stuck her outside the drawing of the barn.

"Even though it doesn't make sense at this point, I think we need to account for everyone who had the knowledge to be our perpetrator."

The color drained from Harriet's face.

"I realize Stella couldn't have been there, but before all this happened, I remember her giving me a really weird look. I haven't been able to shake the feeling that she's somehow involved. I don't know why she'd have any problem with me."

Lauren put a cookie in a mug, poured some milk on it, and added a spoon.

"Here, you look like you could use a little sugar." She handed Harriet the cup. "I can't see any reason *any* of our possible suspects would have a problem with you."

Aunt Beth pointed at the board with her cookie.

"I think one of these people thinks Harriet knows something about them."

"I don't," Harriet complained.

"They think you know something; and maybe you do—you just don't know what it is."

"Where does that leave us?" Mavis asked.

"Let's see if we can eliminate anyone," Robin said.

Harriet used her left hand to point at paper-Stan.

"With Stan's bad leg, I think he'd have trouble doing it."

"When I was hiking around the hay barn, I noticed they have a hay-bale elevator," DeAnn said. "That it would make it easier to get Harriet up to the barn loft."

"I didn't find a door in that room," Harriet reminded them. "I don't know how anyone got me up there."

DeAnn set her cup down.

"There's a door on the back side of the loft where they load hay from the elevator. In the dark, and injured like you were, you might not have been able to tell it was there. Also, there's a ladder up from inside the barn with a trapdoor. There might have been hay covering that."

"I suppose," Harriet said. "Stan asked me to verify he was participating in the horse-therapy program on his application for his housing. I can't imagine he'd want to put that in jeopardy."

Robin took his doll out of the stable and stuck him off to the side under Stella's.

"I'll buy that."

Harriet ate a spoonful of cookie mush.

"I still think JoAnne should be taken down," she said. "Unless she had an issue with Simon we weren't aware of, and likewise Crystal; I just don't see her being our killer or my attacker. I also don't believe she's big enough to have done it without help."

"I'm not so sure," Robin said as she removed JoAnne's doll. "If she can haul bags of horse feed, she can haul you, but you're right—I can't see a motive for her, either. That doesn't mean she doesn't have one, and we just can't see it."

"Who does that leave us?" Mavis said, adjusting her glasses.

"Angela and Emily," Robin answered.

Harriet set her mug of cookie on her side table.

"Are we sure Stella was on her way to Germany on Sunday morning?"

"She told Angela she was leaving Saturday, according to Morse," Aunt Beth said.

"Lauren, could you check with your airport security contacts and verify that she and her husband really did leave Saturday?" Harriet asked.

Lauren sighed. "Sure."

Mavis stood up.

"We can't do anything else here. Let's work on the horse blankets that still need binding or our own projects, if your blanket is done."

Everyone got up and slid their chairs over to the worktable then got out their stitching.

✂ -- ✂ -- ✂

"I'm sorry you're having to finish Major's blanket," Harriet said to no one in particular.

Lauren blew out a breath and stretched her shoulders.

"I don't think any of us has been super-excited about this project, given everything that's happened."

Mavis looked up from her stitching.

"When everyone sees these on the horses, and marvels over how much nicer they look than the storebought version, you're going to feel different about it."

"Maybe," Lauren said and stood up. "Harriet, do you mind if I work at your desk for a few minutes?" She pulled her laptop from her bag. "I thought I'd go ahead and see what I can learn about Stella's travel plans. It might involve a few phone calls, and it's quieter at your desk."

"Of course," Harriet told her. "You can go upstairs in the house, if you want."

Lauren went over to the desk.

"This'll be okay."

Carla cleared her throat.

"I'm sort of surprised the stable is going ahead with the show, given what's been going on."

Harriet moved Cyrano from her lap and set him on the ottoman.

"She probably has to. She's already scheduled judges and workers. At least some of those people would probably have to be paid no matter what happens. And I'm sure she paid for advertising that would be wasted."

Beth stabbed her needle into her blanket binding.

"Honey, she might just need to keep busy so she doesn't have to think about what's happened."

"I guess," Carla mumbled and went back to her stitching.

Robin stood up.

"I need to go pick up kids in half an hour, but let me take your beasts out for a walk before I go."

The dogs both jumped off of Harriet and ran over to her.

DeAnn chuckled. "I guess they understand English."

Harriet shook her head.

"They know the words *go, outside*, and anything to do with food."

Robin went to the kitchen and got their leashes, then took them out through the garage.

Harriet could hear Lauren talking to someone on her cellphone. She watched her make a note and then tap in another number. Judging by the look on her face, she was getting somewhere.

Lauren ended her last call and put her phone in her bag as Robin came back in from the kitchen with the dogs.

"Okay, interesting news," she said.

Everyone stopped sewing and looked up at her, now standing in the middle of the group.

"Stella did not, in fact, leave Saturday night. Her husband has his own jet, which they took over to Germany on Sunday. She is scheduled to fly back with the horse on a regularly scheduled commercial horse transportation flight while her husband will come back with the family jet."

Harriet sat up straighter in her chair, wincing when she repositioned her arm.

"Why would Stella want to get rid of me?"

Mavis set her stitching aside.

"Stella, or whoever, clearly thinks you know something," she insisted. "The question is why would she kill Simon? And why kill Crystal?"

Beth stood up.

"We need to call Morse and make sure she knows about the private jet. Stella fits with our suspect requirements—she knows the stable area well, she's big enough to pick up Harriet, and she probably could drive the ATV."

"And she can come and go from the back side of the stable, since she lives in that neighborhood behind the property," Harriet added.

Robin took out her phone and dialed Morse.

"She's coming back over," she said and put her phone away.

Chapter 54

"**D**o you have any coffee?" Morse asked when she'd entered the studio and removed her coat.

"There's a pod coffee maker in the kitchen," Harriet said. "I'd get it for you, but…"

Aunt Beth stood up.

"You just sit down, Jane, and I'll go get it. Do you like dark, medium, or light roast?"

Morse gave a wry half-smile. "As dark as you've got."

Robin, DeAnn, and Carla had left to pick up their various children, but Mavis, Connie, Beth, and Jenny were still sitting in a circle stitching on their various projects. Lauren was back at Harriet's desk working on her laptop.

Beth returned with a mug of steaming coffee for Morse and sat down in her own chair, picking up Harriet's horse blanket again.

"We'll let Lauren tell you our latest."

Lauren went to the flip chart.

"As you know from when you came by earlier, we've placed paper dolls of all the people who had the knowledge of the property and were known to be at the stable on the Sunday, on the diagram of the barn and surrounding area.

"One of the people who had the knowledge and size to drug Major, drug Harriet, and move her to the hay barn is Stella Bren. The problem we had was Stella supposedly left for Germany to get her new horse on Saturday. I know Harriet's mind has been scrambled, but she thinks Stella gave her a weird look before all this happened. So, we decided to challenge Stella's alibi.

"I repaired and rewrote some security software at the airport, and they are very appreciative. I called one of my contacts and asked if they could verify that Milo Bren's company jet left for Germany Saturday night. After checking, he said it had originally been scheduled to leave Saturday, but in fact, it left mid-morning Sunday, leaving plenty of time for Stella to be Harriet's attacker."

Morse leaned forward in her chair.

"That's an interesting theory. So she had the means and opportunity, but what's her motive?"

Harriet blew out a breath.

"That's what we can't figure out. I've had very little contact with the woman."

Mavis set Harriet's project aside and stood up.

"We think Stella thinks Harriet knows something."

"And that's why she went after her," Beth finished.

"Why would Stella kill Simon and Crystal?" Morse asked.

Harriet squirmed, trying to get comfortable, which was impossible since she was overdue for a pain pill.

"I've been thinking about that. We know Stella's very expensive horse has an injured foot. She told me he was limping, and then he was better, so Simon said she could ride him in a show she had upcoming. She did, and the next day, her horse was limping worse, and when she called the vet in Seattle, he said it was a serious injury, and in fact, the horse might never get over it.

"I found a syringe kit that Simon dropped that was supposedly for pain related to his injuries. What if he injected Stella's horse with a nerve block so she could show him and win the top prize under the banner of the Miller Hill Equestrian Center? The foot injury would intensify, but the horse wouldn't feel it until the block wore off the next day.

"If Stella found out what Simon did, she'd have more than enough motive to want him dead."

"What about Crystal Kelley?" Morse asked.

Beth slid her chair forward.

"Maybe *Crystal* is the one who saw something she shouldn't. According to gossip around the stable, Crystal was known for creeping around in the middle of the night, moving things around, using other people's grooming tools on her daughter's horse."

Morse sipped from her mug while she digested what she'd heard. She pointed at the flip chart.

"This all makes a good story, but…"

"You need evidence," Lauren and Harriet said at the same time.

"You got it. I can't even begin to look for Stella Bren in Germany without solid evidence and a warrant."

Connie shook her head.

"Are you telling us she's going to get away with two murders and Harriet's attack?"

"No, all I'm saying is there's no usable evidence at this point."

"Wait a minute," Harriet said. "As far as she knows, I'm dead. I'm sure that was her intention. Given that, she probably believes she has nothing to worry about. I mean, no one has connected her to Simon and Crystal so far. She'll come back with her horse, convinced that, since she told everyone she was leaving Saturday, she has an alibi."

"Then what?"

"I stay hidden," Harriet said. "Which won't be too hard if she comes home any time soon. Then you write a note, supposedly from one of the barn people—JoAnne, maybe. It will say 'I saw what you did to Harriet in the hay barn. I was out there counting bales and hid when I heard the ATV. I don't want any trouble, and for ten thousand dollars, you'll never see or hear from me again. I just want out of here'."

Morse was quiet.

"Well?" Lauren said.

"It could work. We can set up a meeting site away from the barn and all of you. We can have an officer dress like JoAnne with a hat pulled down covering her face. If Stella shows up with the money and hands it off, we've got her."

"I wonder if her husband is in on it?" Mavis said.

"Her husband is very reclusive. He donates to a number of local charities, but he never shows up for banquets or to receive awards or anything," Jenny advised.

Morse drained her coffee mug.

"Let me go talk this over with my partner, and if he agrees, our boss. Harriet, I'll let you know if you need to play dead. Until then, you all should go about your normal business."

Beth took Morse's empty mug.

"Thank you for listening to us. And we'll understand if your bosses squash the idea."

"I'll be in touch." Morse picked up her coat and left.

"Well, that's that," Mavis said as she gathered up mugs and carried them toward the kitchen.

Beth came over to Harriet's chair.

"You need to go up to your bed and rest."

Harriet sighed. "I'm not going to argue with you on that. You guys can stay and stitch, if you want."

"I've got a dog who needs to go out," Mavis said.

Jenny put her jacket on.

"I need to fill Brian in on what's happening. He'll be glad to know he's no longer a suspect."

"Didn't he already know that?" Lauren asked her.

Jenny shook her head. "Wouldn't believe it as long as they didn't have another one."

Mavis wrapped her knit scarf around her neck.

"I don't blame him for that. I think I'd feel the same way."

"I suppose," Beth said. "Do you need help getting upstairs?" she asked Harriet.

"No, you go on. Nurse Luke will be home soon."

"Call if you need anything," Lauren yelled as she left, following the others out the door.

Chapter 55

"**H**ow is Major doing?" Harriet asked Luke several days later as he came upstairs and joined her in the TV room. He had gone out to the barn with Aunt Beth and Jorge to help work with the veterans' group and to ride.

"He's fine. Dr. Jalbert was there treating a horse who choked on its hay, so I asked him if he'd look at Major. I hope that's okay." He looked worried, and Harriet patted his hand.

"It's fine, sweetie. I should have thought of that sooner."

"He said Major looks great. He doesn't seem to have injured anything when he went down, and you can see the injection site if you look hard enough, but it's fine."

"Emily isn't going out to the barn by herself, is she?"

"No, her parents are barely letting her go to the barn at all. I think they're pressuring her a lot about going to do her 'duty' in India and using the trouble at the barn as an excuse to keep her home and work on her."

"How do you feel about that?"

"I think they've been her parents her whole life, so she's used to dealing with them. She'll have to decide if she's going to stand up to them or not. I can't do that for her."

"Very wise of you."

✄-- ✄-- ✄

"Dinner's ready," James called up the stairs a short while later. "I made stew tonight. I chopped the meat pretty small and cooked it in the slow cooker all day, so hopefully, it'll be soft enough for you."

Harriet came down and sat at the table.

"My throat is much better, and it smells wonderful."

James set a bowl in front of her, while Luke brought a basket of yeast rolls to the table. Harriet had to smile to herself at the sight of James and Luke, both in plaid flannel shirts unbuttoned to the waist with Vancouver Canucks tee-shirts underneath.

"Have you heard from Detective Morse?" James asked as he set down two more bowls of stew.

Harriet buttered her roll with herb butter.

"I haven't heard anything from her. Aunt Beth hasn't heard anything, either. It's possible Stella could decide to stay out of the country for an extended period."

"Can she do that?" Luke asked.

"Sure," Harriet answered. "We don't know that much about her. She might have dual citizenship, in which case she could stay there forever if she wanted."

"So, they might never catch her?" Luke said, his voice rising.

James set his spoon down.

"In America, people are innocent until proven guilty. I want the person responsible for Harriet's attack and the two murders to be caught and put in jail as much as anyone, but if I understand it right, there isn't any evidence against Stella Bren at this point. We all just *think* she did it. It's possible her trip to Germany is a total coincidence."

Luke stared at him. "Do you really believe that?"

"No, but it's still important to keep in mind that we have nothing but a guess at this point."

Harriet adjusted her injured arm in its sling.

"I wonder if the same blackmail ruse could work on Milo Bren. Stella may be able to stay unreachable, but Milo has businesses to run. Someone should be able to get a message to him."

"I'm sure Detective Morse has thought of that," James said.

"I'm not," Harriet insisted. "She has to follow a narrow set of rules, and so far, Foggy Point PD hasn't been known for their ability to think outside the box."

"Don't do anything without including Morse," James said.

"I'll call her after dinner and see what's happening, if anything," Harriet said and ate another bite of roll.

"Mention warm brownies, and maybe she'll come in person," James suggested.

Luke sat up straighter.

"We have brownies?"

James grinned. "I have a secret stash in the freezer for just this sort of occasion."

✂ -- ✂ -- ✂

The bait worked. In just over half an hour, Morse was in the kitchen, coffee was made, and brownies were warming in the oven. She looked up gratefully as James set a steaming mug in front of her.

"What's on your mind?" she asked after savoring a sip.

Harriet looked at James before speaking.

"We were wondering if you'd had any luck with selling our idea of luring Stella out with a fake blackmail note."

Morse shifted her mug from one hand to the other.

"The boss said he'd think about it, but we need Stella back in our jurisdiction before we can do anything. He also had issues with using JoAnne if we do go ahead with the plan. She hasn't been cleared as a suspect yet. I know no one believes she's big enough to do the crimes alone, but she could have an accomplice."

James set a warm brownie on a plate and a fork in front of her.

"What about questioning Milo Bren?"

Morse chuckled.

"You guys must not think very highly of us at the cop shop. Yes, we've thought of questioning Milo Bren. It was one of the first things we did when he got back to town."

"And?" Harriet prompted.

"And nothing. I shouldn't tell you, but I'll use the excuse your brownie bribe is working. Milo either knows nothing, or he should take up acting. He's a busy executive and is happy Stella has her horse to keep her busy. He says his business trip had been planned weeks ago, and it was just convenient for Stella to go along."

"What if I send her a text and ask her to meet me?" Harriet suggested.

"No," James and Luke said simultaneously.

She held up her good hand.

"Just hear me out. I could send her a text saying, 'I know what you did to me, but I have a proposal'. If it wasn't her, she should respond by calling me crazy. If it *was* her, she's going to be shocked I'm alive, and she's going to either want a second chance at me or to at least hear if I have a viable alternative for her."

"And if she agrees to meet, then what?" Morse asked.

"Then she tacitly admits it was her who tried to kill me, and maybe even confesses to killing Simon and Crystal, if I can work it right. You'll be waiting in the wings, listening to the wire I'm wearing…" She cut off James's clear intent to object with a look, "…over my bulletproof vest, although she's not used a gun on anyone. Then, you arrest her."

Morse ate a few bites of her brownie in thoughtful silence. Finally, she put her fork down.

"Let me say, for the record, I hate this idea. It's like a bad movie from the fifties."

Harriet started to protest.

"Wait. I said I hate it, I didn't say I wouldn't do it. I'm going to sell this to my boss. I think he'll buy it because we have a killer running around free who, if she comes back to Foggy Point, will probably try to kill you again."

"What about Luke and me? Don't we get a say in this?"

Harriet reached out and took his hand.

"I have to do this. I can't stay hidden forever hoping someone will find evidence to arrest her."

"What if she doesn't go for it?" Luke asked. "Then she'll know you survived her first attempt and still be free to try again."

"We don't have a large police force," Morse said, "but we have enough people to put round-the-clock surveillance on her if and when she shows her face in town again."

"According to Angela, she's bringing her new horse back later this week," Luke told her.

Harriet took a swallow of her tea. Her throat was slowly getting better, but talking this much was not helping anything. The doctor had said *no talking*, and she was beginning to think she'd better try to do better at that. Maybe whispering would help.

"Angela's been in touch with Stella?"

Luke shrugged.

"I guess. Angela told Emily to clean up and put bedding in the stall next to Essy. Em asked why, and she said Stella was bringing her new horse at the end of the week. As they say, money talks. When Em came to work, horses had been shuffled around to empty that stall."

Morse pulled her notepad from her pocket and made a notation.

"I'll check with Angela in the morning. Given this timeline, I'll need to let the boss know and get you lined up to send the text before Stella gets back."

"You're going to have Harriet protected the whole time, right?" James said as he placed a second brownie in plastic wrap and a napkin beside Morse's plate.

"Nothing is ever guaranteed, but Stella, assuming she's our killer, strangled her victims or used drugs, not guns or knives. That doesn't mean she couldn't start, so we *will* have Harriet in a vest, and I'll have snipers around the meeting place. Harriet will arrive early and won't let Stella get close to her."

James sighed.

"I don't like it, but I'll admit it will be nice to have Stella locked up—if it is her, of course."

Harriet took his hand.

"It's her. I know it is."

Morse stood up, carrying her empty mug to the sink before putting her coat on and picking up her wrapped brownie.

"I'll be in touch," she said, and left.

Chapter 56

Aunt Beth unlocked the outside door to Harriet's studio and stood back to let her enter.

"You go sit in the slipper chair, and I'll make tea." She took Harriet's jacket from around her shoulders and carried it to the kitchen with her.

She'd barely opened the door when Fred, Cyrano, and Scooter squeezed past her and ran to Harriet, jumping onto the ottoman and into her lap.

"Hey, hey. Come on, you guys." She gently pushed Scooter away from her face. "Stop licking."

Aunt Beth returned and removed Scooter, depositing him on the ottoman between Fred and Cyrano.

"I'm glad Brownie doesn't lick like that. I don't know how you stand it."

Harriet reached out her left hand and lifted Scooter back to her lap.

"He can't help it. He had a rough start in life."

"So did Brownie, but she has manners in spite of that."

The whistling of the teakettle interrupted Beth's lecture on dog manners, and she bustled back into the kitchen. The door had barely shut when there was a tap on the outside door and Detective Morse entered.

"How's your arm?"

Harriet wiggled the fingers on her right hand.

"It's getting better. It's mostly my shoulder that's the problem. It's pretty painful if I'm not careful. I still have to keep it immobilized. Enough about me. Do you have news?"

"I do, although I'm not sure whether it's good or bad."

Aunt Beth backed through the door from the kitchen, a mug in each hand.

"I thought I saw your car, Detective," she said and handed Morse a cup of coffee. She set the other cup on the TV tray beside Harriet's chair. The aroma of lavender wafted over to her.

"She has an answer," Harriet told her aunt.

"Let me get my tea, and then you can tell us all about it."

Detective Morse pulled a wheeled chair over and sat down.

"I talked to my boss." She took a swallow of coffee.

"What did he say?" Beth asked. "Did he agree to your plan?"

"Yes…and no. He said I needed to solve this case and do it now, or I'd find myself on traffic detail."

"What about our plan?" Harriet asked her.

"He said he wasn't approving our plan—nor was he disapproving it."

Harriet picked up her tea.

"What does that mean?"

"Basically, if our plan works, he approves. If it doesn't, I'm on traffic detail."

"Will you have other officers to help?" Beth asked.

"Not officially. He said, and I quote, 'If anyone is fool enough to help you, fine. If you fail, they can join you on traffic detail. And you'll be doing it on your own time, all of you.'"

Beth slid her chair closer.

"Did anyone agree to help you?"

Morse blew out a breath.

"Jason, my partner. I can't blame the other guys. Some of them wouldn't help me just because a woman became a detective, and they didn't. Others have families and can't risk losing wages if things go wrong."

Beth pushed her chair back and sat up straight.

"It's off, then."

"No, it's not," Harriet insisted. "We don't need a whole platoon. If Morse and her partner are there, it's enough. I'll be wearing a vest and a wire. Jane and Jason can be on opposite sides of the meeting place, covering me."

"I don't like it," Beth said.

"It seems like Jane is the only one taking a risk. She'll get demoted if it doesn't work, and it sounds like she'll get demoted if she doesn't solve the case."

"I don't think he'll do it unless he absolutely has to," Morse said. "He's under a lot of pressure because of the increase in crime these last couple of years. If he doesn't get a handle on it, he'll be the one on traffic duty. The politicians need a scapegoat. He's willing to give me up if it saves his own hide."

Harriet squirmed in her chair, restoring the circulation to her leg, where Cyrano and Fred were both lying.

"What are you going to do?"

Morse stared into her coffee mug.

"I don't know. Let me think about it and talk to Jason. Can I get back to you later?" She stood up. "Thanks for the coffee."

✂-- ✂-- ✂

James and Luke were home when Morse called.

"I'm putting you on speaker," Harriet told her. "What's the verdict?"

"If you're still willing, Jason and I want to go ahead and try your plan."

"I still don't like it," James grumbled.

"I want this to be over. I don't want to have to look over my shoulder everywhere I go, and I'm sure Luke would like to be able to ride his horse without an escort."

James blew out a breath.

"I get that, but I don't like it. There must be a better way to catch Stella."

"Jason and I have tried to think of one," Morse said, "but with the monetary resources Stella has from her husband, we can't come up with anything. We're afraid she'll hang around in her fortress until things cool down a little, and then take off for parts unknown, never to be seen again. We've done a little digging and it seems Milo Bren has multiple properties around the world, including his own island. They could disappear at any time."

Luke cleared his throat.

"How is Harriet going to wear a bulletproof vest with her arm strapped down?."

"Jason is working on that," Morse said. "He's taking a vest apart and adding some pieces from a dog vest. If Stella tries to approach too near Harriet, we'll close in on her. Likewise if we spot a gun."

James sighed. "I understand why you all want to do this, and I get that you're taking precautions that *should* ensure Harriet's safety, but things have a way of going sideways in this town."

"If you two decide to pull the plug on this, even up to the last minute, I'll understand, no questions asked."

"Not going to happen," Harriet muttered.

Chapter 57

Harriet came downstairs on a cold crisp morning three days later. Another day of waiting stretched in front of her. She'd been practicing stitching with her left hand, but it wasn't going well; and so far nothing else she'd tried off-handed had worked, either.

"What's this?" she said when she entered her kitchen to find Mavis, Connie, and her aunt Beth. They were all dressed in some form of camouflage clothing.

Beth poured hot water into a mug and dropped a teabag into it.

"Lauren ran into Morse and her partner at the coffee shop an hour ago. Stella's back. They were putting the final touches on the note you're going to text to her, and the plan is going down this afternoon. She'll be over when it's time to send the text."

Harriet gestured with her good hand.

"Again, I ask. What is *this*?"

Lauren arrived via the studio as the other three were mumbling and stumbling over their words, trying to come up with a plausible answer.

"They plan on being in the woods around the clearing in front of the hay barn," Lauren supplied, "which is where Morse is having you meet Stella."

Harriet looked from Beth to Connie to Mavis and back to Beth.

"Did Morse agree with this?"

Lauren laughed. "Of course she didn't. She doesn't know about it."

Beth puffed her chest out and straightened her back.

"She won't know we're there unless things go sideways, in which case, we'll be ready to provide backup."

Harriet shook her head. In her mind, she was imagining the trio storming out of the woods in their stylish camo outfits, presenting themselves as targets and making whatever was going on much worse.

"Unbelievable," she finally said.

Mavis sat down and unwrapped a plate of scones Connie had brought. "Don't even think about trying to stop us. If you go, we go."

Harriet's landline rang, and Aunt Beth answered.

"This is Beth," she said. "Uh-huh…uh-huh. She'll be ready."

She hung the phone up and turned to the group.

"That was Morse. She and Jason will be over in an hour to send the text to Stella and get Harriet dressed."

Connie took a scone from the plate.

"We better eat our scones and get out of here."

Beth joined her at the table and took a scone.

"We can finish our tea, but we do need to get out at the equestrian center so we can hide our car and be in position before everyone else gets there."

"I've got to stop by the house and get my binoculars," Connie said after a swallow of tea.

Lauren shook her head and grinned.

"This ought to be good."

"Where are *you* going to be?" Harriet asked her.

"I think I'll go watch Angela's class, if she has one. I'll be nearby, but not interfering with the mission."

Beth harrumphed. "We will not be interfering."

"Merely observing," Mavis added.

Lauren came over and took a scone.

"Whatever," she said and sat down.

✂-- ✂-- ✂

Morse and Martinez had the bulletproof vest with them when they arrived an hour later to send the text that would, hopefully, lure Stella into a confrontation. The text asked Stella to meet an hour after it was sent.

"Let's try on the vest first, just in case we need a do-over," Jason suggested.

Morse agreed. Her face was pale. She had a lot riding on Harriet's performance. If Stella walked away without admitting anything, Morse was facing repercussions. Harriet was pretty sure Stella wouldn't do that, but she also didn't want to be responsible for Morse being demoted.

"Can you raise your good arm?" Jason asked her. She did, and he slid the modified vest over her arm. He'd done a good job of duct-taping a dog vest to a regular vest in such a way that a panel slid under her brace while another piece draped over her immobile arm.

Harriet stood up when he was done.

"Not bad," she said, and twirled around so he and Morse could see the finished effect.

Morse held up Harriet's cellphone, her finger poised over the send button.

"Do we all agree we're ready to send the text? Last chance."

Harriet sat down.

"Do it."

Jason nodded his agreement, and Morse hit the button.

"Now, we wait," he said.

"Now, we wait," Harriet agreed.

✂-- ✂-- ✂

Harriet was staring at her phone, as was everyone else in the kitchen, but she still jumped when it trilled to signal an incoming text.

You alone no one else. This better be good. One hour

"Short and sweet," Morse noted and stood up. "Jason and I will go get in position. Wait thirty minutes for us to get there, and then come to the meeting place."

Lauren chuckled. "Aren't we all forgetting something?"

Morse stopped and turned to her.

"What?"

"Harriet can't drive."

Morse smiled. "Good thing you're planning to be at the equestrian center, right?"

Lauren sighed and got her keys from her pocket, jangling them.

"I guess I'm your taxi," she said to Harriet. "Shall we go by the coffee shop and get a hot cocoa to steel your nerves?"

Harriet attempted a grin but couldn't quite pull it off.

"Yes," Lauren answered her own question, "cocoa would be a good idea, thank you for thinking of it."

"Sorry, I guess I'm a little tense."

"Shall we all meet back here when things are over?" Connie asked.

Beth picked up her purse.

"Sounds good to me."

Mavis agreed and the trio left.

✂-- ✂-- ✂

Lauren helped Harriet into the car.

"I wonder exactly what the Three Amigos are up to in their camo get-ups."

"And whatever other hunting implements they may have dug out of their attics."

"Ah, well, as my grandmother used to say, let's not borrow trouble."

There was nothing else to say after that. They hurried through the drive-in lane to get their cocoa, and then Lauren pointed her car toward Miller Hill Road.

Chapter 58

$\mathcal{L}$ auren drove Harriet as close to the hay barn as she could, then got out and walked with her until she was in the clearing in front of the big doors. She waited for a moment, jingling her car keys in her pocket.

"I guess I'll drive back to the parking area and hang out at the arena until you're done here," she said for the second time. She still couldn't believe everyone had agreed to this plan. She made air quotes with her fingers when she said *done*.

It was twenty minutes before Stella was supposed to show up. Harriet scanned the surrounding woods, but she saw nothing. Nothing, that is, until Detective Morse trotted out from the uphill side of the area.

"We've got a problem. Martinez and I just got called to a reported active crime scene on the other end of town. We need to call this off."

"We can't. Stella should be here in fifteen minutes—or less, if she's early."

"We have to go. Our boss will use us not showing up as a reason to fire us. We tried to keep this quiet, but someone must have told him. I'm sure this will turn out to be a false alarm."

Harriet closed her eyes and took a deep breath. "I'm staying. I want this over with. You can't stop me."

Morse looked back toward the woods where Martinez was easing their car out of its hiding place.

"Come on," he called. "Dispatch wants our ETA."

"Call it off," Morse said one more time.

Harriet shook her head. She knew she was taking a chance, but she also knew she was wearing a bulletproof vest, and that her aunt, Connie, and Mavis were hiding somewhere nearby.

"We'll come back as soon as we can," Morse said and left.

Harriet watched their car drive onto the road and out of sight.

Now what? She was pretty sure Stella only wanted her out of the picture because she thought Harriet was a witness to something. She just needed to convince her that wasn't the case, and that she didn't want anything to do with her business.

No police would pop out of the woods if Stella confessed. On the other hand, she was still wearing the wire, and it would record whatever she said. The difference was, she was going to have to make up a story for Stella. What could she offer?"

Harriet had just decided Morse was right—the gamble wasn't worth it—and was turning to head for the main barn when Stella Bren emerged from the woods.

"Are you going somewhere?" she asked.

"I thought you weren't going to show."

"I have to admit, I'm surprised *you* showed up. I mean, why would you? I tried to kill you."

"Yeah, about that. I've never done anything to make you want to do that. The way I see it, you think I know something that could cause you a problem, but the thing is, I don't. What I do know is my number-one priority is keeping my son safe and happy. And that includes his horse."

"And why should I believe you?"

"Because if you read the papers, you'd know if I knew anything about Simon or Crystal's deaths. I'd have already told the police a long time ago."

"Maybe you know something and don't realize it. It could come back to you. Where would that leave me?"

"First of all, I don't think there is anything to know about you. Second, if there was anything to know about you, we wouldn't be having this conversation because you'd be out of the country."

"Why should I leave the country? All I need to do is get rid of you, and that will be that. No one will be any the wiser. I'll admit you're proving surprisingly difficult to kill."

"Don't you think it'll be a bit suspicious if I'm found dead at the Equestrian Center? The police have a short list of suspects connected to this place as it is."

"You aren't going to be found here. Those homeless people you're so fond of are going to find your body near their camp. You're going to have all sorts of forensic evidence linking you to Stanley Oliver."

"Why can't you leave me alone? I've never done anything to you. Neither has Stan."

Stella shrugged.

"What can I say? Wrong place, wrong time? Unfortunately for Stan, his combat knife went missing from his pack while he was riding Lily this morning." She pulled a wicked-looking combat knife from her belt and pointed it at Harriet. "Turn around."

Harriet heard the sound of an ATV coming toward them from the woods.

"Who's that?"

"That's your transportation. And, actually, your killer. I'm not really into wet work, and as I said, you're tougher than you look. I've brought in a professional to help me. Now, move."

Harriet held her ground, running various options through her mind. She knew you were supposed to run if someone pulled a knife on you, but with her shoulder strapped up, her ability to run was a bit impaired. She could try a sweeping kick and knock Stella to the ground, but the ATV driver might be armed. Besides that, if she lost her balance and landed on her shoulder, it would be her last move—the pain would immobilize her.

As Stella closed in on her, a shot cracked, and the knife flew out of her hand. She grabbed her hand and cried out. A second shot quickly followed by a third exploded the tires on the near side of the approaching ATV, sending it down the slope and onto its side, the driver sprawling.

Three piles of brush stood up and trotted toward Stella, the lead pile holding a rifle. Arms appeared from what Harriet could now see were gillie suits, the netting garments that had brush attached to them that hunters wore to conceal themselves.

She smiled. Her suspicions as to the identity of her rescuers was confirmed when the three removed the hoods to their suits to reveal Connie, Aunt Beth, and, wielding the rifle, Mavis.

"If either of you moves, I'll drop you where you stand," Mavis barked. "Don't think I won't."

Harriet could see Beth fumbling around in the vicinity of her pants pocket—fishing her phone out to dial 911, she assumed.

"Could you at least tell us why we're here?" she asked Stella. "What did Simon and Crystal ever do to you?"

She glanced at Mavis, who was reloading her rifle, and stepped toward Stella in an attempt to distract her from realizing Mavis was temporarily unarmed.

Stella blew out a breath.

"Simple," she said. "Essy hurt his foot, and Simon took it upon himself to put a nerve block into the injured area so Essy could perform without either of us knowing he was damaging his foot further. Why, you might be thinking? All so his stable name will be associated with a win. Nothing more than that.

"The man was a cockroach. He was abusing the teenagers, and they were afraid to report him. And that witch Crystal knew he was abusing her daughter, but she wanted Paige to win trophies so bad she was willing to look the other way. That alone qualified her to leave this world.

"What finally chapped my hide with her was her pathetic attempt to blackmail me. She was always creeping around the stable at night. We could see her walking down to the gate on our security camera at all hours. Anyway, when I asked Simon to meet with me, the lights were out in Crystal's house, so I thought I was clear."

She took a step back and kicked the dirt with the toe of her boot.

"Apparently, Crystal saw me there with Simon. She was hiding in their horse's stall. She heard what happened and decided to ask me to pay for her silence. That never works. Blackmailers are always too greedy. So, we needed a more permanent arrangement."

"Why do you think I know anything about either of those incidents?" Harriet asked. She was watching the woods beyond Stella and could see the woman's confederate creeping toward the ATV.

"I thought you realized I was damaging horses' hooves so no-one would connect Essy's injury with Simon. Then, I thought you recognized me when I pushed you into the stall."

Harriet gave her a wry smile.

"Something about twelve hundred volts to the neck distracted me."

Stella gestured toward Harriet's shoulder.

"Are you telling me we didn't need to do any of this?"

"Sadly, yes,"

"Drop it," a male voice said from the area of the ATV.

Stella's associate had pulled a gun from the vehicle and was pointing it at Mavis. He barely had the words out of his mouth before Mavis shot him in the chest.

"You drop it," she said.

Beth put her phone back in her pocket.

"I already asked the nine-one-one operator to send an ambulance."

"Keelan," Stella shouted. "Shoot them."

A second man came out of the woods, his hands up.

"I'm sorry, Mrs. Bren. You told me you needed protection; you didn't say anything about shooting a bunch of old ladies. I don't know what Lagos agreed to, but I didn't sign up for this."

"But I paid you," she screamed.

"And you're still alive, even though you pulled a knife on an unarmed woman. Job done."

Harriet turned as she heard sirens and in a few minutes saw a Foggy Point Police car come bumping down the track to the barn. Lauren followed the car on foot. She came over to Harriet while the two patrol officers put handcuffs on Stella and Keelan.

"Yet another close call," she said and patted Harriet on the back. "Are you okay?"

Harriet took a deep breath.

"I will be."

Chapter 59

"You'll be happy to know your body cam worked perfectly," Lauren told her. "I got all the action on tape. As an added precaution, I put a wireless camera on that tree." She pointed to a skinny maple at the edge of the woods. "It caught your aunt and her commandos."

Harriet shook her head.

"I'm really glad they were there. I don't know what I was thinking, staying out here to meet Stella alone."

"The rest of us are blaming your pain meds. That's why the commandos were there. In addition, Jenny and Carla are in the barn, in case Stella overpowered you and tried to take you in there.

"Robin and DeAnn are at the gate beyond the woods. They waited until Stella headed this way and had time to get to the barn—I'm not sure if they saw her two companions. Then they parked in front of the gate in case Stella got you and came back this way.

"Of course, no one knew Morse was going to abandon you. We thought we were just there for backup. Except for the commandos, who were pretty sure they would be called into action."

"What's with Mavis and the rifle?"

"Her older boys were in a Four-H shooting club. Since she had to drive the boys to the range every week, she signed up for an adult class and turned out to be quite the competitive shooter."

"Wow," Harriet said, and suddenly felt quite faint.

"You better sit down," Lauren told her and guided her as she sank to the ground. "Can we get some help here?" she shouted.

"I think this has all been a little too much for you." Mary Pierce, whom Harriet had met on a few too many previous occasions like this, checked her vitals. "I suspect you're feeling the after-effects of an adrenaline rush. We can take you to the hospital, but I think you'll be okay if you just go home and lie down."

Morse came over and looked down at Harriet.

"We're going to need all of you down at the station. We have to make sure everything is done by the book. Can you manage that?"

"Just give me a few minutes. I'll be fine," Harriet told her.

"Okay, Martinez and I will see you at the station in…" She looked at her watch. "Forty-five minutes. Can you tell all the others, too?"

"We'll be there."

Harriet sat between Mavis and Aunt Beth, with Connie on Beth's other side, while they waited their turns to be interviewed.

"What were you three thinking?" she demanded.

"We knew you weren't thinking clearly," Aunt Beth answered. "If you had been, you'd have never tried to confront Stella all by yourself."

Mavis slid to the front edge of her chair.

"I thought Stella might have backup with her, so I figured we could even the score."

"And Morse didn't have enough help, even when she was going to be there," Connie added.

Mavis pressed her lips together.

"I hadn't really expected to shoot that man. I knew I was accurate enough to knock a weapon from someone's hand. I've won a number of prizes for sharpshooting," she added with pride.

Connie leaned forward.

"And she's been practicing ever since we first talked about this idea."

Beth chuckled.

"You'd never guess, seeing her now, but Mavis and her oldest boys used to go deer hunting in the fall."

"That was completely from necessity. The widow's benefits didn't start immediately after George…" Mavis paused. "After we thought George was gone. I had five growing boys to feed. We put a couple of deer in the freezer each year. I cried when I shot my first one. Some men who were nearby made fun of me, but I toughened up, and those deer saved us those first winters."

Harriet leaned back.

"I'd have never guessed."

Mavis straightened.

"You should be glad I did, Missy, and that I haven't lost my touch."

Harriet patted her hand.

"I'm very thankful you were there."

Morse broke up their love fest by calling Mavis into the interview room. Robin and DeAnn had followed her out.

Beth looked at her phone.

"Jorge and James are preparing dinner for all of us at Tico's when we're finished here, and want to know if everyone is available."

"I'm headed home first, and the whole clan will come to dinner, if that's okay," Robin said.

"Same," DeAnn echoed.

"Of course it's fine, and I'll let them know," Beth told them.

✂-- ✂-- ✂

James was waiting at home with Luke when Harriet finally returned from the police station. He scooped her carefully into his arms.

"We were so worried about you. When I heard from Jorge that Detective Morse had left you alone with Stella, I went crazy."

"Me, too," Luke said. "I wanted to go to the barn, but James said we had to wait. Aunt Beth had called Jorge, and he called us and said you were okay and so was everyone else."

"Thanks to Mavis," Harriet said with a chuckle and proceeded to tell them about her friend's sharpshooting display.

"Do you feel well enough to go to dinner with the group?"

"Sure. I've been weaning myself off the pain medication, but after all the activity today, I at least need some ibuprofen."

Luke headed for the stairs.

"I'll get it," he said as he took them two at a time.

Harriet leaned into James, and he kissed the top of her head.

"One of these times I really am going to have a heart attack when the phone rings, and someone tells me there's been an incident."

"I'll do my best to make sure it doesn't happen again," she said.

She felt his chuckle against her cheek

"Promises, promises."

✂-- ✂-- ✂

Jorge had prepared tamale pie for dinner, and James had provided green salads and death-by-chocolate cake.

260

"I know chocolate is not the traditional finish to a dinner of tamale pie, but I thought we all might need some after the day a few of us have had," he commented as he and the servers carried in plates of the dense chocolate pastry.

Detective Morse arrived as he finished delivering the desserts.

"Want to start with dessert?" he asked her.

"Why not?" she said, and sat down at the table. She closed her eyes as she savored a bite and then set her fork down.

"I thought you'd all want to know that Stella and her confederates were all arrested, although one is in the hospital nursing a gunshot wound."

"That's a relief," Aunt Beth said.

Morse sipped from the cup of coffee Jorge had set in front of her.

"The elusive Milo Bren came to the station after you all left."

Lauren set her fork down.

"Darn it, we missed him."

Morse smiled.

"You did. He brought a lawyer for Stella as well as a set of divorce papers for her to sign. He shouted at her that she could have bought twelve horses to replace the injured one, and killing people wasn't the answer. He said he was paying for her lawyer and that was the last thing he was doing for her."

"Whoa," Lauren murmured.

"That wasn't the best part," Morse continued. "It turns out Milo isn't really a recluse. His identical twin brother plays a very well-known television detective. When he goes out in public, his brother's fans swarm him along with the paparazzi. He finds it easier not to appear in public unless he has to."

Harriet took another bite of her cake and wiped her mouth.

"What about Mavis?"

Morse turned to look at the newly-revealed sharpshooter.

"Fortunately, Lauren's tape shows a clear image of Keelan's partner pointing his gun and threatening her—a clear case of self-defense."

"What about you and Martinez?" Aunt Beth asked.

Morse laughed.

"We live to fight another day. The boss didn't go so far as to thank us or congratulate us or anything. He just said he'd see us tomorrow, so I guess we still have jobs."

"That's worth a toast," said James, and held up his glass of water. "To Detective Jane Morse."

"To Morse," the group echoed.

Chapter 60

*T*he day of the horse show finally arrived. The blankets were finished, and on the horses, and Luke led the procession into the arena for the opening ceremonies.

James stood in the stands with his arm around Harriet as they watched the horses enter.

"If I'm not mistaken, Major is prancing."

Harriet smiled.

"He knows how to make an entrance."

Lauren stood on Harriet's other side.

"Our blankets look really good. And the weather cooperated and stayed cold enough the horses actually need them."

As the horses filed into the arena, a murmur could be heard from the audience as people commented on the beautiful quilted quarter sheets.

"Where did they get them?" a large woman standing behind Lauren asked aloud.

"I don't know," Lauren said over her shoulder with a straight face. "I guess you have to know a quilter."

END

ACKNOWLEDGMENTS

I'd first like to acknowledge the people who enable my writing habit—first and foremost my husband Jack. Next, my children and grandchildren...I mean, who wouldn't be inspired by their grandgirl proclaiming "Grammy, I'm so proud of you, and I tell all my friends you're an author"?

Of course, my books wouldn't happen without the efforts of Liz at Zumaya Publications and April, the best cover artist ever.

I'd also like to thank Michele Voorhees, horsewomen, trainer and teacher extraordinaire who kept suggesting I write a mystery set at a stable. When I decided to do it, she answered all my questions both in person and in late night texts, and also allowed me to watch her give lessons to Beth (the real Aunt Beth) as well as wander around the barn talking to other people who stable their horses there.

Thank you to Beth, who is not only a dressage rider but volunteers with Courtney Cares, an equine therapeutic program thru Texas A&M University, which includes programs for the disabled as well as veterans. She answered lots of questions and let me tag along to a session to see what goes on.

Thanks to my nephew Chad and his wife Lindsay, who ride, train, and show horses, and recently bought a stable of their own. They also are willing to answer random horse questions.

ABOUT THE AUTHOR

ARLENE SACHITANO decided she'd like to write murder mysteries when she was about eleven years old and read her first Agatha Christie novel. She was already a knitter at that tender age, and started sewing soon after, so it only made sense she'd grow up to write cozy crafting mysteries. A thirty-year side trip into the world of high tech, along with raising multiple children, dogs, and cats, derailed the writing ambitions for a while, but eventually the writing compulsion won out.

Arlene is the author of the Harriet Truman/Loose Threads Mysteries as well as the Permelia O'Brien mysteries. She lives in both Tillamook and Portland, Oregon with her husband Jack and dog Navarre ("No, he's not a min-pin, he's a Manchester terrier").

ABOUT THE ARTIST

APRIL MARTINEZ loves reading and lives in San Diego, California, with her fiancé and his two kids.

CPSIA information can be obtained
at www.ICGtesting.com
Printed in the USA
BVHW070611111121
621201BV00006B/363

9 781612 714295